# A VISION OF POWER

The man said nothing. He was dressed in plain clothing—unadorned leggings, fringed but otherwise unremarkable, a plain buckskin shirt, unpainted and without even beadwork to relieve the ordinariness of its color. His face was unpainted, and he wore a solitary eagle feather in his hair, which hung long and straight. The man turned away for a moment, and Curly noticed a small stone tied behind his ear.

Curly tried to get up, but his body wouldn't work. Gasping for air, he tried to speak, but the man raised a hand to silence him.

"Don't wear a warbonnet," he said. "When you go into battle, leave your horse's tail untied, free to balance him as he leaps across the stones. Before you ride into battle, sprinkle him with dust, let streams of it glide from your curled fingers in streaks and straight lines. Don't paint your war pony."

"Who . . ." Curly croaked.

But again the man raised a hand, cutting him off. "Rub dirt on your skin and hair. Do these things before every battle, and you will never be killed by an enemy or a bullet. Your people must come first. Take nothing for yourself. Your people will know your worth. Know it yourself. Let them celebrate you. It is not necessary for you to boast or sing of your courage."

# Crazy Horse WAR CHIEFS

## BILL DUGAN

# HarperPaperbacks
*A Division of HarperCollinsPublishers*

**HarperPaperbacks**
*A Division of* HarperCollins*Publishers*
10 East 53rd Street, New York, NY 10022-5299

A previous mass market edition of this book was published
in 1992 by HarperCollins*Publishers*.

ISBN 0–06–100448–0

HarperCollins®, 👑®, and HarperPaperbacks™
are trademarks of HarperCollins Publishers Inc.

Cover illustration by Jim Carson

Revised HarperPaperbacks printing: October 1999

Printed in the United States of America

Visit HarperPaperbacks on the World Wide Web at
http://www.harpercollins.com

❖ 10 9 8 7 6

# Chapter 1 ═══════

**September 1841**

IT WAS LATE SEPTEMBER. Far ahead, Bear Butte tow-
ered over the flatlands, its rude, buff-colored face,
flat against the horizon, laced with smoke from
hundreds of fires. Crazy Horse was too far away to
see the individual tipis, but he knew they were
there, thick as needles on a pine limb. The Sioux
were gathering, as they did every autumn, to renew
friendships, see family, and share news. Both good
and bad.

His band was small, just a few families, but it
was from such small groups that the great tide of
the Lakota people was made. They would be coming from every direction, some with news of warfare with the Crow and the Shoshoni, others with
tales of coups counted and battles won, friends lost
and horses stolen.

The Sioux had been gathering here as long as
anyone, even the oldest warrior, could remember.
The winter counts, painstakingly sketched on
tanned leather, soft with years of handling, their
bright paints already beginning to peel in places,
did not go back far enough to show the first time.

Everyone knew that it could not be more than

1

one hundred years, or maybe two. Not that long ago, the Sioux were a woodland people, making their homes on the banks of Minnesota lakes, pulling their lives from the cold, clear blue waters, hunting deer and elk in the thick forests. But that was before the Chippewa had gotten their guns from the white men. Driven westward by the Iroquois, who had their guns first, the Chippewa had passed on the relentless pressure when they got guns of their own.

But the plains were like home now, as comfortable as if they had always been home. There was not a Sioux still living, man or woman, who could remember a time when they did not have horses and follow the buffalo from early spring to early autumn. Nor was there a Sioux still living who could remember a time before the Black Hills were special, a place so nearly perfect that only Wakan Tanka, the Great Spirit, could have fashioned it, made it for the Sioux to venerate the way only a people perfectly in tune with the world around them could venerate so perfect a place.

The weather was almost perfect, too. The worst of the summer heat was already past, and the breeze from the northwest swept away the thick dust kicked up by the ponies and the scraping of the travois. It had been a good late summer hunt, and there was plenty of dried meat to see the small band through the winter. If they were lucky, there would be more buffalo before the first snows forced them into permanent winter camp, but there was plenty of time to worry about such things. At the moment, Crazy Horse wanted to think about the coming reunion.

His wife was expecting her first child at any

time, and Crazy Horse knew it would probably be born at the gathering, in the shadow of Bear Butte. He already had a daughter by his first wife, White Deer's sister, but Laughing Elk Woman was dead two years now. It was still painful, but new life would ease the hurt, only a little, but any relief was welcome. And Bear Butte was a good place to be born, he thought. Not far away, to the south and west, the towering peaks of Paha Sapa, the Black Hills, formed a saw-toothed backdrop for the giant butte. It would be good to visit the Black Hills. The rich valleys and deep woods were full of game. Buffalo and elk seemed to run without number in river valleys. Higher up the slopes, deer and bighorn sheep were plentiful. The water of the Black Hills was the best water he knew, cold and clear and full of fish. Even this late in the year, the hillsides would be covered with a thick carpet of flowers. Staring at the purplish haze of the hills shimmering in the distance, Crazy Horse thought that it was almost as if the Great Spirit had come to him and said, "Tell me what would make the perfect place for you and your people. Tell me, and I will make this place for you, just as you describe it.' That hadn't happened, of course, because the Great Spirit had far too many things to do to worry about what one man thought, even if that one man was a dreamer and a holy man as Crazy Horse was.

But it didn't really matter. Because Crazy Horse, his mind full of fluttering images of those sacred and perfect hills, wouldn't change a single thing about them. They were what he imagined the great place beyond was like, that place where he would go to hunt when his days on earth were finished. They

were a place where there were no Crows and no
Arapahos, no Arikaras and no Pawnee. And most
especially, there were no white men there, no men
with pale skins and cheap whiskey, like those who
had been crossing the Plains for the last few years.
Not many, but more every year.

Just the year before, in fact, there had been several long, curling skeins of wooden boxes with
canvas shells. Wagon trains, the white men called
them, but he preferred to think of them as snakes.
They had come in dribs and drabs, driving their
skinny cattle, with bones poking through their
skins so far a man could count the ribs with his
eyes closed, just by using his fingertips. The
wheels of their wagons gouged deep troughs in
the earth, killed the grass so that it couldn't grow
back. It was a great, ugly scar across the face of the
land. The Oregon Trail, the white men called it,
had divided the great herds of buffalo, who would
not cross it, would not go near it because of the
stink and because the white men killed the buffalo stupidly, uselessly, sometimes even just for
sport.

The whites left mounds of junk behind. Strange
boxes full of metal strings, tall pieces of wood with
glass faces, wagons, broken and wheelless, lying on
their sides like the skeletons of strange beasts.
From time to time, bands of Cheyenne, Sioux, or
Pawnees would attack one of the wagon trains, and
sometimes they would just ride close, until the
white men were so frightened they offered anything and everything, if only the Indians would
leave them alone. Coffee, tobacco, sugar; even
sometimes guns and bullets were offered.

Crazy Horse had no use for those Sioux who had come to depend on the wagon trains and their white man goods. Some of them knew only how to hang around the white man's trading post on the Laramie River, living like parasites on handouts, and drinking the white man's whiskey. They were forgetting the old ways, and that could only mean trouble, one day, if not now.

But he was soon to be a father again, and the white man troubles seemed a small thing on this glorious autumn afternoon. He was close enough now that he could see the tipis, arrayed in a great circle, open to the east and the rising sun. He knew that members of all seven of the great Teton Sioux bands would be there. His own people, the Oglala, his wife's people, the Brule, the Miniconjou and Sans Arc, the Two Kettles and the Hunkpapas and the Blackfeet. More than likely, there would be a few of their friends, the Northern Cheyenne, too.

As his *tiyospe*, or family band, drew near enough to be seen by those already camped, warriors began to ride out to greet him. They were all members of the *akicitas,* the warrior societies that were like the white man's police. They were responsible for the safety of the camp, they set the rules for the hunt, and they took their responsibilities seriously. The Kit Foxes and the Badgers and the Crow-Owners were the best men of the various bands. One did not join one of the *akicitas* just because he felt like it. One had to earn his way in. And once a member, he had better toe the mark, or would not last long. It was no disgrace to be turned down for membership, but it was a great disgrace indeed if, having once earned membership, one were so derelict as to require expulsion.

Once satisfied that Crazy Horse and his band were no threat, the warriors relaxed, bantering with those they knew, teasing the children, and letting their ponies canter along on both sides of the small caravan. Crazy Horse moved away a bit, to ride alongside Two Bows, an Oglala he had known all his life, and ask news of old friends.

It was to be a large gathering, Two Bows told him. Already there were hundreds of lodges. And the hunting had been good. The week before, a large herd of buffalo had been spotted on the eastern edge of the Black Hills. The surround had worked perfectly, and the kill was a large one.

Spotted Tail was there already, and anxiously waiting news of his younger sister and the child she was expecting. Two Bows looked at Crazy Horse expectantly, and when the holy man nodded, he broke into a broad smile. "Soon," Crazy Horse told him. "Any day.'

"It is a great thing to be born so near the Paha Sapa," Two Bows said.

"The best.'

"If the child will be a boy, he will be a great warrior.'

"It is a boy," Crazy Horse said. Once more, his old friend looked quizzically at him. "I have seen. It is true.'

Two Bows knew his friend's reputation as a dreamer and interpreter of visions. He accepted the simple truth of what Crazy Horse had told him. If the holy man said it, it must be so.

The camp was laid out as always. Crazy Horse

knew where to look for the Brule tipis, and waved farewell to Two Bows. As customary, he would camp with his wife's people. He would have to wait a while before going to the Oglala lodges to see his own family. There would be much to do in the next few hours. The great circle was already getting crowded, and fitting the tipis of his *tiyospe* into the camp would keep the whole band busy for the rest of the day. Then there would be socializing. It would be necessary to find Spotted Tail among the Brule. He would want to know how his sister was bearing up under the strain of her pregnancy. But that might have to wait until morning, unless Spotted Tail heard of his arrival and came looking for him.

The tipis were assembled quickly, once a suitable place in the great circle was found. The women did much of the work, and they had done it so often that it appeared to be smooth and almost effortless to an observer. The poles were used for the travois, so the goods of the traveling band had to be unpacked before the tipis could be erected. But everyone knew what to do, and in less than two hours, the frames were in place and the skins ready to be fitted.

Nearly twenty feet across at the base and eighteen feet or so high, the tipis were almost perfect in their economy. Light and easily assembled and disassembled, with a fire they were snug enough in winter and the painted buffalo hides that formed the sides could be rolled up to admit a breeze in warm weather.

Soon the fires were going, their smoke curling lazily up through the smoke holes and mingling

with the haze already hanging above the camp,
draped like a gauzy curtain below the top of Bear
Butte. Even White Deer did her share, refusing to
let her stomach get in the way. The Sioux pulled
their own weight, and pregnancy was no reason to
be excused from the rigors of establishing camp.

It was near sunset when White Deer felt the first
stirrings. She called to Black Calf Woman as she
rushed past the latter's tipi, her hands clutched
against her belly. Together, the two women moved
away from the camp, heading for the bank of a
small stream that fed into the Belle Fourche River a
few miles away. The brush along the stream bank
was still green and the grass was thick, almost lush,
right down to the edge of the water.

Crazy Horse, having no role in the birth, paced
back and forth outside his lodge. He heard the
excited buzz among the women as they made ready
for the new arrival, crushing berries to fill a buffalo
bladder with their juices. This would be the baby's
first meal. According to custom, it would be a day
or so before the mother's milk would be pure
enough.

White Deer felt the pangs deep inside her. The
baby would be her first, and everything was new,
not just the pain, but the terror of the unknown.
She felt as if she would tear in half before the baby
was delivered. But with a rush, things sped to their
conclusion and soon she was holding her child. As
Crazy Horse had foretold, it was a boy. The first
thing she noticed was that he had a full head of
hair, not just any hair, either, but fine hair of a light
brown unlike any she had ever seen on a Sioux.
His skin, too, was light. Not like the whites who

traveled the Holy Road, but lighter than any Sioux or Cheyenne or Pawnee.

The baby started to cry. Her instincts, so finely honed by her life on the Plains, were automatic. She pinched the baby's nose between thumb and forefinger to stop the crying. Despite the size of the camp, there could be Pawnee or Assiniboin about, just waiting for the chance to steal a few horses. Or a Sioux woman and her baby.

There would be time enough for the newborn to learn about such things. He would be a warrior, and if things went on as always, his life would be nothing but such things. While he was young, she would keep him to herself, try to keep him from harm. The world was harsh and unforgiving, their enemies even more so. There would come a time when she would watch him don the war paint and gather his lance and bow to ride out into the plains. And she would sit and do beadwork, her mind always on him, her heart almost still, a clenched fist in her chest, wondering if this time would be the time he would not come back.

But that time was not yet come.

# Chapter 2 ═══════════════════

**August 1844**

THEY CALLED HIM CURLY. He wouldn't have another name until he grew strong, and achieved something worthwhile, perhaps stole a horse belonging to the Crows, or killed a buffalo on his own. For the time being, his appearance would have to give him his name. Maybe, if he were pure enough, and special enough, he would go on a vision quest, and he would receive a sign from the Great Spirit. But that was years away, if it would ever happen at all.

Most of his first year, he spent on a cradle board. Sometimes he would be allowed to crawl around inside the tipi on the floor covered with buffalo robes, or outside with the other children, his hands and knees covered with dirt. He would be free to learn in the Sioux way, by experience. If he thought the fire looked interesting, he was free to reach into the flames and grab a burning brand; free, too, to cry when the pain stabbed up his hand and forearm, his light skin already turning red as White Deer rubbed a coating of buffalo grease on the burn or, if it was winter, wiped it with soothing snow.

The Sioux were very free with their children. The young ones, as soon as they could toddle, were welcome in any tipi, where they would be fed, if they were hungry, or coddled by any adult who happened to be there. Even the warriors, when they had time, loved to play with the children, teasing them, tickling them and teaching them the things they would need to know if they were to survive the hard life that stretched out ahead of them until a stray arrow or, if they were lucky, old age, finally came to take them away.

Curly was no different. The members of his father's band seemed a little bit in awe of him, partly because Crazy Horse was a holy man, in touch with things they could not see, but which they knew existed, and partly because he looked the least bit different. It wasn't just his light skin or the light, curly hair which gave him his name, either. He seemed to understand things beyond his years.

White Deer insisted at least once a week that Curly could speak but simply chose not to, as if his understanding were a great secret he was not quite ready to share with the other members of the band. Two or three times a day she would sense something, look up from her beadwork or stop paying attention to one of the other women, and search the tipi, her eyes darting around the perimeter of the lodge until she found him. And invariably he would be looking at her, his eyes bright with the firelight and fixed on her face, as if wondering why she had stopped what she was doing. At such times, she would squint a little, even lean toward him, maybe to encourage him, she wasn't quite sure, or perhaps to hear the first word as if she were convinced that when it came it would be a whisper, and something she dare not miss hearing.

Crazy Horse, too, knew that his son was special. He spent as much time with the boy as he could. He took Curly on long walks in the open plains, pointing things out to him, showing him where the prairie dogs swarmed in their warrens, pointing out the silent wings of a great eagle high overhead, drifting almost motionless on the air currents far above the summer grass. When he had a dream, he would explain it to his son, sitting alone with the boy, almost whispering, puzzling out the meaning, watching the boy's face as if for some assistance.

Like most of the young ones in the camp, he spent much of the day playing, but the games were serious business. It was important to be strong and to have great endurance. The survival of the band, that of the Oglala and of the Sioux in general, depended on the strong arms and sharp eyes of their warriors. Danger was everywhere. The Pawnees were particularly fierce, and they were not afraid of the Sioux any more than the Sioux were afraid of them. To the west, where the buffalo were increasingly wont to go, there were the Crow, mortal enemies as deadly as the Pawnee and as fierce.

So the games were an extension of the children's education. Often, they combined instinct and physical ability, honing the one and stretching the other, pushing both to their very limits. One game the young Curly came to love had no real name, but everyone called it "Hitting with Fire."

Two mounds of brush would be assembled by some of the older boys, one at either end of the camp. Borrowing a flame from one of the cook fires, the organizers then ignited the brush. Broken into teams, the players grabbed handfuls of burning branches and swarmed over one another, swatting and slashing with the flaming torches. If one of the boys managed to get close enough to hit his opponent, more often than not the first couple of blows were enough to extinguish the flames, and he was left with a blackened stick, its glowing end slowly turning black. More than likely, the opponent still had a torch or two, and unless you were fast enough to get away, you had to take your own swats with the burning wood until it, too, was extinguished.

The game was a great favorite of Curly's by the time he was barely two, still young enough to attach himself to the nearest woman for milk, whether White Deer or some other recent mother. The Sioux shared everything they had, and mother's milk was not exempt from community demands. More often than not, his meals consisted of a piece or two of buffalo meat, softened by his sister's teeth, then dipped in broth which he could suck from the stringy meat before chewing with his first few teeth.

Curly was playing one day when he saw one of the young men who guarded the horses come running toward the camp, his hair flying behind him as if it wanted to stay behind.

"Crows!" he yelled. "The Crows are coming!"

Suddenly, the camp erupted like an anthill disturbed with a sharp stick. Men spilled out of the tipis, some still pulling on their buckskin shirts. They carried their bows and rawhide quivers. The women, too, began running around, gathering up the children and hauling them, most kicking and screaming, toward the nearest tipi, to get them out of harm's way. Crazy Horse rushed from his own tipi and saw Curly in the arms of Black Calf Woman. He carried his own bow, the new one he had made at nights in the last week, Curly sitting on a buffalo robe beside him, asking questions in his halting language. Now his father was going to use the bow, and Curly wondered if it would work well. He wanted to go along, and stretched his arms out to Crazy Horse, who shushed him and waved goodbye as the tipi flap closed between father and son.

Black Calf Woman pulled him down and sat him on her lap. Outside, he could hear the men shouting, their deep voices rising to piercing howls as they cut loose with war whoops, as much to bolster their own spirits as to frighten the enemy, who was still some distance away. The high-pitched voices of the women, still gathering the last few children together, rode above the war whoops like the chattering of frightened birds.

Curly had never experienced anything like this before. He kept squirming in Black Calf Woman's arms, trying to work his way free. Several children huddled around her, and many were starting to cry. The wailing began to fill the tipi, and Curly watched his older friends curiously.

He tugged at Black Calf Woman's hair to get her attention. When she finally noticed him, he pointed to the other children, his eyes wide and his mouth open as if he had just asked a question. "Not now, Curly," she said, leaning forward to reach for one of the smaller children. In that instant, feeling her grip loosen the least little bit, Curly broke free and darted through the circle of children toward the flap which kept out the sunlight and the shouting in the camp.

Black Calf Woman called to him, and he turned once, but didn't slow down as he careened toward the entrance way, tripped, and tumbled against the flap. He rolled on through and out into the open.

Everywhere he looked, adults were running. Most of the men were already on the edge of the camp, their backs to him. Far ahead, he could recognize his father's shirt, and he toddled after him on his short legs.

One woman noticed him and darted after him, but he zigzagged away and kept on in pursuit of the warriors. He could hear her call to him. He recognized her voice. It was Blue Owl, a friend of his mother, but he paid her no mind. It was more exciting away from the camp, and he wanted to see what all the commotion was.

He heard a loud crack far in the distance, then another. He knew enough to recognize the sound as that of a gun. He knew the young man who had sounded the alarm had shouted that the Crows were coming, but he had no idea what that really meant. He knew the Crows were the deadly enemies of the Sioux. He knew, too, that they would steal Sioux horses and Sioux women, but those were alien concepts to him. He had no idea what it meant to be stolen. He knew it was supposed to be a bad thing, but it was too hard to imagine what it would be like to be truly frightened of it.

His legs were beginning to give out, and he was slowing down. He heard the whoops of the Crow warriors far away, and on a ridge above where the

pony herd was grazing, he saw several warriors.
They wore feathers and had their faces painted,
but their hair was not like Sioux hair. Just as he
was deciding that those must be the Crows, an
arm encircled his waist. He started to squirm as
the arm lifted him off his feet. He called to his
father, but Crazy Horse was too far away to hear.
He saw his father kneel to steady his aim as he
drew back the bowstring and let an arrow fly up
the hill over the backs of the frightened ponies,
but he lost it in the flurry of arrows from the other
warriors.

He turned then to see who had captured him,
and found White Deer scowling at him. He started
to cry then, as his mother closed her arms around
him and squeezed him until the air could hardly
get into his lungs.

She was angry at him, he could see that. And
frightened, too. Maybe she thought that he had
been stolen, or that he would be stolen if he had
gone too far. But she would not hit him; he knew
that. He had never seen a Sioux, man or woman,
strike a child.

White Deer turned and hurried to the nearest
tipi, still squeezing him tightly in her arms. He
could feel her legs moving under the deerskin
dress, and her breathing in his ear was very loud.
She made little squeaking sounds, like a mouse,
almost with every step. The sounds made him
laugh, and he tugged on her hair once, then craned
his neck to look over her shoulder up toward the
hillside where his father was doing battle with the
Crows.

White Deer ducked into the tipi and tugged the

flap closed with one hand while her other arm circled under his armpits and dangled him in the air.
Then she sat on the ground right in front of the
entrance flap, to make sure that he could not
escape again.

The noise of the battle was far away now, just
distant echoes of war cries punctuated by an occasional gunshot. The children were beginning to settle down, but the women eyed one another
nervously. They knew that there were not many
Crows and that everything would be all right in the
end, but that did not mean that one of their own
might not be wounded, perhaps even killed. They
would not stop worrying until the attack was beat-
en back and all the men were home safe.

Curly walked over to his mother and stood
beside her, then knelt on her lap, resting his head
on her shoulder. His fingers played idly with the
flap, but he made no attempt to open it. White Deer
stroked his head and cooed in his ear. Some day,
not that far off, he would be out there with the
men, and she would have to worry whether he
would come back.

Watching him, the joy bright in his eyes, his face
curled into a grin, she understood that he would
relish it. For a while.

# Chapter 3

CURLY CONTINUED TO GROW in ways that amazed the members of his father's band. Crazy Horse himself was the most amazed of them all, but he was used to being amazed, to seeing things he could not understand. This led to a kind of serenity in the face of the astounding, one that was rooted not in submission, but in acceptance. There were more things on earth and in the heavens than any one man could possibly understand. Resistance would be of no use, so one learned, if one were wise, to nod and go on with his life. Crazy Horse had done it a thousand times and, if he lived long enough, would do it a thousand more. So, watching his extraordinary son was not something for which he was not prepared.

The boy was nearly eight now, and Crazy Horse sat on a low rise, watching the camp below, his son playing a game with several other boys. It involved one boy, with nerves of steel, holding over his head a huge lobe of cactus out of which the center had been cut. The rest of the boys were armed with bows, small but not toys, and blunted arrows. The boy who held the cactus raced around the village

while the others fired their arrows at him almost as
fast as they could fit them to the string and draw it
back.

The object, of course, was to put an arrow
through the heart of the cactus lobe. But it was the
responsibility of the cactus bearer to make that as
difficult as possible. In the process, he would take
a constant pelting. Arrow after arrow would slam
into his cheeks and head, his shoulders and chest
and back. He was besieged from all sides as the
boys swirled around him, launching volley after
volley. His only solace was the knowledge that, if
someone did manage to hit the bull's-eye, the cactus bearer was free to chase the marksman all over
the village, slapping his buttocks with the cactus.
The lucky marksman would then get to spend several hours yanking the painful spines from his tender parts.

Crazy Horse remembered Curly playing the same
game four or five years before. He had just made
the boy his first bow. Only four years old, Curly
had been watching the older boys with their bows,
and every day would ask when he would have one
of his own.

"You are too young yet, Curly," Crazy Horse
would say. "Wait until you have the strength to
pull back the bowstring. Then I will make you a
bow."

"When?"

"Soon."

"How soon? Tomorrow?"

It had gone on like that every day for nearly a
month. Each day Curly would have a different reason for needing the bow, and each day Crazy Horse

would put him off. It was the first thing on the boy's mind in the morning, and the last thing out of his mouth at night. He would even ask White Deer to ask Crazy Horse when he felt his father was avoiding the issue. Finally, when she could stand it no more, White Deer took Crazy Horse aside.

"I think you should make Curly a bow," she said.

Crazy Horse shook his head. "I keep telling him that he is not ready. I'll make it when he's older."

"He thinks he's ready now."

"I don't think so."

"But until Curly understands that, none of us will have any peace. All day long he asks. He asks everyone he sees who is older than he is. And the other children he tells that he will have a bow that very afternoon. I'm afraid that he will get a bow from someone else. One of the men will make him one just to quiet him. But his first bow should come from you, Crazy Horse. It should come from his father."

The holy man shook his head again, this time in bewildered resignation. He knew his wife was right. Looking back on it now, he couldn't understand why he hadn't seen it sooner, but he hadn't.

Even then, in the back of his mind was the thought that maybe Curly knew something his father didn't. Maybe the boy was ready. Maybe he was ready and he was the only one who realized it.

They had been camped near the Powder River. It was the middle of summer, and the days were long, the sun hanging in the sky off in the west as if reluctant to go down. After the evening meal, he swung Curly up onto his shoulder and grabbed one of the white man's tools, a double-bladed ax, its handle shortened to hatchet length for easy transport, and to lighten the load of carrying it from place to place. When you moved your home and all your worldly possessions on a regular basis, you learned where to cut corners, how to economize.

He ducked under the flap and out into the evening air. Curly, sensing that something important was about to happen, fidgeted on his father's shoulders, his feet tattooing the man's chest, his fists pounding excitedly on Crazy Horse's head.

"Where are we going, Father?" Curly asked.

"You'll see, Curly," Crazy Horse told him. "Just be patient."

Crazy Horse walked toward a small creek that canted to the southwest and flowed into the Powder River. Its banks were lined with stands of cottonwood, and beyond it, a small clump of trees sat in a shallow bowl-shaped depression. More trees were scattered beyond it, on the hillside.

Crazy Horse waded across the creek and headed for the trees. He held the ax with the blade cradled in his fingers, the handle splitting them into pairs. In time to his stride, he tapped the shortened handle against the side of his knee. The boy squirmed so that he almost slipped from his perch, and Crazy Horse was forced to grab him by the feet and hold on.

When he reached the trees, he swung the boy to the ground. Then, almost as if he were alone, he moved from tree to tree, paying particular attention to the smaller ones, the saplings. He tested several, grabbing the trunks above his head and tugging, then letting go, testing for elasticity.

"What are you doing, Father?" Curly asked.

"Looking for a tree, Curly," his father answered.

"There are trees all over the hillside."

"I don't want just any tree. I am looking for a special one."

"Why?"

"You'll see."

The boy darted from tree to tree, touching each with an open palm. "This one? Is this it? This one?" After each question, he would turn to wait for his father's answer and, when it was a negative shake of the head, he would bounce to the next and the next and the one after that.

Watching Crazy Horse, Curly realized that size was a consideration, and soon he touched only saplings. But the holy man was looking not just for a sapling, but an ash sapling. He wanted one that was strong but resilient. He wanted it to be thick enough to contain the perfect bow, but not so thick that the wood would be too hard and too brittle.

Finally, testing one particular ash a third time, leaning into it with all his weight and then letting it go to spring back, he said, "This is the one."

Making sure the boy was out of harm's way, he knelt beside the sapling and began to hack at it. The thud of the ax as it dug into the strong, springy wood seemed to echo among the taller trees, the sound of the blows drifting up, down, and across the hillside and bouncing back from every direction. He could smell the sweet sap now, and chips of wood flew with every bite of the blade.

Soon, he had cut almost all the way through. Still on his knees, he moved around to the opposite side for the last few swings of the ax. The young ash quivered with every blow now, and started to lean. Then, as the blade cut all the way through, the force of the blow pushing the butt of the severed sapling off its base, it thumped to the ground, teetered for a moment, then fell with a swish of its leaves.

The tree was a good one, and Crazy Horse knew he could make more than one bow from the wood, so he measured a length almost eight feet from the butt to the point where the sapling began to get too thin for his purpose, and cut it all the way through.

Lopping off a few short, slender branches little more than shoots, he hefted the eight-foot length of ash. It was heavy, which meant the wood was dense and strong, and then got to his feet. Hoisting the sapling to his shoulder, he called to Curly, who had wandered off among the trees. The boy came scurrying back, stuck his small hand in his father's large palm and smiled when the man's fingers curled over his own.

Crazy Horse took his time on the way back to the village, letting the boy waddle along beside him, his short legs taking three and four steps for every one of his father's. When they reached the creek, Crazy Horse let Curly find his own way across the stones, only once hauling the small boy up when he lost his footing.

White Deer was in front of the tipi when her husband and son returned. She saw the sapling over Crazy Horse's shoulder, but said nothing, in case he hadn't told Curly what it was for. She smiled, and Curly noticed, quickly glancing up at his father for a second, as if to catch some secret meaning on the wing.

Setting the sapling on the ground, Crazy Horse knelt to cut it into two unequal lengths, the smaller for Curly's bow, the larger for his own. Ducking into the lodge, he hauled both pieces of ash with him, set them by the fire, and put away the ax.

He said nothing to Curly, and did not look up, knowing that the boy's curiosity would draw him inside sooner or later. Sitting cross-legged, he took the shorter piece of ash and began to pare away the bark. The process would take several days, perhaps even as much as two weeks, and he hoped that Curly, once he realized what was happening, would find the patience to simply watch and wait.

It was important that the wood dry evenly, and getting the bark out of the way would facilitate the process. He stripped both pieces, then turned his attention to the short one. Turning it over in his hands, he eyed its length, hefted it, balanced it on the surface of one upturned finger, feeling for the inner balance, trying to find the perfect point for the center, where the grip would be carved.

Balance was everything in handling a bow. The movement necessary meant that the bow must function as an extension of its owner's body, move precisely where and how it was supposed to. A fraction of an inch at the point of release would translate into several feet at long range, so accuracy meant that nothing could be left to chance.

Over the next two weeks, Crazy Horse worked both pieces of ash every day, leaving them by the fire, not too close, but close enough, all day long, and taking his steel-bladed white man's knife to the wood every night. Slowly but surely, the shape began to emerge. Curly had not bothered him once, as if he were certain what was happening to the ash.

The holy man remembered his own father telling him that the bow was already in the wood. It was up to the warrior to find it, to cut away all that was not the bow from the bow itself. Only in that way would the weapon be as perfect as it could be and must be. He thought of his father's words as he smoothed the wood, making sure not to pare away too much, coaxing the perfect curves out of the ash.

When Curly's bow was almost done, Crazy Horse pulled the boy onto his lap and held it out to him. He watched as the boy grasped it almost precisely, his short fingers curling around the grip. He adjusted the fingers, then watched as Curly moved the nearly completed bow from side to side, turning his wrist this way and that, the ash almost whispering in the quiet.

Taking it back, Crazy Horse pared a little more away from the grip, then set the small bow on the ground to finish carving the larger one.

That night, when Curly was asleep, Crazy Horse stayed up late, working with a small brush of horsehair, painting the curves of both bows. The front of each was daubed a bright yellow, the inner curve a softer blue. Then, taking the smaller bow in hand, he wrapped the grip in strips of deer hide. He did the same for the larger, and now had a pair, identical in every attribute but length.

Thinking back on it now, it seemed as if it were a lifetime ago. Four winters. Not much, maybe, but when any given day can see life end, impaled on a Pawnee shaft or ground to bloody gristle under the hooves of the buffalo, four years was eternity and then some.

Now, he smiled, watching his son send an arrow through the cactus heart then run, his hands cupped over his buttocks as the boy with the target chased after him, flailing the spiny weapon closer and closer. He looked up then to see White Deer, also watching Curly run for his life.

"Do you remember his first bow?" he asked.

The sad smile she returned told him more than he wanted to know. She remembered the first, and hoped not to live to see the last.

Sighing, Crazy Horse prayed her wish would be granted. Then he said another for himself.

# Chapter 4

**August 1850**

As CURLY GREW OLDER, he found himself spending
more and more time with another boy a few years
older than himself. Named, like almost all Sioux
children, for an aspect of his physical appearance,
the boy was called High Backbone, or Hump, for
short. As they mastered some of the arts of the
Sioux warrior, or so they thought, Curly and Hump
spent more and more time together, wandering farther from the village with each passing month.

Each fed the courage of the other, and their natural curiosity, drawing them into the world outside
the village, seemed to goad them both into behavior
that neither would have risked on his own. Each of
the boys knew that his play with his friend had a
serious purpose. It was training for the harsh and
unforgiving existence that would be their lot for the
rest of their lives.

Armed with bows and quivers made from bobcat
skins, they were learning to understand the world
around them in the only way that really counted—
by direct experience. No amount of firelight story-
telling by the older women, even tales of Wakan
Tanka, the Great Spirit that oversaw the universe,

and cautionary parables about Iktomi, the Trickster, enlightening as they were, could be a substitute for following the zigzagging flight of a rabbit through the buffalo grass, or tracking a coyote to its lair.

Crazy Horse, as a Wicasa Wakan, as the holy men were called, saw the world of the Plains in a broader context, the way all holy men did. To him, each blade of grass had meaning, every pellet in a mound of rabbit droppings had its own significance, a role to play in the great cycles of life and death, the wheels within wheels on which the great plains revolved, taking the Sioux with them on every revolution.

Every night, after the evening meal, Crazy Horse would sit by the fire and ask Curly what he had seen during the day. Curly had a sharp eye, and never failed to have noticed something he had never seen before. Eagerly, he would tell his father everything. Then Crazy Horse would question the boy on what it meant. Sometimes, it was nothing more than an observation of clouds and what kind of weather they might foretell. Other times, it might be some trick played by a *heyoka* on one of the members of the *tiyospe*. The *heyoka* were special people, the clowns of the tribe, but more often than not there was a point to their tricks. Like Shakespearean fools, they always meant something by what they said and did, but it was left to the others to figure it out if they could.

Slowly and steadily, the way a tree grows imperceptibly taller day by day, Curly was getting an education as good as that of anyone in the whole Oglala nation. His mind was curious, but impatient. He jumped from place to place, point to point, zigzagging like a bee in a field of flowers, but sooner or later, as Crazy Horse knew, the boy would pay a visit to every blossom.

The holy man was proud of his son, but frightened for him, too. More than once, he had had a vision, not always the same, but always with the same meaning—Curly was special. Crazy Horse would awaken from one of these dreams with his head spinning. It felt as if the ground were whirling faster and faster beneath him, trying to throw him off. It left him dizzy and a little nauseated. He would feel the cold sweat on his brow, trickling down under his shirt. His breathing would be short and sharp, rasping in his throat. In his ears, his blood beat like thunder and in his chest he could feel the hammering of his heart like an angry fist bashing at the bones that held it prisoner.

And as he would lie there, forcing his breathing back to normal, his hands folded over his chest as if to keep the ribs intact until the heart calmed down, he would try to understand the meaning of the latest dream. Always it centered on Curly, and always its meaning was tantalizing, elusive as a trout in fast water. Curly would achieve great things, for himself and for his people, but he would pay a terrible price. It was never clear what those great things were, and it was never clear what that terrible price might be, only that it was high. The details, Crazy Horse understood, were not meant for him to have, they were for Curly alone.

One day, he knew, his son would wander out into the wilderness and stare at the sky for hours on end, day and night, until Wakan Tanka saw fit to crystallize the vision, make the meaning hard and clear, bright as a bird's eye. And then it would be up to Curly. His son would have to decide whether to accept the weight of the vision with humility or try to fight it off. Such a fight, as Crazy Horse well knew, could not be won, but some men were tempted to try.

Late one summer, when Curly was nine years old, he and Hump, who was almost eleven, followed the tracks of a deer in a forest near the Black Hills. They could see the high peaks of the Paha Sapa in the distance, and the deer was heading that way. Neither boy had seen the deer, but the evidence of the earth was indisputable. The imprints of the hooves were crisp and fresh in the damp earth alongside a creek, where it must have come to drink.

Armed with short bows and the short arrows to match, the two boys followed the tracks deeper into the forest. They knew, by the depth of the prints, that the animal was of good size. And they could tell, by the spacing of the prints, that he was neither frightened nor in a hurry.

The ground was rocky, and the prints were scarce as they started uphill. The slope was long and rather steep. They could not see the Black Hills now, because they were hidden by the ridge above them. Trees, mostly in clumps, were scattered over the hillside, and clusters of large boulders filled many of the open spaces between the stands of trees. Their visibility was as good as they could ask for, but it also gave an advantage to the deer. If they were to get close enough to fire an arrow, they would have to be careful and clever.

Angling across the slope toward the northwest,

they had almost reached the top when Curly
stopped in his tracks. He grabbed Hump by the arm
and hauled him in behind a slab of red rock. Hump
started to argue, but Curly put a finger to his lips
and pointed uphill.

The older boy's jaw went slack when he saw
what his young friend was pointing at. The deer
stood there just beyond a clump of cottonwoods, its
head held high. An enormous rack of antlers
speared the pure blue behind him like the ruins of
an ancient oak.

The buck's ear twitched, and it kept canting its
head to listen. Curly knew it must have heard
something and was trying to decide whether it
should stand and fight or run for its life. The boys
crouched behind the rock, hardly daring to breathe.
They could see sunlight glistening on the damp
nose of the great buck, and when once it turned its
head to look in their direction, its eyes seemed to
be full of fire, where the sunlight reflected from the
huge, dark pupils.

"It's the biggest deer in the world," Hump whispered. The deer seemed to hear even the whisper,
and looked sharply in their direction once more.

Curly clamped a hand over Hump's mouth to
keep him quiet.

At the deer's feet, tall clumps of lush grass
tempted it, and it shook its head, snorting once
before lowering it to graze. Now, even the sharp
tips of the antlers reflected the sunlight, and it
looked to Curly as if lightning were spearing out
from every point.

"I think I can get close enough to shoot him,"
Hump whispered.

Curly shook his head no, but Hump ignored
him. He started to ease out from behind the rock,
and trying to stop him would make too much
noise, so Curly let him go. Since staying where he
was would do no good, he followed Hump, taking
care to place his moccasined feet carefully. Even a
small stone dislodged would make a clatter as it
rolled away, and the deer was already nervous.

Hump worked his way across the hillside, heading for some scrub oak tangled in among a clump of
boulders. If he could reach the cover without
spooking the deer, he would be close enough at
least to try. Already, Hump had three arrows
clutched in his left hand against the bow grip.
Curly knew that the best warriors could fire four,
five, even six arrows so rapidly that the last one
would already be arcing toward the target before
the first one hit.

Hump was good, but not that good. Curly was
better, but he didn't want to shoot the deer in the
first place, so he left his own arrows in their quiver.

When the boys reached the cover, Hump
dropped to his knees and turned to look at his companion. Leaning close, he mouthed the words, "I
think I can hit him from here."

Once more, Curly shook his head. Soundlessly,
he replied, "No. The deer is *wakan*."

"The deer is not holy," Hump insisted. "He is
just a deer. I will bring him down, and then you
will see. If he were *wakan*, I would not be able to
kill him."

Curly nodded, as if in resignation, but that
wasn't what he meant and Hump knew it. But it
didn't deter him. He fitted the first arrow to his

bowstring, then started to rise up from behind the branches of a short oak.

Curly could see the deer, and it seemed as if the animal were waiting for something. It shook its head, snorted, and pawed the ground. The clack of its hooves on the rocks sounded like gunshots, and Hump jumped a little, then gave Curly an embarrassed smile over his shoulder.

"I'm nervous," he said.

"You are right to be nervous," Curly told him. His own smile was more forlorn.

Hump turned back to the buck who was now staring straight downhill toward the boys' hiding place. Hump froze for a moment, his arm pulling back the bowstring until the arrowhead was right against the grip. As he stood up, his arms trembled from the strain of holding the bow at full draw.

With a sudden hum, the string snapped forward and the arrow sped uphill. The buck seemed to watch it, and made no attempt to evade the arrow. It struck his antlers with a sharp crack, then disappeared over the hilltop.

Still, the buck didn't bolt. It continued to stare at the brush where the boys were hidden, took a tentative step in that direction, then stopped. Once more, Hump notched an arrow. This time, he let it fly. The bowstring sang and the arrowhead flashed in the sunlight as it sailed past the buck, passing to its right and sinking into the ground just behind its rear legs. Curly could see the upper half of the shaft and the bright red feathers.

The buck looked at the arrow for a moment, then back downhill. Hump fired a third arrow, and this one fell short.

Curly began to relax, thinking that the buck, whether or not it was truly *wakan*, had nothing to fear from Hump. Suddenly, the buck charged downhill, straight toward them. Hump, caught reaching for a fourth arrow, gave a shout and broke into the open. He was running downhill, the buck thundering behind him and rapidly gaining ground.

Without thinking, Curly notched an arrow, drew and fired, a second arrow already under his fingers as the first struck the buck in the chest. Hump was screaming and the buck was closing. Already, it was almost even with Curly, who aimed and fired his second arrow. It struck the buck with a wet thwacking sound, sank in almost to the feathers, and the buck's knees buckled and it fell to the ground, where it skidded. It turned to look at Curly, its nostrils foaming and bright red blood flecking its lathered lips. It gave a sigh, then its head fell forward and rolled to one side, until the great rack of antlers stopped it.

Hump was already scrambling back up the hill. "That was my deer," he shouted. "You shouldn't have shot him."

"You tried," Curly said. "He would have run you down if I didn't shoot him."

"It was my deer," Hump said again.

"Take it, then. I give it to you."

"I don't want it."

"He is dead because of you. You can't leave him there. It is wasteful."

"I don't want him anymore."

Without a word, Hump turned and stalked downhill, leaving Curly to stare after him in bewilderment. "Hump," he called, "come back!"

But Hump ignored him. He started to run, heading back toward the village. Curly called again and again, but his voice just echoed from the hillside and died away to a whisper. Finally, when he understood that Hump was not coming back, he started after him, his short legs jolting with every step as he ran down the hill.

Hump had a big lead, and the older boy's longer legs were widening the gap with every stride.

By the time the village came into view, Hump had disappeared. Curly, crying now, ran to his tipi. Crazy Horse was sitting by the fire, playing with Little Hawk, his younger son, two years Curly's junior.

He noticed the tears streaming down Curly's face, but said nothing, preferring to wait for the boy to tell him what was wrong.

But Curly said nothing. He went to the farthest recess of the lodge and lay down on his stomach, his face buried against the buffalo skin sheathing of the tipi.

Crazy Horse got to his feet and set Little Hawk on the ground. Patting the boy's head, he told him he would be back shortly, then walked over to sit beside Curly.

"Do you want to tell me what's wrong?"

Curly shook his head and refused to look at his father. "Nothing," he mumbled.

"Then why are you crying?"

Curly didn't answer.

"Was Hump crying for the same reason when he came home? I saw him go past a little before you came in."

Curly turned then and sat up. He looked at his

father, wiped his cheeks with the back of one hand, and nodded.

"What happened?"

He told his father about the deer. "And I thought it was *wakan*."

"Why?" Crazy Horse asked.

"Its antlers were full of fire, like lightning. It knew we were there and yet it was not afraid."

"Does that make it *wakan*?"

"Yes."

The holy man nodded. "Perhaps there were two deer, then," Crazy Horse suggested.

Curly shook his head. "No. There was just one."

"Are you sure?"

Curly nodded. "Yes. I killed it. I saw it there on the ground. There was just one."

"And where is this deer now? Show me." He stood up, extended his hand, and waited for Curly to get to his feet.

Together, they walked back to the hill. "Up there," Curly said, pointing.

"Show me."

Curly tugged his father's hand and pulled him up hill toward where the deer had fallen.

When they got there, the rocky hillside was empty. The buck was gone. Curly looked at his father in bafflement. "It was here. I saw it. It looked at me when it fell. Then it died."

"There is no blood."

"But . . ."

"Each man sees his own thing. The world is full of many strange things, Curly. Wakan Tanka has many faces. This deer had one for you and one for Hump. To him it was just a deer. A big one, but only a deer. For you, it was something else. More than a deer."

"What, then?"

Crazy Horse shrugged. "One day we will know."

"Hump is very angry."

"He will not stay angry long. Not at you. You and Hump are special friends. Like brothers. As close as brothers, but different. Hump is your *kola*. And you are Hump's *kola*. The anger will pass."

Curly was quiet for a long time. Crazy Horse did not want to break the silence. When the boy finally spoke again, he asked, "Do you think the deer was *wakan*?"

"I think so, yes."

"But for me only? I mean, Hump did nothing wrong, wanting to shoot it, did he?"

"No. Hump did nothing wrong."

"And me . . ." he asked, his voice trembling, ". . . did I do something wrong?"

Crazy Horse looked sternly at his older son. Then, with a broad grin, he bent over, snatched him around the waist, and hauled him into his arms. He began to tickle the boy and laughed, "You? Never!"

# Chapter 5 ══════════════

**August 1854**

IN THE SUMMER OF 1845, when Curly was four years
old, white soldiers came to the Sioux lands for the
first time. Led by Col. Stephen Kearny, they had
been dispatched to provide reassurance to the
increasing numbers of settlers who were heading
across the plains for Oregon. Kearny's mandate was
simple—make certain the Sioux knew they would
be punished if they continued to harass the wagon
trains. He was to use friendly persuasion, if possible, but to make known the position of the U.S.
government no matter what it took to do so.

Kearny sent out runners to establish contact
with the Oglalas, and advise them that he wanted
to meet with them on the Laramie River. The desig-
nated rendezvous point was not far from a trading
post established back in 1834 by William Sublette
and christened Fort William. Since Sublette had
chosen his site with an eye to trading, he had
picked a place the Sioux and other plains Indians
had been using for years for their trade meetings,
not only with the whites, but with other Indians
long before the first white man had ever seen the
Laramie.

Kearny had been unequivocal. The white settlers on the Oregon Trail were to be left alone. The Oglala chiefs agreed, but since individual warriors were free to do whatever they wanted, and since stealing horses was a way of life, Kearny's warning had little real impact on the growing friction.

At the time, Curly's family was traveling with a band led by Old Smoke, an Oglala chief who had become enamored of the white man's trading post, principally because he had come to savor the taste of coffee. Supplies could be taken from wagon trains at gunpoint, and often were, but it was easier, and far safer, to frequent Fort William, where it could be had for the asking, part of the price the white men were willing to pay for being unmolested.

But the white men had brought other things, as well—smallpox, measles and, worst of all, cholera. In 1849, an epidemic of cholera took the lives of fully one-half of the Northern Cheyenne nation and hundreds of Sioux. A wave of smallpox took hundreds of additional Sioux and Cheyenne lives in the next few months.

To escape the plague, the Sioux headed north, away from the Platte River country and up into Dakota Territory. As they approached the White River, Curly was riding with a small band of young warriors when they sighted a large Sioux camp. As the warriors approached, they realized the valley was unnaturally quiet. The tipis stood silent. No smoke curled up through the flaps of the lodges. No dogs barked. Nothing moved.

One of the older warriors rode on ahead, calling out to the inhabitants. The rest of the band was not that far behind, now. The warriors' shouts seemed

to be swallowed up, and in their place was only the
sound of the river lapping at the stones. Again he
called, and again there was no answer.

The young warriors dismounted, leaving their
horses in the charge of three or four of the
youngest, Curly among them. All calling out, the
young Sioux spread out among the tipis. Still, there
was nothing but silence in response. A deathly
stillness gripped the warriors now. Curly could see
them looking at one another, their faces confused,
their bodies slack, as if something had sucked out
the bones, leaving them sacs of blood and meat.

One of the warriors ducked down to enter a
tipi. The others watched. Seconds later, they
heard a scream that curdled their blood. For a
long moment, nothing happened. Suddenly, the
warrior backed out of the tipi and ran to a second,
then a third. The others, frozen in place, watched
him, motionless as if they had been rooted to the
earth. Only when he left the third lodge, did they
begin to move again. Curly ran forward, ignoring
Hump's call to come back. Little Hawk, too, sat
his horse, calling after his brother, but Curly paid
no attention.

He ducked into the first tipi he reached. And he
screamed. The stench overwhelmed him, and he
felt his stomach begin to churn. It was as if some
demon were trying to claw its way into his gut
through his nostrils.

Backing out, he looked at Hump, his head shaking, his body beginning to tremble all over. For a
moment, he thought he would be unable to stand,
and caught himself on the verge of crumbling into a
heap on the ground.

He ran back to the horses. Hump jumped down from his mount. "What is it," he asked, "What's wrong?"

"They're dead," Curly said. "All of them."

As abruptly as if someone had sounded a silent signal, all the young warriors raced away from the silent camp, their faces drawn, their mouths slack. No one spoke as they mounted up. When they were all back on their ponies, they exploded in unison, wheeling as one and thundering back up the hill toward the main body of the group.

Old Smoke was at the head of the column as the young warriors roared across the plains toward him, screeching war whoops and shrieking in terror.

The old chief rode ahead to meet them. Some thundered on by, unwilling to stop even there, miles from the village of the dead. But Curly, Hump, and Little Hawk reined in. Old Smoke waited patiently for the story to emerge. When he realized that disease, either cholera or smallpox, had wiped out an entire village, he gave orders for a change of direction. The members of the *akicitas* rode along the straggling column, informing the marchers that they would have to go still farther. They would make a wide detour around the silent village, putting as much distance as possible between themselves and the scene of so much death.

When they finally found a place to camp, north of the Black Hills, the warriors were angry. Some said the diseases were deliberately being spread by the whites. Tales were circulated of blankets being infected with the white man's magic then passed among the Cheyenne. Others didn't bother with such niceties. They simply swore revenge and vowed that they would not permit another white face to cross the plains in safety.

Within two years, the diseases had all but disappeared, but the death toll had been awful, and the Sioux were as angry as they had been at the height of the epidemics. And there were more whites than ever on the Plains. Agents of the government seemed to be everywhere, and settlers flowed in increasing numbers, almost a flood now. Raids on the wagon trains had continued, but some Sioux wanted nothing to do with the whites, not even vengeance.

On orders from the new Indian Commissioner, David Mitchell, the agents tracked down every band they could find to tell them that the Great Father in Washington had a message for them. He wanted peace, they said, and promised that it would be worth their while. There was to be a great council at a new fort on the Laramie River, not far from Fort William, called Fort Laramie.

By August 1851, more than ten thousand Plains Indians had gathered at the fort. Not only Sioux attended, but Shoshoni, Cheyenne, and Crow also put in an appearance. There had never been a larger gathering of Indians on the Plains. None of the old men could remember such a council.

The soldiers at the fort were awed by the huge gathering. For the first time, many of them began to be afraid. They had had no idea that there were so many warriors out there all, so far as they knew or cared, bloodthirsty savages upon whose whims the fate of all white men depended. When they looked around the fort, its rows of buildings open on all sides, surrounded only by adobe walls that looked too feeble for their purpose, they couldn't help but wish they had the safety of a stockade, like Fort William, to interpose between themselves and their charges.

For the Sioux, too, it was a revelation. All of them, but especially the young, had a chance to meet deadly enemies without fear. They were free to play games, to stage mock raids on one another's camps. Despite the language barrier, communication was no problem. Sign language more than compensated for the disparity in tongues.

And the gathering had one primary purpose—to make absolutely certain that the Oregon Trail would not be cut. In order for this to happen, the whites were prepared to make concessions. They would make cash payments to each of the tribes, and agree to present them with huge quantities of trade goods on an annual basis. In exchange, the Sioux and Crow, the Cheyenne and the Shoshoni, would agree not to wage war on the wagon trains, and, a new wrinkle, not to wage war on each other. Intertribal violence was a surefire incitement to continued aggression against the whites, and the government agents were wise enough to understand it.

But the undertaking of the council was sabotaged by the paltry understanding of Plains Indian customs held by the whites. Not only did they not understand the relations between tribes, they also failed to understand the lines of authority, and especially the limits of that authority, within each tribe.

Used to negotiating with kings and diplomats, men authorized to speak for entire nations, they expected the Sioux and the Cheyenne to deal the same way. When Mitchell learned that there was no head chief of the Sioux, he decided to create one. For reasons that no one seemed to understand, he settled on Conquering Bear.

Conquering Bear was a Brule, and a distinguished warrior, but he could no more speak for all the Sioux than he could speak for all the Brule. That wasn't how things worked, but the whites were determined to make it so.

So, after a month of discussions, the chiefs meeting almost daily with Mitchell and the agents, agreement was reached. On the day the treaty was to be signed, all the chiefs, one for each of the tribes represented, appeared at the center of the huge gathering. Each of them wore the uniform of a U.S. Army general, complete with braid and a gilt sword. The military regalia was made somewhat incongruous, however, because the chiefs had elected to make their appearance in full war paint. One by one, the chiefs stepped forward to make their marks on the white man's paper. Without realizing it, they were committing their people to terms that none could live by.

But the piece of paper satisfied the representatives of the Great Father, and was duly taken back to Washington. The tribes went their respective ways, and things returned to normal. The warriors continued to raid the wagon trains, stealing cattle and horses, extorting sugar, coffee, and whatever else caught their fancy in exchange for safe passage, the same train often being hit three and four times before reaching the Northwest and the friendlier domains of the Nez Percé, Yakima, and Umatilla.

Curly, like any young Sioux just coming into his manhood, rode on his share of raids. In addition to his *kola*, Hump, he rode often with his brother, Little Hawk, and another young man called Lone Bear.

By now, Crazy Horse and his family were part of the band led by Man Afraid of His Horses. In Sioux, the chief's name meant that he was so fearsome a warrior that his enemies were frightened even of his ponies. Since his son, a few years older than Curly and also Curly's friend, had the same name, the chief was called Old Man Afraid and his son Young Man Afraid. For three years, the Sioux drifted across the plains, following the buffalo, which already were beginning to decrease in numbers as the whites passing through had taken to shooting them for sport and letting the carcasses of the great beasts rot in the sun.

Time after time, a hunting party would crest a rise only to find itself staring down into a valley of bones, the great racks of ribs looking like the beached ruins of long dead ships. Sometimes they would come upon a killing ground soon after the slaughter. They could see the sky peppered by buzzards and other carrion eaters and, when they drew close enough, smell the stink of the rotting carcasses.

Old Man Afraid, like most of the other Sioux chiefs, was unhappy with the wanton slaughter, but reluctant to confront the army in order to make an issue of it. He believed, as did most of the chiefs, that there were enough buffalo that his people could continue their way of life forever.

But things were changing more rapidly than the Sioux understood. The troops at Fort Laramie were growing more and more restless, even cocky. The soldiers who had seen the great council of 1851, with its thousands of warriors, were long gone. Their places had been taken by new men, who, if they had seen Sioux at all, had seen only small groups, and those tame Indians who were called Loaf About the Forts.

By 1854, there were many who believed that the Sioux and the other plains tribes were too backward a foe to pose much of a threat. That the belief was widely held in the upper echelons of the army could be discerned by the men the high command chose to govern the western plains.

In August, when Old Man Afraid and his band arrived at Fort Laramie, its command officer was Hugh Fleming, a twenty-eight-year-old lieutenant. His second was another lieutenant named John L. Grattan, who was fond of his whiskey, as were most of the soldiers in such lonely outposts and, when in his cups, Grattan was even fonder of boasting what he could do to the Sioux if given half a chance.

"With twenty men and a single field piece," he liked to say, "I could ride through the entire Sioux nation." It might have been an admirable courage the young officer possessed, but wisdom was not one of his outstanding qualities. Fleming was not much better. Neither man understood much of the customs of the people they were meant to supervise.

On August 17, Curly and Hump were returning from a hunt, trailing behind a Mormon wagon train wending its way toward Fort Laramie for a rest and some supplies before continuing on its way west. At the tail end of the train, one would-be settler was walking beside his wagon, driving a lame cow along with assorted yips and an occasional crack of a riding crop on its emaciated flanks. The young men were amused by the settler's actions, and rooting for the cow.

As the train moved past a Sioux village a couple of miles from the fort, the cow, spooked by something or tired of the beating it was taking, broke away from its irate owner and shambled toward the tipis. One of the young warriors, a man by the name of High Forehead, snatched up his bow and, as the cow was about to run through the village, downed it with a single arrow. Hump led a mock charge past the wagon train, frightening all the settlers, and provoking the owner of the cow, who began to shout and curse.

Most of the Sioux ignored him, and those few who didn't were amused by the man's anger and evident frustration. Hump and a couple of the others ran him off, and he sprinted after the wagon train, which hadn't even bothered to slow down. They were still laughing when he disappeared into the cloud of dust kicked up by the wagons.

The following day, it became evident that Lieutenant Fleming did not share the Sioux amusement at the settler's expense. He sent for Conquering Bear. The old chief, annoyed by what he considered foolishness, sent a messenger to tell Fleming that he would not come.

Fleming sent a message in return, insisting that Conquering Bear come into the fort, and that he bring the offending warrior with him.

Conquering Bear, realizing that Fleming would not rest until the matter was disposed of, went into the fort and asked to see Fleming.

Through an interpreter, he said, "I don't understand what all the argument is about. It was a lame cow, good for nothing. Not even a white man could find meat on its bones. It was scrawny and useless. Besides, it did not belong in our village. Children were playing in front of the lodges. They could have been hurt."

Fleming got right to the point. "Did you bring High Forehead with you?"

The old chief shook his head. "No, I did not."

"I want him arrested. If you don't bring him in, I'll have to come and get him."

"That is crazy. Show me the man who owned the cow. I will take him to my herd and he can pick out any horse he wants. That is more than enough payment for so sad a cow. The worst horse in my herd would pay for ten such cows. I will make an even exchange."

"You can't buy me off that easily, Chief. Your man did something wrong and he has to pay for it."

"He did nothing wrong."

"He killed an animal that did not belong to him. How would you like it if the man went to your herd and killed one of your horses?"

Conquering Bear was at a loss. "I can't give you High Forehead."

"Why not? Has he run away? Then tell me where he went. I'll go get him myself."

"No, he has not run off. I don't have the right to give him up. He is a Miniconjou. I am a Brule."

"But you're the chief of all the Sioux . . ."

"I am Brule. He is Miniconjou."

"Chief, I'll give you twenty-four hours. You have him here tomorrow, or I will see to it that he comes in, whether you like it or not. And I don't give a damn which way it is. You understand?"

The old chief said nothing. Instead, he turned and left Fleming's office, wondering how things could have gotten so far out of hand. He mounted his horse and rode back to the village, knowing that something was about to happen that he could not prevent. When he explained to the other chiefs and warriors what Fleming had said, many of them wanted to attack the fort. Old Man Afraid, though, counseled patience. Conquering Bear, too, urged them to be calm.

The following morning, Lieutenant Grattan got his chance to ride through the whole Sioux nation, or at least, a small part of it. At the moment, there were more than six hundred lodges in the area, more than a thousand warriors, and they were in no mood for Grattan's abuse. On the way to Conquering Bear's camp, Grattan stopped at the trading post. James Bordeaux, the trader, was known to the Sioux. They trusted him, and he was fluent in their language.

Bordeaux greeted the lieutenant coolly. "Good morning," he said. "I see you are prepared for war."

Grattan waved grandly. "Thirty-one men. That's all I need. I got a field piece and a mountain howitzer. We'll get the job done."

"You're a goddamned fool, Lieutenant. It was just a cow. Forget about it."

Grattan bristled. "Look, if it matters to you so much, why don't you come along. You can interpret. Maybe it'll help."

"You don't need help. You need to go home and think about what you're doing, Lieutenant. You are about to make a very big mistake."

"I can handle anything that comes along, Bordeaux. With you or without you."

"Does Lieutenant Fleming know what you're doing?"

Grattan nodded. "He knows."

"Then you're both fools."

"I take it you won't come along . . . ?"

"Hell no, I won't come along. And if you know what's good for . . ."

"Savages, Bordeaux. Undisciplined savages. Do you really think they can stand . . ."

"Have you ever seen the Sioux fight, Lieutenant?"

Grattan hesitated for a moment, before answering. "No, I haven't."

"Have you ever seen combat of any kind?"

Grattan shook his head.

"Well, you go ahead with this, and you'll see more than you want to. Talk to me afterward."

The men were getting restless, and Grattan was afraid that Bordeaux's words might inhibit them. Brusquely, he remounted. "I'll see you this afternoon. And I think Lieutenant Fleming will not be happy you refused to help."

"Fleming can go to hell." He turned and went back into the trading post.

Grattan pushed on. He passed a large Oglala camp on his way to Conquering Bear's Brule village. All the Oglala ponies had been brought in. If he noticed, he didn't understand the significance. The Oglala were ready for war. Young Man Afraid, son of the chief, and himself a warrior of rising influence, rode along with the soldiers. On the way, he tried to convince Grattan that there would be trouble. Auguste Lucien, the Frenchman who was to serve as interpreter, kept shouting insults at the Sioux warriors as they rode past the Oglala lodges. Between shouts, he drank from a bottle of whiskey. Another bottle was being passed among the soldiers.

Grattan listened to Young Man Afraid, but waved off his warnings. "I will have High Forehead in the jail, or I will die trying."

"There are many Sioux," Young Man Afraid said. "Too many for you."

Grattan shook his head. "No, not too many. It will work out. Just make sure that the Oglala stay out of it if a fight starts." Lucien was babbling his interpretations, and neither Grattan nor Young Man Afraid was convinced the other was being told his words exactly.

By the time they reached the Brule camp, a large open circle at the foot of a small bluff, most of the warriors had hidden themselves in the trees under the bluff. Conquering Bear came out to meet Grattan. It was obvious that he wanted to prevent trouble.

"Why all the fuss?" he asked. "It was a lame cow, no good to anybody."

Grattan said, "I want High Forehead. If you won't bring him to me, tell me where he is."

Some of the Sioux standing behind the chief said

that High Forehead had gone, but one man pointed
to a lodge and said, "There. That is his tipi."

Again and again, Conquering Bear tried to talk
Grattan out of his purpose, but the lieutenant was
adamant. All the while, Lucien kept riding back
and forth behind the soldiers, shouting insults and
threats at the Sioux. Grattan seemed to sense that
trouble was brewing, but he didn't know how to get
out of it.

He ordered his men to aim and to fire on his
command. A messenger sent to High Forehead's
lodge returned with word that the Miniconjou had
five men with him, and they were all prepared to
fight, even to die, if necessary.

Conquering Bear once more offered to pay for
the cow with horses from his own herd, but Grattan
would not be put off. The chief, realizing that the
chance of avoiding a fight had gone, turned to walk
away. At that moment, one of the troopers fired,
hitting a warrior in the chest and killing him.

The Miniconjou appeared at the door to High
Forehead's lodge. Grattan ordered his two big guns
fired, and the shells went high, nipping the tips of
some lodge poles, but doing no other damage. The
Miniconjous opened fire then, and Grattan gave the
order to fire. In an instant, a flurry of arrows
poured out of the village. Grattan and four other
soldiers, three of them artillerymen, were hit. At
almost the same moment, the Brule hidden at the
base of the bluff thundered down on the village.

Young Man Afraid looked on in horror, yelling
for the Oglalas to intercede, to help the soldiers
before it was too late.

But there was nothing to be done. The fury of

the Brule had been unleashed. The soldiers turned and ran, but the warriors pursued them on horseback and on foot. The soldiers' single shot rifles were too cumbersome, and almost useless against the speed and deadly accuracy of the Sioux bowmen. Volley after volley of arrows poured into the fleeing troops. One by one they fell.

And then it was over. The village fell strangely silent. Grattan and all thirty-one of his men lay dead. In a frenzy, the Sioux swarmed over the two gun carriages, set them on fire, and destroyed the howitzers.

Conquering Bear had been badly wounded, shot in the back, the leg, and the side. He lay bleeding in the dust for several minutes before the warriors gathered him up and helped him to his tent.

Back at the Oglala village, the warriors, Young Man Afraid and Old Man Afraid at their head, stood silently and watched. Curly and Hump and Little Hawk had gotten their first look at a conflict that would shape the rest of their lives.

# Chapter 6

**September 1854**

AFTER THE FIGHT with Grattan's men, the Sioux
seemed disorganized. Some wanted to ride on the
fort and kill the rest of the soldiers, burn Fort
Laramie to the ground, and take control of the
Plains. Others, frightened that the whites would
just send more and more soldiers, until there were
too many for the Sioux to fight, wanted to stay
where they were. They thought that the Great
Father would understand that what had happened
was not their fault.

The vast majority, though, just wanted to get
away from Fort Laramie. They wanted their lives to
continue as they had always been. If hanging
around the Fort meant dependence on the white
man's goods, then they would leave. They had fed
themselves long before anyone had seen a white
man. They had more than held their own against
the Pawnee and pushed the Crow far enough west
that they had all the breathing room they could
want. There was the beauty of the Paha Sapa and
the wide open expanse of the plains where they
could spend the rest of their lives without ever seeing another white man.

Old Man Afraid, though, knew that something had changed forever. In the first major armed conflict with the whites, the Sioux had won a victory, but it was hollow and, the chief suspected, likely to be shortlived.

The Oglala moved on, and the Brule, too. Curly and his family rode east with the Brule, his mother's people. On the long trek, Conquering Bear continued to suffer from his wounds. Unable to ride, he was borne on a travois. Often, Curly and Hump would ride along behind the gravely wounded chief. Sometimes, at night, they would peek into the chief's lodge. He would be lying there, more often than not asleep, wrapped in a buffalo robe. He was losing weight, wasting away from his wounds. No one wanted to say it aloud, but it was obvious that Conquering Bear was dying.

Confused by the events, upset over Conquering Bear's condition, Curly rode out onto the prairie by himself. He was determined to seek a vision, but he was not playing by the rules. The vision quest was the central event of a Sioux warrior's life. It was what gave him his adult name, and its cryptic intelligence would guide him for the rest of his life, if he were lucky enough to have a vision at all.

In order to be ready, custom required that the young man about to seek his vision receive intensive instruction for many weeks from a holy man. This would prepare his mind to receive the critical information the vision would impart. It was also a prerequisite to undergo a ritual of purification. Since purification was deemed essential before attempting to establish contact with the controlling spirits, the forces in nature and above it that con-

trolled men's lives, a shaman would officiate at a
purifying sweat bath, held in a dome-shaped sweat
lodge built for this purpose. A shaman would
accompany the prospective seeker to supervise the
purification. Fasting was a part of the preparation,
as well.

But Curly was impatient. Desperate for an explanation of the confusing things around him, he
decided to seek his vision on his own. He rode into
the hills of western Nebraska without telling anyone where he was going. Deep in the Sand Hills, he
found a lake, overlooked by a steep hill. Tethering
his horse at the lakeside, giving it enough lead to
feed itself on the thick grasses on the shore, he
climbed the hill until he reached the top, where a
flat table of unbroken stone jutted out toward the
lake far below.

He lay down on the stone and began to fast.
Determined to keep himself awake, he placed sharp
stones under him. The points digging into his back
and shoulders, the backs of his thighs, and his
calves were torture, but they served their purpose.
For two days with no food or water he lay there,
staring at the sun in the daytime and the stars at
night.

On the third day, his body sore, his lips cracked
and his throat parched, he was beginning to fear
that he would not have a vision after all. He began
to worry that his lack of preparation had doomed
his quest. Maybe it wasn't right to seek so powerful
a thing without the right prayers being said. Maybe
he wasn't pure enough. These thoughts, sharper
than any of the stones poking into his flesh, tor-
tured him for the rest of the day.

Getting to his feet, Curly looked at the lake far below. It seemed to shimmer in the sunlight, as if the waters were trying to part, giving birth to something deep beneath the surface. Dejected, he backed away from the rim and started down the hill. His head spun, and as he looked at the sky, the clouds began to swirl. Bright light seemed to pour like liquid out of them, thick waves of it sweeping toward him. The light rippled like the sea of grass far across the lake, shifting, undulating. He shook his head, but the sensation wouldn't leave him.

He stumbled, fell to one knee, and reached out to catch himself. A sharp pain stabbed through his hand, the shock made his elbow buckle, and he gasped with the pain, fell headlong and began to slide over the rocks and gravel. The hiss of sand in his ears was like the voice of a rattler, and he twisted his head from side to side, trying to see where it came from. His arms spread like wings, he clawed at the ground, but kept on sliding.

Halfway down the hill, on a little belly ledge in the slope, he slowed enough to arrest his fall. Rolling onto his back, he looked up to see a man on horseback. The man shimmered, his horse pawing the earth. Curly blinked, trying to clear his vision, but everything looked watery, as if the world were dissolving.

The great horse began to change colors, first a dark roan, then a brilliant, almost silvery gray. It turned dark again, black as night, a white blaze on its forehead, then it turned colors Curly had never seen anywhere, not on a horse, not on a bird's wing or the wings of a butterfly.

The man on horseback said nothing. He was

dressed in plain clothing—unadorned leggings, fringed but otherwise unremarkable, a plain buckskin shirt, unpainted and without even beadwork to relieve the ordinariness of its color. His face was unpainted, and he wore a solitary eagle feather in his hair, which hung long and straight. Light brown in color, it reminded Curly of his own hair. The man turned away for a moment, and Curly noticed a small stone tied behind his ear.

Curly tried to get up, but his body wouldn't work. His joints seemed to have dissolved in his skin, leaving only jelly where the bone had been. Gasping for air, he tried to speak, but the man raised a hand to silence him.

"Don't wear a warbonnet," he said. "When you go into battle, leave your horse's tail untied, free to balance him as he leaps across the stones. Before you ride into battle, sprinkle him with dust, let streams of it glide from your curled fingers in streaks and straight lines. Don't paint your war pony."

"Who . . ." Curly croaked.

But again the man raised a hand, cutting him off. "Rub dirt on your skin and hair. Do these things before every battle, and you will never be killed by an enemy or a bullet. Your people must come first. Take nothing for yourself. Your people will know your worth. Know it yourself. Let them celebrate you. It is not necessary for you to boast or sing of your courage."

As the man spoke, he seemed to be doing battle with ghosts. He wheeled on his horse then and rode as if into battle. Strange blurs and shadows swirled around him, darting close, darkening as if about to become solid, then vanishing when the man waved his hand to chase them off. Arrows swarmed around him in clouds, like angry bees, but none struck him. Bullets sang as they flew past, sometimes close enough to raise the fine hairs on his skin as they passed. Most disappeared as they were about to strike him.

Curly felt his head spinning, his eyes bugging out. His throat was so parched that he could only rasp as he tried once more to speak, trying desperately to call out to the phantom warrior. A new wave of enemies swarmed around the strange man, and one of his own people, no face, just a shadow behind the strange warrior, grabbed his arms from behind, holding him back, preventing him from raising a hand to defend himself.

Thunder cracked then, as if the sky had split in two, the earth about to follow, rumbling beneath Curly, his body swallowing the tremors whole, quaking with the rattling of the earth and with terror. It grew dark, then darker still. Lightning flashed across the dark face of the clouds and it began to storm. Huge drops of water spattered Curly's face, swept in torrents across the sky, almost blurring the man, blotting him out as the wind howled and hail began to rattle on the rocks around him. The man rode past once more, his horse pounding the earth. His face seemed to loom up out of the storm, and Curly saw that it was painted with a single bolt of lightning. A handful of white hail spots was sprinkled on his chest and shoulders.

Then, as suddenly as he had come, he was gone. Curly closed his eyes for a moment, then opened them. He was gasping like a fish, his body sucking air in huge gulps. He closed his eyes again, still listening to the storm as it swirled around him. The clatter of hail was gone, but the hammering of the rain on his chest and skull sounded like drums. He opened his eyes to a brightening sky. A single hawk soared high above him, its cry distant and desperate.

Then everything went black.

When he awoke, his vision was blurred. Great shadows speared the ground beside him as he blinked away the sun. He thought for a moment the rider had come back. As he tried to move his arms, he realized they worked normally, and he pushed himself up. His vision cleared, and he found himself staring into his father's scowl. Hump stood a little behind, as if to be out of reach of his father's wrath.

"What is wrong with you, boy?" his father shouted. "Conquering Bear is dying. You run off where no one can find you, except the Pawnee or the Crow."

Curly swallowed hard. "I was seeking a vision, Father."

"Without purification? Without instruction? Why?"

Curly shook his head. "I don't know. I just wanted . . ."

His father was even angrier now. Curly decided it was better to say nothing of his dream. He got slowly to his feet. His father was already halfway down the hill. Hump tried to hang back, but Curly's father kept calling to them both.

Maybe it was not a good dream, Curly thought. Maybe I will have another one.

All the way back to camp, he debated whether to tell his father what he had seen, but he knew now was not the time. And judging from the look on his father's face, maybe that time would never come.

Two days later, Conquering Bear died, and the Brules wrapped the old chief in a buffalo robe, placed him on a burial scaffold, and left for the fall buffalo hunt. Curly had still said nothing, not even to Hump. He was biding his time. But the more he thought about it, the more he realized that the dream was meant for him, that it was something he had to understand. One day, he knew, he would have to tell his father about it, and let the holy man tell him what it meant.

He would try to understand on his own, to puzzle his way through the meaning the way he puzzled his way through everything else, thinking for himself, learning, always learning. And if that didn't work, if he was unable to piece together the meaning of the strange visitation, he could ask his father.

But not while his father was in such a mood. Not just yet.

# Chapter 7 ═══════════

## June 1855

AFTER THE DEATH of Conquering Bear, the Sioux decided that the Fort Laramie area was too uncomfortable. Some of the chiefs still wanted to stay close, in order to get the yearly annuities the government had promised them in the 1851 treaty. But most of the chiefs and warriors called such men Loaf About the Forts or Laramie Loafers. To their way of thinking, the freedom of the plains was preferable to a dependence on handouts.

But they also knew that there would be more soldiers coming. The river of settlers seemed to grow in force each year, and it was only natural to assume that more and more soldiers would come to protect them. So, following the buffalo would serve two purposes—it would allow them to live as they had always lived, and it would also keep them away from the Holy Road. Warriors, especially the young ones, were still fond of raiding the wagon trains, and would make long trips for that express purpose. The chiefs tried to stop them, but since the Sioux had no centralized authority, each man was expected to decide such things for himself.

Curly and his family traveled south, in a band

led by the great Brule war chief, Spotted Tail, who was Curly's uncle. Their purpose was to attack the Pawnee, steal some horses, and put the Grattan situation behind them.

But when they finally found a Pawnee village, it was deserted. In order to salvage the long trek, Spotted Tail decided to shift his attention to the Omahas. It would not be as rewarding as hitting the hated Pawnee, but it was better than nothing.

When they finally found an Omaha camp, they struck at once. Curly was in the raid, putting himself to the final test as a Sioux warrior. So far, he had hunted animals, but never killed a human being. In the Sioux custom, killing was less important than touching, or counting coup. It was, in fact, a more significant achievement to confront a living enemy and touch him with an extended lance or bow or, best of all, the bare hand. Such a feat would get one's praises sung in the village. It entitled the warrior to wear a feather in his hair as well—the more coups, the more feathers.

With Hump and Lone Bear, Curly was looking forward to the battle. Hump, being older, had already counted his first coup. Curly hoped to join him soon. He looked up to the older warrior, and wanted to be like him. He was goaded, too, by the vision, which he still kept to himself. He had not even told Little Hawk of his dream.

When the assault began, the Omahas scattered in every direction. They had been taken completely by surprise, and warriors ran into the trees, trying to mount their horses while waging a desperate rear-guard action.

On his first pass through the Omaha village,

Curly narrowly missed a running man with the tip of his bow, leaning far out over the left side of the pony in his effort. On the second pass, there was some resistance. Some of the Omaha warriors had managed to recover from the surprise, and were beginning to loose volleys of arrows in the general direction of the advancing Sioux.

Just beyond the village, a thick band of brush paralleled the creek on which the camp had been established, and Curly caught a glimpse of movement in the leaves. Aiming quickly, he launched an arrow, heard it strike, and heard a groan. He knew he had hit his target, and jumped from his pony, knife in hand, to take his first scalp.

Crouching as he entered the brush, he swept branches aside with one forearm, holding his knife ready in the other hand. At first, he saw nothing. There had been no further sound from the thick undergrowth, and he was beginning to think that after all, he had missed altogether.

The sounds of battle behind him faded away, the war whoops of Sioux and Omaha both faint, as he concentrated his attention on the possible danger just ahead.

Just as he was about to give up, he saw a swatch of color, cloth of some kind, and plunged through the intervening brush, his knife waving back and forth in front of him.

He saw the body then, lying on its stomach, and he dropped to one knee. Grabbing his target by the shoulder, he yanked the body over, grabbed a fistful of long black hair, and froze. It was a woman, a young woman, he had killed. And pretty. She reminded him of his sister, and he turned away

then, trying not to smell the blood, trying to blot
out the bright red stain on the side of her dress,
where the shattered shaft of his arrow protruded
like broken bone.

His stomach churned, and he bent over. He tried
to stop it, but he was powerless, and the churning
erupted into a spew of vomit. He gagged, choking
on the bitter bilge. Coughing and sputtering, he
backed away from the body, wiping his mouth with
the back of his hand. He could see the glitter of the
blade in front of him, and shoved the knife back
into its sheath. Movement behind him spun him
around. He found himself staring into the eyes of
another Sioux, Horned Owl, a friend of Hump's.

Horned Owl looked past him, and Curly stepped
sidewise, trying to get between the warrior's gaze
and the body of the young woman. But he was too
slow. Horned Owl saw what had happened, and
broke into a grin.

Then, his nose twitching in comic exaggeration,
he said, "Weak stomach, Curly?" He laughed and
turned away. Curly stood there for a long moment,
ashamed to go out into the open. There was no prohibition of killing women, but it made Curly sick,
and he wondered whether it was right, law or no.
He would have to ask his father.

The battle was already over. The Omaha had
abandoned the field, and everything they owned
except the few horses and weapons they had managed to grab in their flight. Curly jumped back on
his pony and rode toward the main body of Sioux.
Already, Horned Owl was circulating among them,
telling them of Curly's achievement. The warriors
who knew grinned at him, some lifting their hair

and making a slashing motion across their fore-heads, then giving vent to piercing whoops.

It was tempting to run, but Curly knew he could only postpone, not avoid, the teasing. Better to endure it now. The sooner he put it behind him, the sooner he could live it down.

After the raid, Spotted Tail decided that it would be a good idea to head north, and establish a winter camp near the Black Hills. All the way back, Curly was teased unmercifully by the older warriors. Hump tried to ease the pain, but Curly faced it head-on, letting the men say what they wanted. Part of him thought they were right. What had happened was funny. But part of him believed that he had been right to be revolted. The young woman had done no one any harm.

Had he known who he was shooting at, he realized, he might not have loosed the arrow. It would have been easier then to hide from the truth, because no one would have known, but he would have had an unanswered question eating at him. Such a question, and the uncertainty it bred, could get him killed.

Unknown to Spotted Tail or his people, things were changing fast. The government had appointed a new agent to the Sioux. Thomas S. Twiss was a West Point graduate with white whiskers worthy of a prophet, and a passion to see the Indian troubles resolved quickly and, by his own limited lights, fairly.

At the same time, a new military commander had been appointed by Jefferson Davis, the Secretary of War. William S. Harney was a giant of a man at six feet four inches. A gifted athlete, he was the fastest man in his command, and was known to challenge all comers, red and white alike, to footraces. On at least one occasion, he had challenged an Indian warrior, who had been convicted of some minor offense, to a race, promising him a hundred-yard lead, and that if the warrior won, Harney would spare him the punishment the warrior had earned by his conduct. The race took place on a frozen lake. At the last minute, Harney gaining with every stride, the wily brave spotted a section of thin ice, veered toward it, and Harney followed. The big man's greater weight plunged him into the freezing waters. Harney lost the race. And kept his word.

But he was known for his intolerance for nonsense. He didn't like fancy talk or unnecessary regulation. Given a job, he wanted to do it his way, with no interference from his superiors. More often than not, he got it done.

Now, in the aftermath of the Grattan massacre, he was expected to punish the Sioux. Anxious to avoid bloodshed, Twiss sent out runners, demanding attendance at a council at Fort Laramie. At the same time, the chiefs were advised to move their people south of the Platte River or face the army's wrath.

Harney assembled a command of seven hundred men at Fort Leavenworth in Kansas and began his march to Fort Laramie, following the Oregon Trail. He intended to inflict heavy damage on any Sioux he encountered along the way. Once at Laramie, Harney planned to turn northeast, and follow the road to Fort Pierre in Dakota Territory.

When Spotted Tail arrived in the vicinity of the

Bluewater River a little more than a hundred miles from Fort Laramie, he found a village led by Little Thunder, a Brule chief. Little Thunder was widely considered to be a friend of the whites, but he was a powerful and courageous man, and Spotted Tail and his warriors decided to join the group. A large herd of buffalo was nearby, and the warriors managed to bring down huge numbers, enough to provide food for the whole winter.

Curly managed four kills on his own, and his hunting success enabled him to get over the embarrassment of the Omaha raid. Besides, with so much work dressing and drying the meat and preparing the hides, drying and tanning them, there was little time for anyone to tease him. By spring, he hoped, it would all be forgotten.

Most of the work was done by the women, and many of the warriors headed out again to raid along the Oregon Trail. They had not gotten news of Harney's advance, or the size of his force. Even if they had, the young hotheads, still preening themselves on the success of the Grattan affair, would not have given it a second thought. They were, after all, Sioux warriors, good enough to stand up to anybody, red or white.

Curly was out hunting when a messenger from Agent Twiss reached Little Thunder's camp. The chief, knowing that there was still much work to be done on the buffalo meat, that the hides still had to be tanned, and that if the work were not done immediately, the food and skins would spoil, was not willing to go.

"Tell the Agent Twiss that I am not unfriendly," Little Thunder told the runner. "But my people have much work to do. We cannot come for many weeks. When the work is finished, we will come to Fort Laramie."

The messenger, knowing that this was not what Twiss wanted to hear, insisted. "If you do not come right away, you will be considered hostile," he told the chief. "Any soldiers who find you will have the right, even the duty, to make war on you."

"But we are not enemies," Little Thunder argued.

"I only know what I am told," the messenger said, watching the chief's face as he waited for his words to be translated.

But Little Thunder would not budge. The messenger went away only with the chief's promise to come in within three months. When the messenger reached Fort Laramie, the news upset James Bordeaux, who sent a messenger of his own. He knew Little Thunder, liked him, and wanted to avoid bloodshed, which he believed to be inevitable if Harney should stumble on the Brule camp. But Little Thunder still refused to come in early.

The camp was not a large one, and with so many warriors out hunting or raiding the Oregon Trail, fewer than one hundred warriors were left to defend the village. But Little Thunder wasn't concerned, since he knew he had nothing but peaceful intentions.

On September 2, Harney reached the Bluewater River. His scouts found Little Thunder's camp, which was still peaceably going about the business of preparing for winter. Seeing an opportunity to make a point, a chance to vent some of the frustration building on the long, arduous and, so far, uneventful march, Harney drew up a plan of attack.

As far as he knew, the Indians had no idea they had been discovered. Regular scout runs kept him apprised of comings and goings while he deployed his troops. He had significant numbers of cavalry, infantry, and artillery. With his adjutant, Philip St. George Cooke, he went over every angle again and again.

"Captain," he said, "I know what happened to Grattan. I won't have that happen here."

"I don't think we have to worry about anything like that, General," Cooke said. "We have twenty times the men. We are much better armed and, frankly, a lieutenant is hardly your equal in strategy and tactics, General."

"Don't you bullshit me, Phil. That's not what I mean, and you damn well know it. I want to make sure the Sioux get the message. If we hit them hard, bloody their noses, they'll think twice before they hit another wagon train. There's a lot we can teach these red rascals, but first we have to get their attention. I mean to do just that tomorrow."

The general then proceeded to outline his plan, and gave Cooke command of a sizable cavalry unit. Cooke was to move his troops around to the far side of Little Thunder's village. Harney hoped to provoke a reckless retreat, which would bring the disorganized warriors under Cook's guns.

The troops moved out before dawn, but secrecy was critical to the plan's success. Accordingly, Cooke took his men on an elaborate detour, making a very wide loop to avoid being spotted. Once he had gotten past the village, he had to double back to take up his position on the top of a steep bluff.

At dawn, Harney's troops were very near Little Thunder's camp. But Cooke was not yet in position. At almost the same moment, a small band of warriors stumbled on Harney and his force, raced back to the village, and alerted the chief.

Little Thunder immediately mounted his horse and rode out to meet the general, Spotted Tail beside him carrying a white flag. Harney was grateful for the chance to delay his attack, knowing that it would be likely to fail unless Cooke was in position.

"I do not wish to fight you," Little Thunder told the general. "Agent Twiss sent for me and my people, and I told him that I would come in to Fort Laramie as soon as we were done preparing our food and hides for the winter. We need the food or we will starve. Without the buffalo robes, my people will freeze to death."

"Your warriors have been raiding the Holy Road," Harney said. "Some of your men attacked a mail train and killed several innocent civilians."

"I know about those things, and I have tried to stop them, but . . ." He shrugged. "You have your wild young men, just as I do. You know what it is like to try to break them, to put a bit in their mouths."

"You mean Lieutenant Grattan, don't you?" Harney asked. He'd read the report filed by Fleming, and by Fleming's successor, Lieutenant Colonel Hoffman. "You mean you are not to blame for failing to control your young bucks, and I am not to blame for the mistakes my young soldiers make, don't you?"

Little Thunder nodded. "It is hard to be a chief.

You must try to make your people see the right thing, but there is just so much you can do to make them behave the way they should. When they do, you receive praise, and when they do not, you are blamed. I am blamed, and I accept it. But these people here with me, they have bothered no one. They have attacked no whites, stolen nothing except horses from the Crows and the Pawnees, which is what we have always done."

Harney was getting nervous. The scout from Cooke was overdue, but he dare not move on the village until he was certain Cooke was deployed.

"I don't want any of your people hurt, but you should have thought of that before now, Chief. You know that Agent Twiss said any Sioux north of the Platte will be considered hostile. That means you and your people are to be considered hostile."

As he waited for the chief's reply, he saw the dust cloud of a rider approaching at a full gallop. Crossing his fingers that it was Cooke's scout, he excused himself and moved aside to wait for the rider. It was indeed Cooke's messenger. Everything was ready. He was in place and waiting for the expected retreat.

Harney spurred his mount back toward Little Thunder. The chief watched him closely, as if he suspected something.

"I came here to fight you, Chief. Those are my orders," Harney told him. "And I mean to follow them to the letter."

"But there is no reason to fight. We will go in when we are ready."

"No, now, that isn't the way it's going to be. I came to fight and you must fight."

Little Thunder looked at Spotted Tail, who shook his head as he listened to the interpreter's words. As their meaning sank in, he let the white flag fall to his side, turned his horse, and headed back toward the village at a gallop.

Little Thunder looked sadly at Harney. "I will fight if I must, but . . ." He couldn't finish, turned slowly, and rode back toward the camp.

Harney waited patiently until Little Thunder was almost at the edge of the village, then gave the order to charge. His men moved ahead with fixed bayonets. The field pieces opened up, showering explosive shells into the middle of the camp. Suddenly, like a hornet's nest poked with a sharp stick, the place came alive. Sioux were everywhere, running in every conceivable direction. Most of them were women and children.

The advancing troops waited for the artillery to let up, then charged ahead, firing their rifles, stopping to reload, then charging ahead again. Over and over, they fired in ranks, leapfrogging and laying down an incessant hail of fire.

As Harney expected, most of the Sioux scattered. Unused to organized fighting, they were helpless in front of Harney's onslaught.

Those who ran up the draw behind the village fell under Cooke's guns. Many of the Indians tried to climb up the steep face of the bluff to get at Cooke's men, but the artillery was brought to bear, and shell after shell thundered into the scrambling warriors.

It was over as suddenly as it had begun. The village was a shambles. Most of the tipis had been destroyed. Systematically torched, they spewed smoke into the sky until a pall hung over the battle site. The campground was littered with dead and dying Sioux, many women among them.

Harney's men moved among the fallen. Women had their dresses yanked over their heads. If they were living they were raped and if dead, their pubic hair was cut out as if it were a scalp. The remaining Sioux who managed to escape ran for Fort Laramie, believing it was their only chance to survive.

Curly saw the smoke from miles away. He and Hump and Little Hawk lashed their ponies, fearing the worst as they sprinted for the village. As they drew closer, they could see the ruined lodges, some still blazing, others already reduced to ashes.

Dismounting on the edge of the silent, abandoned camp, they walked gingerly among the dead. One by one they checked the bodies, hoping to find survivors. The mutilated women lay everywhere. Curly choked back a sob, trying to control his rage. He thought of the young woman he had killed, and was glad that he had been unable to scalp her. Seeing the women of his own tribe brutalized this way convinced him that he had been right. Women and children should not be victims of the war.

Hump was calling for him to mount up, when Curly heard a sound from the far side of a tipi that lay on its side, the skin walls scorched but not burned through.

Stepping around the upended lodge, he saw a woman, a baby in her arms, lying on her side, curled into a ball. The baby was whimpering. He moved closer and knelt beside her, only to realize it was not the baby but the woman who cried so pitifully. He lifted the baby from her arms and saw that it was dead.

Trying to comfort her, he shouted for Little Hawk to make a travois. When it was ready, he wrapped the woman in a buffalo robe. Leaving Hump and Little Hawk, he rode out onto the prairie. Over and over, he asked her name, but she could only stare at him, strange, childlike sobs wracking her slender body.

That night, she was able to speak. She said her name was Yellow Woman. She was a Cheyenne, the niece of Ice, a great shaman, and had been visiting with the Brule.

"I'll take you home," Curly told her. She looked at him as if she did not believe him or worse, as if she did not care. She just sat across the fire from him, her eyes black as the sky overhead, swallowing the firelight as it danced between them.

Once more, he said, "I'll take you home."

And he knew she didn't care.

# Chapter 8 ═══════════

**July 1857**

THE NEXT TWO YEARS were hard ones. Curly wandered from place to place, sometimes with Hump, sometimes with Young Man Afraid, sometimes with both and sometimes with neither. Sioux and Cheyenne alike made him welcome, but something gnawed at him. It was as if he had swallowed a small, vicious beast that chewed on his insides, not to get out, but simply for the pleasure of tormenting him.

On his long rides across the plains, he said little, even to his *kola*. Hump respected the silence and did not press him. Both young men knew that things were changing in ways they could not see and could not understand even if they could see. The Sioux way of life was being bombarded from all sides. Soldier chiefs like Harney attacked them, some of the Sioux had given up, their spirits broken, and hung around the forts until the yearly white man gifts were distributed, then wandered off, their heads down, their hearts numb.

Curly envied them that numbness. He felt too many things, and wanted to feel none of them. Better, he sometimes thought, to feel nothing at all

than to feel the empty ache in his belly. It was like
the ache he felt when he watched Black Buffalo
Woman carry water to her mother's lodge, or when
he would catch her staring at him as she sat in
front of the lodge doing beadwork that everyone
said was the best they had ever seen. She looked at
him, and he looked back. And it seemed that that
was all that would ever happen between them.

Yellow Woman's uncle Ice understood these
things. He was a wise man, like Curly's father, a
shaman who saw with more eyes than other men.
He could see things they could not see, and knew
things they would never know, no matter how
many times they were told.

Like all shamans, he was custodian of the past
and intermediary to the world beyond the plains
and the endless blue sky. He could talk to Wakan
Tanka. He could talk to the animals, and even to
the clouds. He was less a man of the world than a
man in it. He understood, too, that things were
changing, and this understanding made him sad
and silent. Often, he and Curly would sit together
for hours, sometimes deep into the night, saying
nothing.

But even during these long silences, Curly
learned. The hoot of a great owl would break the
silence, and Ice would get up, waving for Curly to
follow him out of the lodge. On a clear night, they
would walk away from the village, even out
beyond the pony herd, where nothing would disturb them, and the voices of the night would whisper things to Ice, things he would relate to Curly.
The ways of the Cheyenne were passing, he would
begin. "The Cheyenne themselves are passing. The

Oglala and the Brule are passing, too. But none of them, not the Cheyenne or the Oglala, the Brule or the Miniconjou, understand. But I think that you understand."

Curly would feel a profound sadness roll over him like a dark flood at these words, but he knew that Ice was right, and that there was nothing he could say to argue with the holy man.

But he refused to give up. There had to be a way to keep things as they always had been, and as they should continue to be. There had to be a way to make the white man go away, leave the Sioux and the Cheyenne in peace.

But Ice would not wait for these thoughts to lure Curly away into some dark wood where he would lose his way altogether. Instead, he would begin to talk of the old ways, tell him how things were before the white man came, and how they could be again, if only the white man would go away and leave them in peace. Neither the old holy man nor the young warrior knew how to make such a thing happen, but both believed it was the only way for their peoples to survive.

In the summer of 1857, Curly was fifteen years old. The Cheyenne were keeping to themselves in Kansas, but white soldiers were everywhere, looking for them and for the Sioux. Occasional fights between small bands of Cheyenne and small cavalry patrols had punctuated the spring months, and the Sioux they encountered warned them that great numbers of white soldiers were coming.

In late July, Ice and his band were camped on the Solomon River in northern Kansas. And the Sioux prediction came true. Six cavalry troops, under the command of Col. E.V. Sumner, found them. Ice had had the warriors dip their hands in the cold waters of a lake to make themselves bullet-proof, and they were confident as they rode out to meet the soldiers.

Curly, like the others, was almost casual. He let his bow hang on his shoulder, feeling the string tight against his skin. He looked around him, and saw that most of the Cheyenne were making no preparations to use their weapons. Instead, they formed a battle line after sprinting their horses back and forth to give them a second wind, as they always did before combat.

The soldiers seemed confused by the Indian tactics, but formed up in ranks three deep. As they moved forward, they held their fire. Sumner, wondering what was happening, waited until the forces were almost face to face, then gave the command for sabers to be drawn. The sudden flash of the arcing blades in the bright sun confused the Cheyenne warriors. They were expecting to catch bullets in the air like small bugs, and toss them harmlessly away, but Ice had said nothing about the long knives.

The Cheyenne line broke in disarray and the warriors raced back to their village to get the women and children. Leaving everything they owned behind, they scattered to the four winds. The soldiers, still baffled by the Cheyenne behavior, never fired a single shot. An hour later, the plains were empty of Cheyenne, except for the four men killed by the saber charge.

Curly decided to head north, to rejoin his family. On the solitary ride, he mulled over what he had seen in the past few years. He was starting to put together pieces that did not seem to belong to the same puzzle. Starting with the things that Ice had taught him, and adding the evidence of his own eyes, he was beginning to understand.

The whites were too strong for any small village. Whenever there was a battle, it was the Indian village that was destroyed, the Indian women and children who were killed or left homeless, the Indian warriors who bled to death in the grass. The only success he had seen was at Grattan's attack on Conquering Bear, and there the numbers had been so much in the Sioux favor, thirty soldiers against a thousand Sioux and more, that he had to face the fact that the Sioux could only win their battles with the white soldiers if they could work together in large numbers.

The white man's guns were powerful weapons, and not one Sioux in a hundred had a rifle. The wagon guns tore lodges to pieces, and destroyed villages from long range the way no Sioux weapon could ever do.

All these things were tumbling over and over in his mind, like leaves in a flooded creek. He had to stop the water long enough to pull the leaves together and see what they would tell him.

A great council of all the Sioux was being planned at Bear Butte, and that is where Curly headed. It was where he had been born, in the very shadow of the butte, and as he drew near, he began to wonder whether he would ever see the great butte again. It seemed as if the Sioux were being sucked into a whirlwind. No one knew the numbers, but everyone knew that the flood of whites was increasing month by month. Towns were springing up all over Kansas and Nebraska territories, newly created by Congress, although the Sioux did not know this. They knew only that where once there had been grass, rippling like water in the wind, stretching as far as the eye could see, and buffalo like black oceans rolling across the land, now there were houses made of sod, fences, and farms springing up like weeds.

When he reached Bear Butte, he was one of the last to arrive. More than seven thousand Teton Sioux had already gathered. All the bands were there except the Brule. Little Thunder and Spotted Tail, taking to heart the message of Harney's assault on the Bluewater, had chosen to stay away. But the six other bands were well represented. The greatest Sioux warriors were there, men like Red Cloud and Sitting Bull, Crow Feather and Old Man Afraid. Touch the Clouds, over seven feet tall, was there, too. These were men who loomed up like heroes out of the past, men whose names would live as long as there was a Sioux nation, men about whom he would listen to tales, mouth agape, around the campfire.

And friends he had not seen for months, even years, were there as well. Hump, Young Man Afraid, and Lone Bear. But best of all, he got to see his family for the first time in two years. Little Hawk spotted him coming along the great circle toward the Oglala lodges. He ran to get his father, and the holy man emerged from the tipi, squinting away the sun, shielding his eyes with one hand.

He started to run toward his son, then, as if ashamed, held back, choosing to walk slowly as

Curly dismounted and sprinted toward him, letting his pony follow in his wake at its own speed.

Curly threw his arms around his father, who squeezed him hard enough to force the air from his lungs, then held him back at arm's length to look him over. Curly was tall now, almost six feet, but slender. At one hundred and forty pounds or so, the boy had filled out. He was still light-haired but sculpted now of lean muscle, his black eyes like hard chips of obsidian set in his light-skinned face.

"It has been a long time, Curly. Two winters since I have seen you, son. I have been worried about you. Are you well?"

Curly nodded. "I am well. I see that you are, too, and Little Hawk."

"Where have you been?"

Curly shrugged. "Many places. I have seen much that I need to talk to you about."

"Tonight we will talk, and you will tell me everything." He turned then and led the way back to his lodge. Curly ducked to pull aside the flap, held it for his father, then followed the holy man inside.

Little Hawk was sitting by the fire, his face split by a broad grin. "I didn't know if I would ever see you again," he said.

"How could you doubt it? Someone has to keep you in line. Father is too busy for such things, so I will have to do it." He threw himself at the younger boy, wrapped him in a bear hug, and rolled over and over on the buffalo robes spread around the fire.

Finally, letting his brother up and smacking him playfully on the cheek, he said, "You are strong now."

"Not as strong as you, though," Little Hawk said, pleased by the compliment.

"Soon you will be."

"Then I will have to take care of you, I think."

"Each of us will always take care of the other. That is what brothers do," Curly said.

The council was drawing to a close, and Curly decided to wait until it was over, when he could have his father's undivided attention before telling him of his dream. On the last day of the council, the young man and the old man rode off alone. They made a small camp beside a branch of the Belle Fourche River.

That night, sitting by the fire, Curly waited for his father to say what was on his mind. After the evening meal, the old man finally spoke. "You are getting to be a full-grown warrior now, and there are many things I should tell you, things I would have told you before now if you had been with me. But it is still not too late."

"What sort of things?" Curly asked, wondering whether there would be an opening for him to tell of his vision.

"A warrior has many burdens to carry. It is not an easy thing to care for the old, and to see that everyone has enough to eat. It is important that you understand that your people come first. Only when everyone else has enough food do you feed yourself. When you capture horses from the Crows or the Pawnees, see that you give them to the people. Keep only the horses you need to hunt and to make war for yourself."

Curly said nothing for a long time. He was about to break the silence, when his father stood up.

"Come with me," he said, walking toward the creek.

Curly sprinted after him. "Where are we going?"

"I think we should build a sweat lodge. You should purify yourself. It is important to set things right with the Wakan Tanka. Only after a sweat bath can you expect to see things you need to see to be a good man."

They gathered several willow branches and arranged them in a dome, planting them in the ground and bending the slender, supple wood toward the center, where they were tied together. Then the willow frame was covered with skins.

Pointing to the center of the floor, the holy man said, "You dig the *iniowaspe*, and I will gather the stones. Not too deep, but deep enough."

Curly did as he was told. His father arranged the entrance and gathered a number of dry stones from the creek bank, and enough wood for a good-size fire, then started to heat the rocks. Normally, the holy man would have an assistant to carry the heated stones, but this was special, and he would do it himself. While the stones heated, the two of them moved along the watercourse, gathering sage to cover the floor of the sweat lodge.

When the stones were heated well enough, he took four of them inside, using a forked stick to carry them, placed them in the *iniowaspe*, and draped a water bag over his shoulder. Using a horn spoon, he sprinkled water on the hot rocks. While Curly took off his clothes, the lodge filled with swirling clouds of dense steam.

The sacred pipe was ready, and he touched it to one of the stones, then offered it to Curly. The fragrant willow bark in the bowl filled the steamy lodge. Curly handed the pipe back and the holy man offered a benediction to each of the four directions.

After the appropriate prayers of purification, the holy man said, "I know there is something that you want to tell me."

Curly started to tell his father about the vision he had had. It was a great relief, after keeping it to himself for so long, to share it with someone, especially someone who could tell him what it meant.

When he was finished, the old man said nothing for several minutes.

"What does it mean?" Curly asked, when he could endure the silence no longer.

"You are the man in the vision," his father answered. "You must do exactly as the dream instructed you. Wear no paint except the lightning and the hail spots. Do not paint your horse. Pass the dust over your horse and your body before battle, just the way the man in the dream did. And, most important, take nothing for yourself. If you do these things, then it will be as the dream says. Your enemies will not be able to kill you with their bullets."

Curly nodded, not sure he understood.

The next morning, they rejoined a band of Sioux. Curly knew the ceremony was only a prelude, but he wasn't sure what to expect. While hunting buffalo that afternoon, Curly, Hump, and Lone Bear ran into a small band of Arapaho. The Arapaho charged, and a short, furious battle ensued, in the course of which an arrow hit Curly and embedded itself in his leg. But Hump removed it, and the Sioux succeeded in driving off the attackers. Back in the village, Curly's father dressed the wound. Then, wrapped in a ceremonial blanket and carrying his sacred pipe, he moved out of the lodge and circled the village. He began to sing.

The Sioux gathered around, listening to the holy man, who concluded his song and looked long and hard into the faces of the people. In the long pause, Curly hobbled to the lodge entrance and stepped outside. He watched his father curiously, uncertain what was coming.

Then the holy man began to speak. "From this day forward, I will have a new name. I will be called Worm. And my son . . . my son will have a great name. The name of his father, of my father, and of his father. He will be called Crazy Horse."

# Chapter 9 =====================

CRAZY HORSE AND WORM were riding hard. The
scent of buffalo was in the air. The summer had
been lean, and the herds had been sparse. With the
winter snows just weeks away, they needed meat
and they needed it soon, while there would still be
time to dry it, and pound the berries and herbs into
it to make the winter supply.

The sky overhead was a deep blue, deeper even
than the water of the lakes. Crazy Horse thought
he heard the bellowing of a bull far in the distance. He tried to push his pony to its limit. A better rider than Worm, he was gradually pulling
ahead. Every rise would let him gain a few yards
on his father, until he was nearly three hundred
yards ahead.

There was no doubt about it now. He could hear
the lowing of the buffalo, maybe a large herd, but
any herd at all would be a blessing from Wakan
Tanka. He looked back at Worm and waved. The
joy of the hunt was smeared on his face like war
paint. Grinning from ear to ear, he teased the older
man, challenging him to ride harder, to close the
gap. It was almost like the horse races his people

loved so much, but if he was right, there was much more at stake than a few trinkets.

As he charged up a steep slope, his pony slowed, almost as if it sensed something, and Crazy Horse let the animal choose its own pace. As he reached the ridge, he reined in. Far below, spread out all across the floor of a broad valley, a herd of buffalo was grazing. The sound was almost unbelievable now, welling up from the valley floor in one continuous muttering. The buffalo drifted slowly along, munching the grass, switching their tails to keep away the small green flies that swarmed in clouds around them.

Here and there, birds trotted along behind the animals, pecking at the bugs dislodged by their wrenching of the grass. He shifted his weight to turn on one hip and wait for Worm, who had slowed now that he knew the quarry was in sight.

When he reached the top of the ridge, he broke into a smile. "Good," he said. "As much as we will need. We are lucky to find them. Blessed. Maybe we are living right."

"We should get the others," Crazy Horse said.

But Worm shook his head. "No. There is no hurry. As long as we have found them, we will be all right. But it is too soon to hunt them."

"But why?" Crazy Horse asked. He was still learning, and every day taught him something that he was amazed he had not realized on his own. But nature was so complicated, so vast and incomprehensible a thing. The Sioux were as the flies, a small cloud around the great beasts below. Balance was critical. Without it, they would perish. And every year there were fewer buffalo as the white men continued to decimate their numbers. Every year they were driven farther and farther to the West, closer and closer to the land of the Crows, as the white farmers conquered more and more of the land with their plows, ripping open the earth until it bled.

If they were not careful, the Sioux would be forced to find some other source of food. They had to husband the buffalo, care for them like they did the old ones. Because the wisest among them knew, and tried to teach the others, once the buffalo were gone, they would not be back.

Worm extended an arm and pointed. "Look at the hides."

Crazy Horse did as he was told.

"What do you see?"

"Buffalo."

"Look at the hair. Do you see?"

Crazy Horse shook his head. "No. I see buffalo, that's all. They look as they always look."

"The hair is too short. If we kill them now, the hides will not make good robes. They will not be warm enough for the winter. We will have to wait, follow them, herd them, like the white men do their scrawny cows. When the hair thickens, then we will hunt them."

"Hou!" Crazy Horse understood now. He was disappointed that he had not understood without having to be told. But at least now he knew.

"You stay and watch," Worm said. "If they move, follow them, and leave a sign. I will get the others. We will catch up to you as soon as we can, maybe by night."

Crazy Horse nodded. His father waved, turned

his horse, and started back the way they had come. Dismounting, Crazy Horse sat in the grass, his legs folded beneath him. He did not want to get too close for fear of frightening the herd. The longer they stayed where they were, the sooner they would be under the control of his people.

All day, he stayed on the ridge, watching the animals drift back and forth across the floor of the great valley. He remembered when there were so many no man could see the far side of a herd. It was a time when you did not have to ride for weeks to find the buffalo. But that time was gone now. Ice had been right. Things were changing faster than the Indian could follow. And it was the fault of the white man, who would not leave either the Indian or the buffalo alone.

He knew that the rest of his life would be spent warring with the white man. It was fine to stay away from the Holy Road, and pretend that only the Pawnee and the Crow were the enemy, but that was to pretend that the biggest enemy of them all did not exist. A wise man would open his ears and eyes, hear what the white man was telling him, see what the white man was doing. The difference between what was said and what was done would tell him all he needed to know.

The sun was low in the sky when Hump and Little Hawk appeared on the rise overlooking the valley behind him. He waved, then got to his feet and mounted his pony, heading downhill to meet them.

"The rest of the people will be here before morning," Hump said. "It is a good thing you found them."

"It is a good thing my father was here to tell me what to do," Crazy Horse answered.

Hump nodded. "It is late. We should camp here for the night. The herd will not move after dark. And we can keep watch for the others from the hilltop."

Crazy Horse was not in the mood for idle chatter, so the others left him to himself. It was well on toward morning before more of the band showed up. Black Shield was the chief, and he immediately took charge, dispatching several of the warriors to the far side of the next valley, with instructions to make a wide circle to make certain they could get around the herd without stampeding it.

As the sun rose, the village was almost completely in place, two valleys away, by the bank of a wide, shallow stream. Crazy Horse was exhausted from his long vigil, and wrapped himself in a buffalo robe in his father's lodge to sleep. No sooner had he closed his eyes, however, than one of the warriors sent to watch the herd came riding into the village, calling for Black Shield.

Rousing himself immediately, Crazy Horse ran outside.

The warrior, Tall Eagle, was already in the middle of his story. White soldiers, but not many, had camped a few miles away. As they were moving in to take up their positions on the far side of the herd, the warriors had stumbled on the camp. An argument ensued, some of the warriors arguing that the whites had no business in the Black Hills and should be killed. But Tall Eagle had argued that that was a decision for the headmen to make, and had extracted promise that nothing would be done until he had a chance to tell Black Shield and Worm and the others.

Black Shield agreed that the whites had no business being here, but he knew that an attack might lead to General Harney taking to the warpath again. That was something that should be avoided, if at all possible. He decided that he, Worm, Crazy Horse, and Hump, along with a few other warriors, should try to convince the soldiers to leave.

It was an hour after sunrise when the Sioux rode into the center of the camp. Tall Eagle had been right, there were not many. Their commander, a young lieutenant by the name of Gouverneur Warren, was conciliatory.

"Why are you here?" Black Shield demanded, the others crowding in around him.

"I am making a survey. Maps. That's all."

"Why do you need maps? This is Sioux land. No white men are supposed to be here. We agreed to leave the Holy Road alone. We said that it could stay. We said that the road from Fort Laramie to Fort Pierre could remain. But that is all. If you build more roads, more whites will come here."

"I am not planning to build a road. The Great Father just wants to have maps of all the land, that's all."

"And if you have your maps, then it will be easy for other whites to come to Paha Sapa. Is that so?"

Warren couldn't lie to the chief. He recognized the legitimacy of Black Shield's concern. He nodded. "That is so," he said.

"We were told there would be no more roads, and every year there are more. And every year more and more whites come on the roads. If we cannot have the land that is supposed to be ours, there will be no place for us to hunt the buffalo. Then we will die. My people think it is better to die fighting than to waste away."

Warren shook his head. "Nobody wants that," he said. "The Great Father does not want that."

"But it will happen, if the Great Father has his maps."

Warren was badly outnumbered, and knew the Sioux were getting edgy. A quick survey of the foreboding faces arrayed behind Black Shield told him that the ice he was skating on was very thin, and beginning to melt.

"Suppose," he said, "we just finish making our maps and . . ."

"No maps," Black Shield insisted. "No maps. Just go."

"All right, Chief. We'll go back to Fort Laramie."

"You cannot go west," the chief said.

"But that is where we came from. That's the way to Fort Laramie."

"No. There is a herd of buffalo that way." Black Shield pointed in the general direction of the herd. "If you go that way, you will frighten them off. We can't hunt them yet, but we have to keep them where they are. Your wagons will stampede them."

"What do you want us to do?"

Black Shield held up a hand, then stepped aside a few paces to confer with Worm, Hump, and Crazy Horse. Warren watched apprehensively, not entirely convinced that the Sioux were not discussing how to get the jump on the small detachment. He had some cavalry, and they were well armed, but they were no match in numbers for the warriors, and he guessed there had to be more nearby, perhaps lying in wait for a signal to swarm down on them and wipe them out.

Finally, Black Shield had forged some sort of consensus, and he came back toward Warren. "You can go north to Bear Butte, then turn east. That way you can circle behind the Paha Sapa. You will not bother the buffalo, and we will not bother you."

"All right. We'll leave tomorrow morning."

"Today," Black Shield said. "My people are angry that you are here. It is not just the buffalo, it is Paha Sapa. This land is sacred to my people. No whites are supposed to be here. That is the law. That is the treaty that was signed at Fort Laramie."

"You're right, Chief. I know that. I'm sorry."

"I will believe that if I never see another blue-coat in Paha Sapa."

"I hope you never do, Chief. I honestly do."

Black Shield shook his head sadly. "But you know and I know that there will be more bluecoats. Even if I do not live to be a very old man, there will be more."

# Chapter 10 ═══════════

**June 1861**

FOR NEARLY THREE YEARS after the encounter with
Lieutenant Warren's survey party, the Oglala
worked at forcing their lives back into the patterns
they had always known. The white soldiers were
staying at their forts. No whites were coming to
Paha Sapa, and the warriors were free to concentrate their energies on what mattered most to them,
hunting and warfare with the Crows and Shoshoni.

Crazy Horse was happier than most to see this
development. Always solitary, now he spent much
of his time hunting. Nothing gave him more joy
than bringing in an elk or a deer to feed the hungry,
or a string of ducks or geese to lighten the steady
diet of buffalo meat for an old woman.

For weeks at a time, he was away from the village, more often than not by himself. On these long
trips, he had nothing but time, time to think about
the Sioux way of life and his place in it. But it
wasn't all solitude. There were war parties, too,
raids to steal horses from the Crows, opportunities
to count coup without riding under the muzzle of a
wagon gun, or darting from rock to rock to avoid
the long range rifles of the bluecoats.

There was danger and, occasionally, the death of a close friend, but nothing like the carnage that warfare with the white soldiers brought with it. It was the kind of combat a warrior could relish, one man against another, fighting for pride and horses, fighting as it had always been done, before the guns of the white man had found their way into Chippewa hands.

Already, his name was being celebrated in the lodges, not by himself, which was the custom, but by those who received the fruit of his labor. An old man with two new horses thanks to Crazy Horse would sing his praises around the campfire. An old woman, with no one to care for her, would tell of his gift of a deer to help her through the long winter ahead of her. Among the Oglala, he was regarded as the best and most generous hunter and the bravest warrior, with more coups than men twice his age.

Still, he preferred to spend his time alone by the fire, fashioning more arrows, fitting the heads to the shafts or working on a new bow. He talked some, but only as much as he had to. His younger brother, Little Hawk, was a free spirit, and teased him, sometimes even making him laugh, but the less attention he received, the happier he seemed to be.

When it came to a war party, though, Crazy Horse was always among the first to sign on. When word that he was going spread among the lodges, dozens of warriors were eager to go along. For three years, left alone by the whites, the Sioux had been exerting a steady pressure on the tribes to the west, particularly in the valley of the Powder River, where the largest buffalo herds and the best hunting were.

The Crows and Shoshoni were pushed steadily backward, and by 1861, the Sioux were preeminent in the region. Although they didn't realize it, the Sioux were simply reenacting a pattern that had begun when the first permanent white settlement had been established on the Atlantic coast. The coastal tribes, pushed inland by the settlers, had pushed western peoples ahead of them. It was this constant pressure that had driven the Sioux themselves from their former lands in Minnesota. But now, with their horses, they had become the most fearsome presence on the plains, and they were able to go where they wanted and when. Already, the Crows and Shoshoni had been driven to the far side of the Bighorn Mountains. But the pressure from the whites was no less constant.

In late June, after the Sun Dance, Sioux scouts found a large Shoshoni hunting party camped on the Sweetwater River. It was several days' march, but Crazy Horse was anxious for the first war party of the year. The winter was no time to fight, and hunting to replenish the food stocks more than filled the spring, so it had been a long wait, and he was looking forward to the raid. The scouts said the Shoshoni were led by Washakie, a chief as famous on the plains as Red Cloud or Conquering Bear.

Dozens of men were ready to go, and the scouts led the way. After five days, the scouts called a halt and crept ahead to make certain the Shoshoni were still there. After the long winter, the *akicitas* had their hands full, maintaining discipline among the younger warriors.

When the scouts returned, the Sioux arrayed themselves just below the last ridge before the Shoshoni camp. The enemy pony herd was on the far side of the village, but the plan, which Crazy Horse suggested, was to drive downhill at first light, charge straight through the village, and drive off as many as possible of the war-horses tethered beside their owners' lodges. On the plains, it had become a widespread practice to keep a favorite pony close at hand for just such emergencies, and Crazy Horse sought to neutralize the advantage by striking first at the defense of the Shoshoni.

When the sky began to turn gray, the Sioux were already on their ponies. When Crazy Horse raised a hand, the warriors watched tensely, waiting for the hand to drop. They twisted the bridle ropes in their hands, drawing them taut, and poised their knees to dig them into the ponies' flanks. Finally, the hand fell, and they were off, war whoops rippling along the line like cresting waves of earsplitting thunder.

The downhill plunge was detected almost immediately by the old women of the camp, who were already up and about, preparing for the morning meal. The Shoshoni dogs, too, joined the uproar, but the Sioux thundered on downhill and reached the first lodges as the defenders scurried from their sleep, scrambling for lances and bows. Most of the war-horses were driven off in a single charge through the village.

Many coup were counted on staggering Shoshoni warriors, who seemed disoriented as they tried to organize resistance. Plunging on across the open space in the center of the camp and on out the far side of the circle, the Sioux reached the

Shoshoni pony herd, nearly a thousand animals milling around under only token guard.

There was little fire from the few young men watching the herd, and Crazy Horse and his followers plunged on into its heart, cutting it in half and driving off more than four hundred animals. The Shoshoni, Washakie himself at their head, were racing toward the herd, most of them on foot, bows and lances waving angrily as the Sioux pushed their booty up the far hill, then curled to the left and back past the village, nearly a mile upstream.

Some of the defenders ran down frightened mounts still milling in the remainder of the herd. It took them some time to get the horses under control and more time still to organize a pursuit.

Crazy Horse, Little Hawk, and a handful of Sioux warriors formed a rear guard to slow Washakie's pursuit. The sheer numbers of stolen ponies made driving them a problem. The escape was going slowly, and as the Shoshoni gathered their senses, they were determined to get back the horses and punish the invaders.

Crazy Horse and the others would find cover and fire as many arrows as they could to scatter the defenders and keep them off balance. At one point Crazy Horse became separated from the others because of his habit of dismounting before shooting. This made his aim more accurate, but it slowed him down and exposed him to the charging Shoshoni. Little Hawk, seeing that the Shoshoni were closing in on Crazy Horse, charged back, dismounted, and stood beside his brother.

Together they halted the pursuit, but they were now far from the herd, and almost as far from the rest of the rear guard. And they were running out of arrows. As the Shoshoni rained volley after volley toward them, the brothers gathered undamaged shafts, plucking them from the ground like women harvesting stalks of grain, fitted them to their bowstrings and sent them back toward their owners.

But Washakie led a flanking movement, and suddenly they were surrounded by eight or nine Shoshoni. Both their ponies were wounded and unable to carry them. Circling for the kill at some distance, the Shoshoni taunted them, but neither man broke and ran. One of the braver defenders charged headlong toward Crazy Horse, who shouted to Little Hawk, "You watch the others, I'll take care of the fancy stuff." The Shoshoni carried a lance along the right side of his horse.

The brave was almost on him, his eyes betraying his confusion. He'd expected Crazy Horse to try to dodge out of the way, probably to the opposite side of the pony to avoid the lance, but Crazy Horse stood his ground. With the gap down to a few yards, Crazy Horse feinted to the left, causing the advancing horseman to shift his lance to that side, but Crazy Horse ducked back the other way. The lance was now out of line, high over the pony's head, and Crazy Horse darted in, catching the Shoshoni by the leg and jerking him from his horse. The Shoshoni's head cracked on the ground and he rolled over once and lay still.

Swinging onto the Shoshoni horse, he turned to see Little Hawk loose an arrow at a second defender. The arrow struck the warrior in the chest with a wet thwack, knocked him from the horse, and Little Hawk vaulted up to take his place.

Confused by their lack of success, and enraged by the apparent success of the raiders, the Shoshoni started to string out in a long line as they chased after Crazy Horse and Little Hawk. The men with the faster horses were getting out in front, anxious to get their revenge. This made it easier for the rear guard, who could take their pursuers on one at a time instead of having to withstand an organized assault.

One man, leaving his comrades in his dust, charged toward the main body of the Sioux rear guard. He carried a pistol in each hand and barreled ahead, whooping nonstop. The small knot of Sioux stood their ground, amazed at the Shoshoni's courage, even admiring him a little, as he drew close enough to fire both pistols. The bullets went wide, but he charged on, tucking the guns in his belt and shifting to his bow.

One of the Sioux braced himself, legs wide apart, his lance extended, and jabbed suddenly as the Shoshoni thundered by. The impact knocked the Sioux to the ground, and left the lance, its shaft shattered, embedded in the defender's chest. He lay on the ground, clutching at the bloody wood for a moment, then closed his eyes and lay still.

The lance bearer scrambled to his feet and snatched a knife from his hip to take the warrior's scalp. Not until later did they learn it was Washakie's oldest son. To honor his son's great courage, they returned the scalp to Washakie.

Far across the valley, Washakie himself had led a small band of his warriors at an angle, enabling him to catch up to the stolen ponies. Charging into the herd and whooping, they lashed at the ponies with their lances and bows, managing to split it in half and then wheel the recovered stock back toward the village.

Content with their captured ponies, the Sioux, able to drive the smaller number more swiftly, headed for home. The Shoshoni gave up the pursuit.

Four days later, back at the village, Crazy Horse was sitting in his lodge when someone called to him. Crazy Horse told the man to enter. He looked up in surprise to see his friend Chips, a medicine man.

"I heard about your raid on the Shoshonis," Chips said. "You take many risks."

"It is what I do," Crazy Horse answered with a shrug.

"I know. That's why I made you this." Chips reached into his shirt and pulled out a small charm, a small white stone, holed in its middle, and attached to a buckskin thong. He thrust it toward his friend. "Here, wear this when you go into battle."

"What is it?" Crazy Horse asked.

"Two or three times, you have been wounded. But if you wear this, you will not be wounded in battle again. Loop it over your shoulder, and keep the stone under your arm."

Chips dropped the stone dangling from its thong into his friend's hand, then curled Crazy Horse's fingers around it. "We have been friends for a long time, Crazy Horse," he said. "I want us to be old men together, and let the young men bring us our meat."

Crazy Horse looked at his hand silently, hefted the charm, then put it on. He hadn't said a word. Only when the charm was in place did he say, "I want that, too, Chips. But I don't think it will happen."

# Chapter 11 ====

ON A LONG WALK with his son one May evening,
Worm led the way to a stand of willows a mile or
so above the village. It was obvious that Worm had
something on his mind, but Crazy Horse, try as he
might, was unable to guess what it might be. As
usual, his approach was to wait for Worm to open
the discussion. He knew from long experience that
Worm would talk when he was ready, and not
before. No amount of prompting, pleading, or
threatening would coax a solitary word from his
lips until he was ready to let it fly.

The older man took a seat on the sand at the
edge of the stream, shielded from the village, and
from a casual passerby, by the dense foliage of
the willows. Leaning forward and snatching at a
reed at the water's edge, he patted the ground
beside him, and waited for Crazy Horse to sit
down.

Worm twirled the reed in his hand, took a knife
from his hip and sliced it through cleanly at both
ends, leaving himself with about eighteen inches of
the hollow stem. Holding it to his eyes, he peered
through it for a long moment, his son silent at his

side. Then, cutting several small sections from one side of the reed, he blew through one end. A delicate moan emanated from the reed. Covering the holes with his fingers one at a time, he changed the pitch of the sound. Since he had not tried to be careful, cutting the small lozenges from the edge of the stem the way a farmer would cut chips from a whittling stick, there was no relation between the tones. The music, if such it could be called, was sour, the sounds random as hole after hole was covered by Worm's fingers.

Then, tapping his thigh with the reed, he looked at Crazy Horse. "Not a very good flute, is it?"

Crazy Horse, knowing the question was only preamble, smiled, but said nothing.

"I used to be able to make a very good one. But you have to have just the right reed. It must be big enough around, the walls thick enough, but not too thick, or the sound is muddy. But then, I am not really a musician."

"Neither am I," Crazy Horse said.

"No. You are a warrior. Maybe the best there is. I know that some would say Red Cloud, and some would say Spotted Tail. They are great men, both of them. And there are others, too. They all would have their defenders, but I guess I am partial to you."

"You are my father."

Worm nodded. "I am. Still, I have another son, also a warrior, and also a very great one. But Little Hawk is not Crazy Horse. Only you are Crazy Horse. You alone. Alone."

"Yes. I am alone in many ways, but that is not a bad thing."

"Yes, it is. It is a bad thing. It is not right for a man to be alone. It is not right for so great a warrior to have no one to tend him when he is ill, to cook for him, to give him sons as White Deer, and her sister before her, gave me children. That is only proper."

"I am away often. Sometimes I am gone for weeks at a time. That is hard on a woman."

Worm nodded. "That is true." He seemed to mull that over for a moment, but Crazy Horse knew that Worm was not ready to abandon his theme just yet. Instead, the son guessed, his father was probably trying to find another way to approach it, the same way a warrior would try to attack an enemy and, being repulsed, would try again from another direction. Try again and again, if he were courageous and a great warrior, until he found the way to do what he had come to do. So would Worm persist until he found the way to make his argument.

"You have seen twenty-one winters, son."

"Yes.

"If the Great Spirit is willing, you will see many more; twice, three times that number. I hope that will be your time. And that is a long time."

"Yes, it is a long time."

"A long time to be alone."

"I have my work."

"Your work is to care for the people. But you, Crazy Horse, are you not one of the people? Who will care for you?"

"I need no one to care for me."

"Not now, maybe, but . . . Listen, you have seen the old ones. You have seen how, when they can no longer go into battle, they have other things to do, children to teach, even children's children. That is a good thing. I have enjoyed watching my children grow."

"That is not something a man has to do. It is something he chooses to do."

"And you choose not to?"

"I didn't say that, Father. I don't know. I just think that it wouldn't be right, to leave a woman alone all the time. I would worry about her when I was on the warpath. Who would protect her from the Crow . . . and from the white soldiers? I have seen what happens to the women and the children. I once . . ."

Worm nodded. "I remember. I know how much that hurt you, the teasing, the jokes at your expense. But I know that what hurt you most was not what the other warriors said, but what you felt in your heart. You thought it a bad thing to kill a woman."

"I did. I do now. And I have never done it again. And I never will. But the Crow are not like that. The Pawnee don't mind killing women. And the white men seem to like it. I remember at Ash Hollow, what they did. I saw the dresses pulled up, the dried blood between the legs where there should have been soft hair. That was not right. That was not what a warrior ought to do. It is something I would never do, and that I have never seen any Lakota do."

"But that is no reason to deprive yourself of the comfort a woman can bring. Why suffer alone when you can have someone to share the suffering? It makes it easier to bear. Even the worst suffering can be endured if you have someone to share it with."

"It is not my way."

Again, Worm paused for a long time. When he spoke again, he was more direct. "If there were a woman you would wish to take to your lodge, who would she be?"

"I have never thought about it."

"Yes, you have. I even know who she is. Why not speak her name yourself?"

"What would be the point?"

"All right, then *I'll* say it—Black Buffalo Woman. I think maybe you should court her. I think maybe she would be a good wife to you, and you a good husband to her."

Crazy Horse shook his head. "No. She is from a great family. Red Cloud is her uncle. There is . . ."

"My own family is not nothing, you know." He clapped his son on the shoulder. "Try it. What have you got to lose? If she refuses you, well, you say you don't wish to be married. But if she says yes, then . . . I know what you feel for her in here." He reached out and tapped his son on the chest. "It is what I felt for White Deer. It is what I still feel for White Deer, even after all these winters together."

And so Crazy Horse was left with no way out. In the evening, according to the custom, he would show himself at the door to Black Buffalo Woman's lodge. She was permitted to come out and sit with her suitors. The young man and woman would wrap themselves completely in a buffalo robe. It was the only way they were permitted to be alone. But there was little time for anything more than small talk. And since Black Buffalo Woman was beautiful, and from a good family, she had many suitors. If another would show up, one she preferred to the man with whom she was wrapped in the robe, it was permitted for her to make a change.

During the day, and during the long nights after his visits, Crazy Horse would think about her. He had known her most of his life. He could still see her as a child, her braids trailing in the breeze as she ran through the grass. Later, when she was old enough to work, he would watch her bringing water to the village, or tanning buffalo hides or sitting with the other women, talking about whatever it was the women talked about. None of the men knew or, if he did, he was not sharing his secret knowledge.

Once again, Crazy Horse became the butt of jokes. Hump teased him unmercifully. Little Hawk, too, would raise the issue at every opportunity. And Pretty One, the *winkte*, who now went by the name Woman's Dress, would tease him, too. But he didn't mind so much.

He enjoyed his time wrapped in the robe with Black Buffalo Woman. It seemed to fly by, and the long days waiting for another chance to court her seemed to stab him with a thousand knives. Sometimes he couldn't breathe for thinking of her. But in the back of his mind was a worry. She had several suitors who had more to offer her. No Water was one of them. His family was powerful, and his brother, Black Twin, was already a member of the council, though not much older than Crazy Horse.

All Crazy Horse had to offer her was the life of a warrior's woman. And that meant long periods without seeing each other. It meant the torture, all the time he was away, of wondering whether or not he would come back. It might mean early widow-hood, perhaps with children to care for and worry about. She was young and beautiful, and she would find someone who could offer her so much more than he could. Because of his vision, Crazy Horse did not have much at all to offer her father. He had only a few horses, the ones he needed for war par-ties. Beyond that, he had nothing. And he was sure that it made a difference. Why wouldn't it?

After two months of courting, it came as a relief when Red Cloud announced that he was going to lead a war party against the Crows. Hump was going, Black Twin and No Water, too. And Crazy Horse signed on without hesitation. Little Hawk, too, would go along. On the warpath, Crazy Horse knew that he could forget about his fears. He would not see Black Buffalo Woman for many weeks, but that was almost better than seeing her so much with so little he could offer her.

But on the morning they were scheduled to depart, No Water was in agony. He had a terrible toothache. In itself, this was no great thing. But for No Water, it was everything. No Water's spe-cial medicine was from the long incisors of the grizzly bear. The toothache meant that his medicine sign was not favorable. It would be fool-ish, could even be fatal, to risk the warpath in such circumstances.

They were gone two weeks. The raid was a suc-cess, although they found few Crows and stole few horses. None of the Sioux were wounded, and they had managed to kill one enemy warrior, so there was every reason to feel satisfied.

On the long ride home, without the anticipation of battle to occupy his mind, Crazy Horse found himself thinking about Black Buffalo Woman almost constantly. When the wind blew through the trees, he thought it was her voice whispering to him. When he looked at the sky, he saw her face in the clouds. At night, with nothing but the deep black of the heavens and the tiny points of the stars to see, he imagined the twinkling of her eyes. She was everywhere. He couldn't wait to see her again.

He hadn't realized until the separation how much she meant to him. He was willing to do anything, endure any humiliation, make any sacrifice, if only he could succeed in winning her. He knew that Red Cloud had no objection, because he had overheard Hump and the great war chief talking about it. That gave him hope. But he knew, too, that the final decision was not for Red Cloud to make. It wasn't even for her father to make. It was up to the woman herself. And in his heart he had to admit that he just didn't know what she would decide.

As they drew near the village, Woman's Dress ran out to meet the warriors. Taking Crazy Horse by the leg, he pulled him, still on his pony, to one side. Crazy Horse watched the *winkte* in bafflement. "What do . . . ?"

But Woman's Dress shook his head. "Wait." He held a hand to his lips and waited for the rest of the warriors to pass by. Little Hawk looked quizzically at the two of them, but Woman's Dress waved him on impatiently.

Only when the rest of the warriors were inside the village circle did Woman's Dress speak. "I wanted to be the one to tell you. I think it is best if . . ."

"Tell me what?"

Woman's Dress rubbed a hand over his chin. The beadwork on his dress, the best anyone had ever seen, which he had done himself, shimmered in the afternoon sunlight. It looked as if sheets of white fire were coursing down his body as he breathed.

"Black Buffalo Woman . . ."

Crazy Horse jumped from his pony. "What has happened to her? Is she . . ."

Woman's Dress shook his head. "No. Nothing like that. It's just . . . she's married."

"Married? Who?"

"No Water."

"But she can't have done that. She wouldn't do that. She . . ."

"She has, Crazy Horse."

"It was planned, wasn't it? No Water didn't have a toothache. He had this planned all along. Even Red Cloud . . . this must have been his idea. He . . ."

Woman's Dress shook his head vigorously. "No. Red Cloud knew nothing of this. He will be as surprised as you. And as angry at No Water for this cowardly way of dealing."

"No, he won't. No one can be that angry, my friend." Crazy Horse slumped to the ground and let his head hang to his lap. Woman's Dress tried to comfort him, but the great warrior just pushed his friend away. "Leave me alone," he said. Then, without a word to anyone, he got to his feet, climbed onto his pony, and rode off into the plains. Lashing the war-horse's flanks with his reins, he drove it to a full gallop, its hooves thudding dully on the grass until they could no longer be heard in the village. Woman's Dress watched him until he was out of sight.

Crazy Horse never looked back.

# Chapter 12

**June 1863**

Lt. Caspar Collins nodded to the sentry standing at parade rest beside the entrance to the commanding officer's office at Fort Laramie. Glancing over his shoulder at Peter Bordeaux, who gave him the thumbs-up, he tried to smile. Then he stepped into the office, wiping sweaty palms on the trousers of his uniform. He cleared his throat and clicked his heels as he stopped in front of the commander's desk.

"At ease, Lieutenant," the colonel said. "What can I do for you."

Collins cleared his throat a second time, then curled the fingers of both hands into his palms. He could feel a new sheen of sweat already beginning to glaze them, but he ignored it, afraid the commander would catch the gesture, and having caught it, would realize its significance.

"I was wondering, Colonel, if . . ." he stopped in midsentence, not quite sure he had made the right beginning. "That is, I . . ."

"Spit it out, Lieutenant." The colonel leaned back in his chair. His whiskers, still black despite his age, nearly fifty, bunched under his chin as he tilted his head forward a bit to peer at the young lieutenant over his spectacles.

Taking a deep breath, Collins tried again. "Well, sir, I was wondering if you would have any objection to my visiting a Sioux village . . . ? Unofficially, I mean."

"Oh? Do you mind if I ask why?"

"No, sir. It's, well, I find them fascinating. I'd like to learn more about them. Curiosity, I guess."

"What do you plan to do, Lieutenant, put them under a microscope, examine them like bugs?"

"No, sir. I just want to understand them better, the way they think, the way they see things. I mean, if I'm going to be posted in the West for the next few years, I think it would help me to be a better officer."

"They're human beings, just like we are, Lieutenant. You know that, don't you."

"Of course I know that, sir. I don't mean that I'll be obtrusive. I mean, I'll only do what they'll let me do. I won't interfere in their affairs. I'd like to learn their language if I could."

"To help you be a better officer?"

Collins nodded. "Yes, sir. I think maybe it's important to be able to speak to them directly, to understand what they really mean. Some of these interpreters aren't the most reliable men, sir. Half the time you can't find one when you need him, and the half of the time you do, he's got a snootful of whiskey. I don't think that's in anyone's interest, Colonel."

The colonel nodded. "You're right, Lieutenant, it isn't. But how do you propose to communicate with the Sioux?"

"Peter Bordeaux, the son of the trader, has agreed to help me."

"Very well . . ."

"Then you have no objection?"

The colonel shook his head. "No, I have no objection. But I think I ought to warn you, Lieutenant. These people are not fools. They will know that you are an army officer. They don't much trust white men of any kind, let alone soldiers, and I can't say I blame them for that. It wouldn't surprise me if they didn't want anything to do with you."

"I'll take that chance, sir, if I may."

"You may."

"Thank you, Colonel." Collins snapped to attention, saluted, and spun smartly on his heel. He was already on his way to the door when the colonel called to him.

"One more thing, Lieutenant . . ."

Collins stopped and turned. "Sir?"

"You might be putting yourself at some risk. That's something I want you to consider before you go. Eventually, if they don't know it already, they will know that you're also my son."

"I'll be careful, Colonel."

"See that you are. For all our sakes."

As he stepped outside, Bordeaux, who was sitting on the boardwalk, talking to the sentry, said, "Well, how did it go?"

"He said all right," Collins said, breaking into a broad grin.

"When do you want to start?"

"What's wrong with right now?"

"Christ, you're eager, aren't you? You sure you don't want to think it over for a day or so, now that it's approved, I mean?"

"No. I might change my mind."

"You get into this, you still might. In fact, you might wish you never got started."

Collins nodded. "I know that, Peter. But if I don't do it, I might wish I had. So, better to seize the day."

"You're in charge, Lieutenant. I'll meet you at the stable in fifteen minutes."

Collins waved, watched Bordeaux cross the compound to the general store, then walked to the stable and ordered his horse saddled. He waited impatiently for the trader's son, and checked his rifle twice before Bordeaux finally reappeared.

Collins swung into the saddle while Bordeaux went into the stable to get his own mount. Bordeaux rode out, looked at Collins, and said, "I thought you might change out of that uniform, Lieutenant."

Collins shook his head. "No. I am what I am, Peter. I can't change that. And the last thing I want to do is go out there and pretend I'm something else. If anything is to come of this, they're going to have to trust me."

Bordeaux sucked his cheeks in and gnawed at the flesh on their insides for a moment. Then, clicking his tongue against the roof of his mouth, he nodded. "You're right, Lieutenant. You ready?"

Without waiting for an answer, Bordeaux rode across the compound and out onto the plains. He headed for the Laramie River, Collins riding to his left and slightly to the rear. "Where we heading?" Collins shouted.

"Closest village makes the most sense. It ain't like we're in real demand. This might not work at all, you know. Lot of them Indians don't have no use for a white man, even one like you."

"And what kind am I, Peter?"

Bordeaux turned to look at him before answering. "I don't rightly know. And if *I* don't, it's for damn sure the Sioux won't, neither."

Red Cloud and many of his people were camped about ten miles upstream from the fort. They were no longer taking the annuities, and seldom came near the fort itself, but the hunting was good in the area, and the reduced army presence reduced the chances of being attacked by the troops. Back in the East, the Civil War was at its height, and the government had its mind on a more immediate enemy. The Sioux and the other plains tribes were still raiding wagon trains, but the raids were almost always by small groups, and usually the raiders left the people alone as long as the settlers were willing to part with some coffee or sugar or ammunition for the rifles that had been finding their way into Sioux hands.

The sun was well up in the sky by the time the pair reached a bluff overlooking the Sioux village on the river below. Collins stayed there for a long time, his hands draped over the saddle horn, staring at the great circle of lodges. There were nearly a hundred tipis, and Bordeaux estimated that seven or eight hundred Sioux called the village home.

"Reckon we might as well go on down, Lieutenant. They ain't likely to come on up with a cup of tea for you."

"You know any of the Indians who live here?" Collins asked, as they backed off the bluff and found a way down that took them out of sight of the village.

Bordeaux nodded. "Quite a few. Most of them have been through the fort at one time or another. I'm half Sioux myself, so I guess it's easier for me. But it sure don't seem easy."

"I didn't know you were . . ."

"My mother was a Brule Sioux. She died a few years ago. But she taught me a lot. And most of the chiefs know my father. They even like him, I think. I know they trust him."

"How do you know that?"

"Still alive, ain't he?"

"Why is it difficult for you, then?"

"Because the Sioux think I'm more white than Indian, and a lot of whites, most in fact, think a little bit of Indian blood goes a long way. You can imagine how they feel about a half-breed."

Collins nudged his horse close enough to grab Bordeaux's arm. "Look, Peter, if this is going to cause you any pain, make you uncomfortable in any way, then . . ."

Bordeaux shook his head. "Don't worry about me, Lieutenant. Sooner or later, the Sioux are gonna have to learn to live with the white man. The sooner they do, the fewer innocent people will die. On both sides. If you can help make that happen, then I'm all for it. Besides, it ain't likely you could make things much worse than they already are. Most of the officers they send out here are clowns. Hell, there was one colonel sent a letter back East talking about the Winnibigoshish being on the warpath."

"Never heard of them."

"Neither did anyone else, Lieutenant. It's a god-damned lake. You ever see a lake on the warpath?"

Collins laughed, but Bordeaux never cracked a smile.

When they hit the flats leading into the village, Collins felt his shoulders go stiff, as if he were a clock and someone had overwound him. Everything inside was tight. He was breathing rapidly, shallow drafts that seemed to catch in his throat. He had never been this close to a Sioux village before, and realized that he knew next to nothing about these people. But he forced himself to stay calm.

Some of the warriors nearest him glared at him or, he hoped, at his uniform. But most of the men paid no attention to him. Either they found him uninteresting or they felt that he posed no threat and therefore could safely be ignored.

Some of the warriors waved to Bordeaux, while looking curiously at the white man wearing the uniform of the bluecoats. Bordeaux dismounted, and motioned for Collins to do the same. The lieu-tenant took a deep breath and slid from his saddle, curling the reins in his hand and squeezing them until his knuckles whitened.

"Well," Bordeaux said, flashing him a grin, "here we are."

"What now?"

"You tell me, Lieutenant. This was your idea."

"Can you introduce me? I don't know what the protocol is."

"Protocol?"

"You know, good manners. Should I meet the chief first?"

"Absolutely."

"Where is he?"

"He'll be along. Just relax."

A moment later, some of the more curious among the Sioux began to gather in a circle around the two men. They were keeping their distance, but their faces were not unfriendly. Collins, trying to conceal his nervousness, nodded politely, smiling and waving with his free hand.

The circle grew in thickness as more Sioux lined up behind the first. Then the circle parted abruptly, and a tall, vigorous-looking man, his hair hanging in long braids down over his shoulders, stepped through. The circle immediately closed around him.

Collins looked to Bordeaux. "Red Cloud," the trader said.

He then turned to the chief and conversed for several moments in Red Cloud's tongue. Collins, knowing it was foolish even as he did so, tried to translate the conversation. He noticed that Red Cloud kept looking at him, darting glances that seemed to linger, while still paying attention to Bordeaux. Then the trader turned to Collins and waved him closer.

"Lieutenant Collins, this is Red Cloud. Chief, this is Lieutenant Caspar Collins."

Red Cloud was watching Bordeaux closely now. He said something, and Bordeaux nodded, then responded.

Turning to Collins, he said, "The chief wanted to know if you are related to the colonel who rules over Fort Laramie."

"What did you tell him?"

"The truth."

"Good. Does he have any objection to my being here?"

"No. He says as long as you behave properly, you are welcome."

At that, Red Cloud stepped up to the young soldier and extended his hand. Collins clasped it and almost winced at the older man's grip. Red Cloud pumped the hand vigorously, almost a parody of the conventional white man's greeting, then said that he had things to do. By the time Bordeaux had translated, Red Cloud was gone.

"Let's have a look around, then, Peter," Collins suggested. "I'd like to meet some of the warriors. We are all soldiers, so we will have at least that in common."

"Don't count on that meaning much, Lieutenant." Bordeaux said something to the circle, which had drawn still closer after Red Cloud left, and the Indians parted to let the visitors through.

They walked into the middle of the camp, several children following close behind, some of the others keeping a little distance, almost as if they wished to keep an eye on the young bluecoat who had come to their village.

Collins walked halfway around the camp, looking at the lodges and admiring the paintings on the skins covering them. Some of them were rolled partway up to let in fresh air, and Collins bent over from time to time to peer inside. He kept looking at Bordeaux, his head swiveling back and forth. "Let me know if I'm being rude, Peter," he said.

"You bet your ass I will, Lieutenant."

Across the large circle, Collins spotted a young warrior sitting on the ground, working on a bow.

"How about that fellow?" he asked, gesturing toward the warrior. "Do you think he'd talk to me?"

"I doubt it."

"It won't hurt to ask, will it?"

Bordeaux shrugged. "Wait here," he said. He walked over to the young warrior and squatted beside him. The young man didn't look up, but canted an ear to Bordeaux. When the trader was finished speaking, the warrior grunted, then looked at Collins. The lieutenant smiled.

The warrior straightened up gracefully, and Bordeaux gestured for Collins to join him. "He says he'll talk to you."

"Do you know him?"

"Hell, yes. And you don't know how lucky you are, Lieutenant. This man is as good as it gets. Meet Crazy Horse."

The warrior looked intently at his visitor, then extended a hand. Collins shook it, then laughed.

# Chapter 13 ═══════

**October 1863**

CASPAR COLLINS LOOKED AT HIMSELF in the mirror and wondered what was happening to him. He no longer felt as comfortable in his uniform as he used to. The buckskin pants felt natural to him now, the shirt as if it were an extension of his body. Many of the troops, members of the 11th Ohio Volunteer Cavalry regiment, had adopted frontiersman garb, too, but for reasons he did not share.

The troops, disappointed at being sent west, to a region they regarded as the most desolate and god-forsaken spot imaginable on the continent, had expected to be fighting rebels in Virginia and Tennessee. Spoiling for a fight, frustrated at not getting one, they felt as if their time was being wasted, so they emulated the white men they saw most frequently, the hunters and scouts, pretending they were ready to take on any damn bunch of Indians the plains had to offer. Their arrogance was that of the late Lieutenant Grattan. It didn't seem to matter that that attitude had gotten Grattan killed.

But Caspar Collins was irresistibly going native for other reasons entirely. He had spent several months, off and on, with Crazy Horse. The Sioux

was given to long silent stretches, and Collins had
come to accept them, but when he did talk, he
proved to be articulate and intelligent, displaying
an understanding, and a kind of sad resignation at
the future, of his people. But he was devoted to the
old ways, and Collins was starting to agree with
him.

There was something criminal in forcing a way
of life on a people that was as far as imaginable
from the one they already had, the one that had
allowed them to flourish in land that belonged to
them, if it belonged to anyone, and it seemed to
Collins that Sioux belief was not that acquisitive.
The land, along with everything in it, was there to
be used, to be lived on, to be loved and feared.

This morning, he was going hunting with Crazy
Horse for the first time. He had been making
progress in studying the Lakota language, enough
that he no longer needed Peter Bordeaux along to
interpret, although he was far from fluent. Crazy
Horse proved to have a sly sense of humor, and
delighted in teasing him about his mispronuncia-
tion and limited vocabulary, two aspects of his
shaky command of the language that often led him
to turn right when instructed to turn left, or to
think a conversation was about the Great Spirit
when it was about a buffalo.

There was a kind of pantheistic embrace of the
universe in Sioux thought that saw holiness everywhere, meaning in the eye of a butterfly and the
whole wheeling shield of midnight stars. The
approach was one Collins had found congenial,
even persuasive, and in the few conversations he'd
had with Crazy Horse's father, Worm, he had

learned a great deal about respect for the land and, especially, for the animals and plants on which Sioux existence depended much more directly and completely than any white man's did.

Stepping back from the mirror, he ran a hand across his features, delicate under the light brown hair, almost the color of his Sioux friend's hair, and recognized that his face was aging, as if the weight of the Sioux future were impressing itself on him, too. The colonel had asked him once whether he might not be getting too close to the Sioux, a people who, after all, he was here to supervise. But the colonel was almost as impressed with the Sioux as he was, and had meant the question not as a rebuke but as an expression of parental concern. It was a kind of warning that his heart might be broken in a way he could not anticipate. Caspar acknowledged the risk, but thought it one eminently worth taking. In any case, it was too late to do anything about it—he was smitten.

Turning away from the mirror, he glanced once over his shoulder, and it seemed for a moment as if the figure in the glass were someone else. Maybe, he thought, it is, but he turned away and headed for the door. Stopping for a second to grab a new pair of Springfield rifles, he stepped outside and closed the door. His horse was already saddled, standing nervously at the hitching post in front of the officers' quarters, and he mounted up with a wave to a couple of his men.

"Where you goin', Lieutenant?" one of them called.

"Hunting."

"For Injuns?"

Collins shook his head. "No, Timmy. *With* Indians."

The soldier waved derisively, but Collins, knowing the man probably would not understand and if he did, would disapprove, waved back and kicked his horse into a trot.

He felt better once he got away from the fort. It had come to symbolize something that he could not justify much longer, if he still could. He felt like he were trapped between two great stones. Both seemed solid, and each pressed flush against him. If either moved, he would be ground to fine powder, and it was beginning to seem that there was no way out, no way to slide away from the stones because any attempt to do so would cause one or the other to shift, not much, but enough to do him in entirely.

The ride to Red Cloud's camp was second nature now. The Sioux were accustomed to his presence, and barely noticed him when he arrived. Some of the other warriors waved a greeting, and, as always, he stopped by the chief's lodge to pay his respects, then walked his mount around the outside of the village circle to hobble it behind Crazy Horse's tipi. He took one of the new Springfields from the back of his saddle and held it behind his back as he moved around to the front of the lodge.

The warrior was expecting him. They hadn't seen each other for more than two weeks, and Collins was curious about where the Sioux had been. As he entered the lodge, he waited a moment for his eyes to adjust to the firelight. Crazy Horse was sitting in front of the fire, working on a new bow. He looked up and nodded at Collins.

In greeting, Collins tried the creaky mechanism

of his Lakota, and drew a smile from the warrior. "I brought something for you," Collins said.

He brought out the rifle and offered it to Crazy Horse. The warrior looked skeptical, but Collins pressed the gift on him. "It's brand new," he said. "I have one just like it for myself."

Crazy Horse took the rifle and examined it. Most of the guns the Sioux had, and they didn't have many, were old throwaways. Many had their barrels bound in rawhide to hold them together, their stocks cracked and scarred, decorated with brass tacks driven into the wood.

"Thank you," the warrior said.

"I thought we might use them on our hunt."

Crazy Horse grunted, looking at the unfinished bow where he had left it beside the fire. "No," he said. "We both know how to use guns. But you do not know how to use the bow. We will hunt with bow and arrow."

"I'm not sure I . . ."

Crazy Horse shook his head vigorously. "You want to learn the way we live. That is how we live. To understand it, you should learn to do it. Just be happy that your life does not depend on the bow, as ours does."

Crazy Horse held the gun for a long moment. "Thank you, my friend. I hope that I never have to look at you over the sights of this rifle."

"No chance of that, Crazy Horse," Collins said.

"We should go now." The Sioux led the way out of the lodge, and Collins followed behind him, meek as a child, glancing longingly back once at the rifle, where Crazy Horse had placed it against the wall of the lodge.

Mounting their horses, they rode away from the village, heading up into the hills away from the river. "What are we hunting for?" Collins asked.

"Food. And wisdom."

"I have enough food but not nearly enough wisdom."

"No man has enough wisdom, Caspar. My father is the wisest man I know. And Sitting Bull, the Hunkpapa medicine man. But even they together don't know half of what there is to know."

"Will we go far?"

"That depends."

"On what?"

"When one hunts, one must go where the prey is to be found. One never knows that until he gets there."

The rolling grassland of the river bottom was falling away behind them as they moved up into the hills. As they reached the high rise ahead, Crazy Horse turned on his pony and pointed back down toward the river, which caught the sunlight and seemed to be on fire. The lodges of the Sioux village seemed like toys, and the warrior nodded, then said, "The Lakota are a very small thing. The world is very large. Sometimes I wonder why there does not seem to be enough room."

"You mean the white men?" Collins asked.

Crazy Horse nodded. "Yes. And the Crow and the Pawnee and the Arapaho and the Shoshoni." He paused for a long moment, then added. "And the Sioux."

Collins didn't know what to say, so he said nothing. After a pause in which the warrior's face seemed to betray a thousand ghostly sorrows that swept in wave after wave across his features, he turned and nudged his pony forward with his knees.

Collins knew this was no ordinary man he followed. But he was still surprised by some new revelation every time they were alone together. It seemed almost as if there were some secret Crazy Horse that he reserved for rare moments of confidence, times when he could tell Collins things he dared not share with his own people.

And Collins felt himself changing almost daily. Going about the performance of his everyday duties, he would catch himself, suddenly wondering what he was doing. It didn't take much to set off the doubts. Maybe he heard one of the other officers say something about the Sioux that struck him as woefully ignorant, or maybe it would be just a little thing, like a ladybug landing on his wrist triggering a recollection of something Crazy Horse or Worm had said. No matter what it might have been, once triggered, the doubt was almost impossible to brush aside. It would haunt him all day long, leave him tossing under his blanket at night.

Once, he tried to explain to his father what was happening to him, but the colonel just smiled sadly, as if he had expected as much. There was resignation in that smile, as if one had just heard a death sentence pronounced on a loved one, a sentence with no appeal.

It was well after noon before Crazy Horse called a halt for food and to give the horses a rest. The two men ate in silence. Only after the meal was finished, did Collins break it. "Why do you fight the Crow?"

Crazy Horse looked at his friend as if he could not understand the question. When he was certain that he had not misheard, he said, "Why do the white men fight the Lakota?"

Collins shrugged. "I don't know."

"Yes, you do know."

"Tell me, then."

"Land. The white man wants the land the Sioux depend on for their lives and the lives of their families. Every year they take more. We fight the Crow for the same reason. What you take from us has to be replaced. We cannot go east, so we go west, where the Crow are. If we beat them, they will turn west, too, and make war on whoever lives there."

"I . . ."

Crazy Horse shook his head. "I know what you are thinking. You are thinking that you wish it was not like that. But it is. It has always been that way, as long as I can remember. As long as the oldest Lakota can remember. Your people gave guns to the Chippewas and we were forced off our land to the north and east of the Black Hills. Now it is not the Chippewa who force us, but your own people. It can be no other way. If we are strong, then we will win and the Crow will lose. If not, we will be ground up between the white man and the Crow the way grain is ground between two stones."

"I'm sorry it has to be that way."

"Is the wolf sorry it has to hunt the deer? Does the bear feel sad that it eats a fish? It is the way things are. We are what we are. There is no time to be sorry."

After the meal, they mounted up and headed uphill. Over the rise, Crazy Horse had said, was a valley full of forest. It was the best place for hunting for miles in any direction. Reining in, the Sioux said, "We will ride partway down the hill, then leave the horses. It is best to hunt deer on foot."

Collins nodded, then waited for Crazy Horse to lead the way.

Once into the trees, it seemed to Collins that the forest filled the whole world. There was no direction in which he could see anything but trees. Cottonwoods, pines, ash and maple, oak and elm. It seemed as if every tree he had ever seen was represented.

Entering a clearing, Crazy Horse dismounted and hobbled his pony. Collins emulated his friend. "Just the bow and arrow," Crazy Horse reminded him.

"But I've never used a bow at all. Not even to practice."

"We will practice if we see a deer."

"He'll get away for sure."

"Today it is more important to hunt than to kill a deer. There has to be a first time for everything, Caspar Collins."

The lieutenant shook his head meekly, glanced longingly at the stock of his rifle, then took the bow and a quiver full of arrows from his saddle. He slipped the quiver over his shoulder then draped the bow on the other shoulder, as Crazy Horse had done.

The Sioux stepped away from the ponies and into the trees, the soldier right behind him. Overhead, patches of bright blue sky brought fitful illumination to the deep shade of the forest. Already, Crazy Horse had found tracks. He pointed to scuff marks in the leaf mulch littering the forest floor.

"How do you know that's a deer track?" Collins asked.

Crazy Horse just smiled. He moved off after the deer, finding the trail where Collins could see nothing at all, even from hands and knees while leaning close to the earth. When they had gone several hundred yards, Crazy Horse stopped, turned, and placed a finger to his lips. Then he pointed. Peering through the trees, Collins followed the extended arm. He could see nothing but the dark trunks of trees and masses of shadowy underbrush.

But he knew better than to question his friend.

Moving lightly, Crazy Horse led the way until the underbrush thinned a little. Something glittered through an opening in the brush, and Collins soon realized it was sunlight on bright water. A spring of some kind, maybe a brook. Then, almost as if it hadn't been there at all until a moment before, a deer materialized. It was a large one, a female, Collins thought.

Pointing to his bow, Crazy Horse nodded. The lieutenant removed the bow from his shoulder, then an arrow from the brand new quiver. He fitted the arrow's notch to the bowstring, struggled to hold the arrow in place against the bow grip. It rattled several times until he tilted the bow and let gravity hold it in place. Crazy Horse shook his head the way one does at a child's prank.

"You do it," Collins said, but Crazy Horse shook his head.

"It is your deer," he whispered. "Or it is no one's."

Collins drew the bowstring back as far as he could. He felt his arms tremble as he tried to hold the powerful bow at full draw. He watched Crazy Horse for a signal. Then it came. The deer had heard something and raised its head, water running in silvery filigrees from its muzzle.

The string snapped, the arrow sailed, glanced off a tree and clattered on into the brush.

The deer was gone.

"Now," Crazy Horse said, "you are starting to see how hard it is to be Lakota. And when the deer and buffalo are gone, what will we do?"

Collins made no answer. He knew there was none.

# Chapter 14 ═══════════

## June 1865

ON NOVEMBER 29, 1864, a thousand troops from the Department of Colorado, under the command of Col. J. M. Chivington, attacked a village under the leadership of the Cheyenne chief Black Kettle. Black Kettle had been a friend of the white man for years, and his band was perfectly peaceful, but Colonel Chivington was not a man to let facts trouble him. When his butchers were done, nearly two hundred Cheyenne, mostly women and children, lay dead. Their bodies were mutilated, scalps taken and savagery almost unparalleled had been visited upon the women, living and dead alike.

It did not take long for news of the slaughter to spread across the plains. When word reached Fort Laramie, one of the Laramie Loafers told Maj. George O'Brien, "You have set the prairie on fire."

And so indeed it happened. Furious at the carnage, feeling betrayed and foolish, even a peaceful Sioux chief like Spotted Tail was moved to go on the warpath. A great council was held on Cherry Creek, and in its aftermath, the plains Indians cooperated like never before. Cheyenne and

Arapaho joined forces with the Sioux, even friendly Brules, and the result was the most intense and
sustained warfare the plains had yet seen.

Rather than form a massive force to sweep down
on the forts and settlements, the leaders opted for a
less concentrated and more effective kind of warfare. Crazy Horse led one of dozens of bands of
warriors, sometimes with as few as ten members,
sometimes nearly a hundred, which fanned out
across the plains.

The troops were widely scattered, their outposts
separated from one another by miles of open space,
and that space belonged to the Sioux. Communication
was sporadic at best, limited to telegraph and, when
that was not possible, by courier. Realizing how
dependent the army was on the "talking wire," Crazy
Horse made one of his principal aims the disruption
of the telegraphy system.

Stations were burned, wires cut and, when there
were enough warriors available, long sections of
the wire removed and the poles toppled and
burned. The mails, too, came in for their share of
attention, as did the stagecoach lines. One after
another, stage stations were burned to the ground.
Remote, even isolated, many of them were manned
by a handful of defenders, often enough to drive off
the raiders but not to save the stations themselves.
Pursuit of attacking bands was out of the question.

By early spring, it was apparent that the Sioux
were not about to forget Sand Creek. The incessant
raids were taking an enormous toll on supplies
and, more importantly, on military morale. Many
of the soldiers were unfamiliar with plains Indian
warfare and contemptuous of their adversaries.

Like Grattan before them, they felt as if they were being held back by reluctant commanders, prevented from putting a permanent, expedient end to the Sioux depredations.

With the Civil War ending, Maj. Gen. Grenville Dodge, fresh from Sherman's march, was given command of the Department of the Missouri. Two months of harassment of stage and telegraph lines by the Sioux brought Dodge west to Fort Riley with a sheaf of orders to wage war on the Sioux and restore order to the Platte River Territory.

The winter was severe, even more severe than usual when Dodge reached Kansas and, true to his mission, he started immediately, despite the intense cold and the unremitting snowstorms. He lost thirteen men to the weather on his way to Fort Kearney. He took a stagecoach, making his way from post to post and finding, without exception, that his post commanders were bound to their installations. The Sioux were everywhere, and the troops were reluctant to travel beyond a quick sprint back to their stockades.

Not one to tolerate cowardice, or anything which in his rather severe definition even approximated it, he issued orders at fort after fort. His commanders were told in no uncertain terms to send their men out and not to readmit them until the telegraph lines were up and working. Whether afraid of Dodge or the Sioux, the men worked fast, and full communications were restored within two months.

During this period, there were very few significant clashes with the Sioux, and Dodge congratulated himself on striking terror into their hearts.

What he didn't realize is that the Sioux were interested only in harassment. They were on their way
to the last remaining good buffalo hunting territory
north of the Platte, in the Powder River country
and the vicinity of the Black Hills.

Unfortunately for both Dodge and the Sioux,
Colonel Collins, the only military commander in
the Department of the Missouri who seemed to
have a grasp of Sioux mentality, had completed his
three years' service on the frontier, mustered out
and retired. His place was taken by Col. Thomas
Moonlight, whose sole claim to fame was having
replaced Colonel Chivington as the commander of
the Department of Colorado. That left Dodge with
no counsel worth having. Firebrands were a dime a
dozen in the army, and most didn't need a match to
ignite their quick tempers. Dodge was not the least
among them, and he was determined to discharge
his duties with the unremitting zeal for which he
had become known. The attitude percolated
throughout the Department.

While Dodge was trying to reinvigorate his
forces, Spotted Tail and the Brule, and the Oglala
under Old Man Afraid, were ensconced in the buffalo country. But the Cheyenne, furious over the
betrayal at Sand Creek, rode north in an effort to
entice their Sioux allies to join them in a full-scale
war against the white soldiers. Spotted Tail
declined the Cheyenne request, but Old Man
Afraid, while still opposed to war, knew that his
young warriors could not be held back and, reluctantly, accepted the war pipe, as did Red Cloud.

Using the Powder River valley as a base of oper-
ations, the Sioux resumed their attacks on the out-

posts west of Fort Laramie. Crazy Horse, with Young Man Afraid, Hump, and Red Cloud, led raid after raid, trying to pound the bluecoats into submission. Using new tactics devised in large part by Crazy Horse, the Sioux would stage a raid as a diversionary tactic. When the raid managed to draw out a cavalry column to relieve the besieged station, the Sioux, watching from concealment, then swooped down on the post the cavalry had left lightly defended. Again and again, they attacked, feinted, and fell back. All the soldiers could do was race across the plains arriving hours, even days, late, only to find that somewhere behind them yet another raid had taken place.

Throughout the spring, the guerrilla war raged across Colorado Territory. Moonlight, like so many of his fellow officers, was in the dark about his adversaries, and yielded little to Lieutenant Grattan when it came to impetuousness. Sensing Moonlight's belligerence, the soldiers in his command allowed themselves to take a more aggressive attitude toward the Sioux, even the Laramie Loafers who clung like barnacles to the Fort. But the constant barrage of muttering and threats was beginning to make the Loafers nervous.

It seemed to Smoke and the other peaceful Sioux settled near the fort that Moonlight and his men did not know the difference between friendly and hostile Sioux or, if they did, did not care. The one ray of sunshine in the Loafers' lot was the presence of Capt. Charlie Elliston, who was married to a Sioux woman, and given command of a detachment of Indian police, charged with keeping the peace in the Oglala settlement, which Colonel

Collins had had the foresight to move a few miles farther away from Fort Laramie before retiring.

But Elliston was derided as a "squaw man" by the white soldiers, and the lack of respect with which he was regarded gave him little influence among them.

By the middle of May, the tinder was already beginning to smolder. But no one noticed the tiny curls of smoke. On the eighteenth, a Sioux sub-chief named Two Face showed up at the gates of Fort Laramie. With him was a white woman, Naomi Eubanks, and her daughter. The two women had been prisoners of the Cheyenne for several months. Two Face, thinking to make some headway in his quest for peace with the bluecoats, ransomed the two women from the Cheyenne, and brought them in.

When Two Face had arrived at Bordeaux's trading post, it was apparent that Mrs. Eubanks had fared badly at Cheyenne hands. Her clothes were torn and dirty, her face showed bruises and other signs of abuse, and her tale of rape at Cheyenne hands inflamed all the whites, soldiers and settlers alike. One of the women at Bordeaux's gave her a change of clothes, and George Beauvais, one of Bordeaux's men, accompanied the Sioux and the two women on to the Fort.

A raft was sent over for Two Face, the women, and Beauvais, who was to translate for Two Face, and try to explain what the Sioux's purpose had been. But once across the river, Mrs. Eubanks, whether from malice or the inability to tell one Indian from another, accused not only the Cheyenne but Two Face himself of having raped her. She also accused another Sioux subchief, Blackfoot, living in a village on the White River. Captain Elliston was dispatched to bring Blackfoot in, against his better judgment.

When Ellison returned with Blackfoot in tow, both Sioux were clapped in irons and locked in the Laramie guardhouse. Beauvais protested, explaining again and again that Two Face had done nothing wrong, nothing but try to help Mrs. Eubanks.

"Why would he have come in here," Beauvais argued, "if he had done what the woman says he did?"

"He's a redskin, Beauvais," Moonlight countered. "How the hell am I supposed to know what goes on in his mind."

"Look, Colonel, no man, red or white, would put himself in the way of trouble like that. Not if he'd done anything like what that poor woman says he's done."

"Then why did that poor woman, as you call her, accuse him?"

"How the hell do I know? She's scared to death. Maybe all Indians are the same to her. Maybe she just wants to see some poor Indian suffer, pay back for what happened to her."

"And maybe she's telling the truth. Did you consider that possibility?"

"I know the man. No way on God's green earth he done what she says."

"Well, I think he did, and I'm going to make an example out of him. I'll string the bastards to a tall tree. Maybe then the other Sioux'll get the message."

"That's a bad idea, Colonel, a real bad idea."

"I don't give a damn what you say, Beauvais. Hell, you're not much better'n a redskin yourself."

"You hurt those men, Colonel, especially for something they didn't do, and this whole country will explode. You're cutting off your nose to spite your face."

"It's my nose, Beauvais. And my face. I'll do what I want with them."

Moonlight would not listen to reason, and word soon spread. The sutler's agent at Laramie, retired Col. W. G. Bullock, heard what Moonlight was planning, and rushed to the fort. He was ushered into Moonlight's office and started speaking before the colonel even had a chance to look up from his desk.

"You better think about what you're doing, Colonel," Bullock warned. "You hang those men and every hostile Indian for a hundred miles will come thundering down on this fort. There's thousands of 'em, and they'll overrun this place in the wink of an eye."

"They're Indians, Mister Bullock. We have more and better weapons. That more than makes up for their numbers. And I'll be damned if I will let anybody, even you, tell me how to run my command."

"You better let somebody tell you, Colonel, or your widow will get a short letter from the Secretary of War right quick."

"Get out of my office."

"Listen to me, Colonel. You . . ."

"I've already heard enough, Mister Bullock. You think there's going to be a massacre here at the fort, do you? Well, let me tell you, the Sioux will be shorthanded by two, massacre or no. And that's a fact."

"You're mad."

"You're damn right I am, Mister Bullock. Mad as hell. And those damned savages are going to pay the price."

Bullock started to argue, but Moonlight held up a hand. "No more, Mister Bullock. No more. You will not dissuade me. Don't even try."

On May 26, the two Sioux prisoners were escorted to a hilltop overlooking the river. A gallows had already been built and, without ceremony, iron balls were attached to their legs and the two innocent Sioux were hanged. Moonlight would not permit the bodies to be taken down, and they stayed there on the hilltop, swaying in the breeze, until the bodies rotted and the heavy iron balls pulled the legs from the torsos.

The Sioux were furious. General Dodge, when apprised of that anger, and that there was a Sioux camp located so close to Fort Laramie, ordered that the village be moved to Fort Kearney, deeper in white-controlled territory. But the Sioux had long memories. They recalled that Conquering Bear had been a friend to the whites and had been shot down for his troubles. They remembered that Harney had attacked Little Thunder's Brule camp without provocation, despite assurances from the chief that his people were not hostile.

When word of the enforced removal reached Sioux ears, it didn't take long for the resentment to boil over. And when they realized that they were to be moved, disarmed, to a camp in the heart of Pawnee territory, the thought of being at the mercy of their hated enemies was more than they could tolerate. Spotted Tail, despite his commitment to peace, was determined that he would not go. The tame Oglala, used to handouts and long removed from independence, were resolved that they would not go, either.

On June 11, the caravan moved out. Nearly two thousand Oglala and Brule, toting everything they owned in the world on their horses and travois, started to march down the Platte River. But word of the forced march had reached other bands of Sioux, and Crazy Horse slipped into the temporary camp on the first night, past the lackadaisical troopers under the command of Capt. W. D. Fouts.

Fouts, like Moonlight, was contemptuous of the Sioux and their fighting ability. So much, in fact, that he refused to issue ammunition to half his men, those marching in the rear of the caravan. Their picketing was porous, to say the least, and Crazy Horse had little trouble slipping in and out of the village.

It didn't take much to convince Spotted Tail and the others that escape was desirable and, with Crazy Horse urging them on, possible. The next day, as the caravan moved slowly along the river bottom, the young warriors, to ease the passage of time and vent a little of their pent-up energy and simmering frustration, raced their ponies back and forth along the line of march. Fouts was furious, and ordered them to stop. The warriors ignored him.

The following day, the warriors again raced along the route, and smoke signals began to appear in the hills rolling away from the river. That night,

Fouts called the chiefs together and read them the riot act. He threatened that any warrior who chose to disregard the prohibition on racing his pony would be tied to a wagon wheel and whipped.

They were camped within a stone's throw of the campground for the Great Council of 1851, and the proximity became a goad to the more irascible among the Sioux. They remembered the promises made to them at the Council, and could now see for themselves how good the white man's word might be. Well after dark, Crazy Horse reappeared in the camp and told Spotted Tail that warriors had marked a route through the quicksands of the Platte, using willow poles driven into the river bottom. The plan called for the warriors to hold the troopers at bay while the women and children made a break across the river. Once the women and children had reached the far side, the warriors would follow. The Sioux knew that most of the troopers were unable to swim, and were counting on the river protecting them from pursuit, once they managed their crossing.

The following morning, the Sioux were laggard in breaking camp. Fouts, impatient to be going, left word that they should catch up to him as soon as possible, then moved his men on out. As soon as the last trooper was out of sight, the Sioux broke for the riverbank. Fouts reappeared a few minutes later, and, when he saw the waters of the Platte teeming with women and children, demanded to know what was going on.

A rifle cracked, and Fouts fell dead. As if the gunshot had been a signal, the rest of the Sioux stampeded for the river. The rear guard troops saw

what was happening but, without ammunition,
they were powerless to interfere. Several warriors,
Crazy Horse and Black Wolf among them, spurred
their people on, prowling the riverbank with their
arms whirling, urging everyone to cross.

"Come on, hurry, hurry," Black Wolf shouted.

Crazy Horse spotted more troops coming. Some
of Fouts's advance guard had apparently heard the
gunshots and come to see what was happening.
Fouts's second in command, Capt. John Wilcox,
rode up and, when he saw the melee, demanded to
know why the rear guard had done nothing. When
he learned they had no ammunition, he had it
issued, then deployed his wagons for defense and
sent Captain Ellison to tell the Sioux that those who
were not hostile could return without punishment.

The resultant charge of massed Sioux warriors
convinced him in short order that all of the Sioux
were hostile. The warriors charged the wagons, and
nearly overran them. The troopers fell back under
the onslaught, but the Sioux were less interested in
attacking than in buying time. As soon as the
women and children were safely across, the warriors turned their mounts and followed them.

By nine o'clock, all two thousand had crossed
the river, leaving the troopers, and all their worldly
possessions, on the south bank of the Platte.

# Chapter 15 ════════

THE COUNCIL WAS THE LARGEST IN YEARS. Sioux came from all over, Cheyennes, too, and even Arapaho. The plains were in turmoil. News of the Sand Creek massacre of Black Kettle's friendly village ran like prairie fire from village to village. The chiefs inclined to go on the warpath argued that Chivington's cowardly attack on a peaceful village proved that the white men would never allow the Sioux to live in peace.

Red Cloud was the most articulate spokesman for the war party. "The white man makes promises but he does not keep them," he said. The council nodded.

Even Spotted Tail knew it was true. He was a proud man, one who wanted peace, but refused to surrender his dignity. A great warrior, he had the respect of many of the fence straddlers. "Red Cloud is right. But he should know that there are many more white soldiers than there are Sioux and Cheyenne. He has heard the stories, just as I have, just as we all have, of armies of a hundred thousand men fighting in the great white man's war."

Red Cloud nodded his agreement. "I have heard

those stories. But I have never seen those armies. Has Spotted Tail seen them?"

"No. But I believe the stories. The trader, Bordeaux, says they are true. He has no reason to lie. He has showed stories to me in the paper with writing."

"He is a white man. What more reason does he need. He makes money by selling his goods to the soldiers, and he makes money by trading his goods to the Loaf About the Forts. The Great Father pays him well to keep the Lakota people quiet. But I am tired of being quiet. The white man has taken our land, ruined the buffalo hunting, and built his forts where we used to make our villages. It has to stop."

Old Man Afraid took the floor. "You know me. You know I have counted coup on Crow and Shoshoni, on Pawnee and the bluecoat." Around the fire, the chiefs looked at one another, some saying "Hou," assenting to the truth of what Old Man Afraid was saying. Others, knowing he was just beginning, waited to see what he would say next.

"Our Cheyenne brothers know how cruel the white soldiers can be." He paused to look at Roman Nose, the great Cheyenne war chief, who nodded. "He can tell you about the children lying in the mud made by their own blood mixing with the earth. He can tell you of the women, their scalps taken and their private parts butchered by the white soldiers. I don't want that for our children and our women."

Red Cloud interrupted. "Then Old Man Afraid should go on the warpath to kill the bluecoats before they can kill his people. If we kill them before they kill us, our women and children will be safe. We can take back our lands."

"And will the buffalo come back?" Spotted Tail demanded. "If not, how will we live?"

"Does Spotted Tail wish to hang around the fort on his knees, his hands out like a beggar, waiting for crumbs? Is that how a warrior should live? On his own land?"

Stung by the charge, Spotted Tail got to his feet. "You are supposed to be leaders. But a leader does not lead his people to slaughter. He does not put his pride above the safety of those who depend on him. We have all heard of Sand Creek. We have all seen the wagon guns that kill ten warriors with one shot. We have all seen the river of whites that flows without end year after year. We cannot win a war with the whites. Better that we ask for peace while we are still strong, while we can still get something in exchange."

Red Cloud laughed then. "What we will get is promises, promises that change like the moon. If we take the path of peace, we will walk into slaughter like the buffalo, with nothing to do but wait for the bullets that will surely come. If we do not fight now when we are strong, then we will lose everything."

Old Man Afraid started to speak, but Red Cloud cut him off. "Look around this council, my brothers. The chiefs we have assembled here are the best chiefs. They lead the best warriors. We are not afraid, and I say we should not act as if we are afraid. The white man is afraid of us, too. Did we not cut his talking wire? Did we not win every battle we fought with the bluecoats this past year?

Why should we give up when we are winning? Let the white man ask for peace. Maybe we will give it to him, and maybe we will push him back where he came from, and he will leave us alone."

Crazy Horse was sitting in the back, next to Hump and Little Hawk. Worm was in the main council circle, and looked at his son, who seemed restless. When Red Cloud finished speaking, there was a long silence. It seemed as if no one wanted to agree with him, but no one wanted to argue for peace, either. Spotted Tail and Old Man Afraid were isolated, and no one wanted to speak for their side.

Finally, Crazy Horse asked for permission to speak. Red Cloud nodded, and no one objected. "Always," the young warrior said, "when we fight, we fight the same way. The bluecoats know how we fight, and they are ready for us. If we are to fight, we will have to fight like the white man does. We will have to have discipline, and the warriors will have to follow their chiefs, do what they say, not fight when they feel like fighting. We must make plans and follow them. If we are to win a war with the white soldiers, that is the way we will have to do it."

Since he had become so prominent, Crazy Horse was respected not just for his courage but for his wisdom, and his words now provoked a buzz of discussion.

"Does Crazy Horse think we can defeat the white soldiers?" Old Man Afraid asked.

"I don't know," Crazy Horse answered. "But I know we cannot win if we fight as we have always fought. If we change, if we fight like the white man fights . . ."—he shrugged—". . . then, maybe we can."

"Will you fight?"

"Yes."

Old Man Afraid shook his head sadly. He knew that Crazy Horse spoke for many of the young warriors, most of them, more than likely. Even his own son. He believed that fighting would come to no good, but he also knew that that was a painful lesson that would only be learned under the muzzle of the soldier guns.

"Will you tell us how to fight the bluecoats?" Old Man Afraid asked.

Crazy Horse nodded. "Yes."

Spotted Tail was not ready to give up. "Would you follow this stripling? Would you let him lead you into battle, when there are many here twice his age?"

"Perhaps you are too old to fight, Spotted Tail," Red Cloud suggested. "Perhaps you are an old dog that cannot learn new ways."

Spotted Tail snorted in disgust. "I *have* learned new ways. That is why I believe that fighting is useless. I have learned not to fight."

Red Cloud smiled. There was no derision in the look, just a tinge of sadness. "Perhaps you are right. But I do not believe it. I will fight."

One by one, the chiefs around the council fire nodded their agreement. In the end, Spotted Tail stood alone against the warpath. Even Old Man Afraid, who was opposed to war, sided with Red Cloud, thinking that it would be better if there were someone in the war party who could argue for peace when the time came. And he knew that, if he fought, his arguments for peace would be the stronger for it.

"I am leaving," Spotted Tail announced.

Red Cloud nodded. "Hou!" he said. "I wish you well. Where will you go?"

"First, I will go to Fort Laramie and tell the white soldiers that my people are on the path of peace. Then"—he shrugged—"maybe to the Black Hills."

The council continued its deliberations after Spotted Tail said goodbye to his friends. Crazy Horse started to outline his plans, and asked to meet with the chiefs again the following morning, after he'd had a chance to consider the best way to proceed.

Spotted Tail left at sunrise. Crazy Horse walked a way with his uncle, talking quietly under the bustle of the moving village. "If you change your mind, you are always welcome among your mother's people, Crazy Horse."

"I know." He looked at the sky, at the almost unclouded blue, a blue so deep he thought he could swim up and away in it, the way he would in a deep lake. "Maybe, some day . . ."

"Goodbye," his uncle said, then swung up onto his pony.

Walking back to the council lodge, he wondered whether he was making a mistake. He knew that Spotted Tail was wise, and that he might even be right. But it galled him to think of living in the shadow of a stockade, his hand out for a bag of coffee, learning to eat the white man's beef. It was more than he could stand. More than he should have to stand.

He ducked into the lodge, where the chiefs were already waiting for him. It took him an hour to outline his plan, and another hour to convince the chiefs that it was the only way. Most of them saw the wisdom of his argument, but the old ways were a powerful magnet. They wanted to fight as they had always fought. This new way of fighting would be difficult, especially for the wild young men who were not used to taking orders. The Sioux way had always been individual combat. Plans were not something they were used to following. And now, flushed with the success of the raids, and angered by the Sand Creek massacre, the young men would not be easy to control.

The plan was a simple one. Crazy Horse wanted to cut the white soldiers' line apart piece by piece. He would start with the small fort guarding the last bridge over the Platte River. If the Sioux could gain control of the bridge, the forts beyond it would be cut off from their supplies. It would be simple to overrun the forts then. Once that first step had been taken, they could then begin to chew their way back along the Oregon Trail until they had forced the white soldiers all the way out of Sioux Territory.

The young men were told to stop raiding. Crazy Horse wanted the soldiers to feel secure. They might get sloppy, but even if they didn't, they would not be calling for more troops. Better to take them on now, before their strength increased. In the middle of July, nearly two thousand warriors headed for the Platte River. The column was two miles long.

On the morning of the twenty-fourth, scouts

went out to see what sort of force the whites could command, while the rest of the warriors took up their positions. The small fort was on the south side of the Platte River. The day's plan called for a decoy to lure the troops out and across the bridge, where they could be cut off. But Crazy Horse was worried. Red Cloud and some of the other older men had added embellishments. They were planning to concentrate too many warriors in too small an area. Crazy Horse feared they would get in one another's way, but the old chiefs refused to listen to him, and after one final try, he was forced to hold his tongue.

Most of the Indian force took up a position two miles away, hidden behind the rolling hills that swept down toward the river. Passing a pair of army binoculars around, the chiefs kept watch on the bridge and the small party of warriors sent out as bait.

The commander of Platte Bridge Station, Maj. Martin Anderson, was not going to be lured easily. Again and again, the decoys approached the bridge, taunting the soldiers and trying to provoke them into pursuit, but again and again, Anderson held his men back. Twice, he sent howitzer shells across the river, but they did no damage, and the decoys fell back out of range with nothing to show for their efforts.

The following morning, the decoys tried again, and again had no success. More decoys approached the bridge that afternoon, thinking that a larger party might be enough to spring the trap. The main war party was showing its new discipline, keeping out of sight, and giving the plan a chance to work.

Crazy Horse watched quietly, wondering just how long that discipline would hold. He knew it wouldn't last forever.

But then the Sioux luck turned. Unknown to them, a wagon train loaded with guns and ammunition was approaching. With the telegraph lines cut, the commander of the wagon train, Sgt. Amos Custard, had left Fort Laramie without being informed of the presence of the Indians. Major Anderson had no idea of the force hidden in the hills, but he sensed that something was about to happen, and would have halted the supply train had he been able to.

Some of the younger officers in the fort wanted to ride out to meet the train, but Anderson was wary. He was bothered by the repeated forays of the small bands, and something seemed odd to him. He couldn't put his finger on what it was, and the younger officers were starting to suspect that he was frightened.

The following morning, Anderson's hand was forced. The wagon train would arrive in a few hours, and Anderson was worried. He called a conference of the officers to try and decide how to handle the situation. Caspar Collins, on the way to his permanent post at Sweetwater Station, was among them. There was much debate, some of the more rash among the younger officers wanting to ride out to meet the supply train and escort it in. Others, like Anderson, suspicious of the frequent appearance of small parties of Sioux, argued for prudence.

While the conference ground on, the Indians took up their positions. Four hundred Cheyenne rode down to the river and hid themselves in the brush along the waterline, just west of the bridge. Several hundred Sioux positioned themselves in a dry wash that led to the river on the east of the station. Several hundred Arapaho took up a third position, in Casper Creek. The rest of the Sioux, several hundred more, flooded into the canyons that crisscrossed the road farther to the west.

The plan was simple. Once the decoys had lured the troopers out of the fort, the Cheyenne would launch their attack. At the same time, the Arapaho and the smaller contingent of the Sioux would block their retreat, forcing them to head west along the road. They would ride right into the arms of the waiting Sioux hordes. All the Sioux needed for that to happen was for the decoy party to do its job, and the rest would be easy.

In the fort, Anderson was concerned about how poorly armed his men were. Almost a third of the one hundred and twenty men didn't even have rifles. They were armed with revolvers only, or had no guns at all. The weather had kept the road muddy for months, and supplies had been slow in coming. Stores of ammunition were dangerously depleted. Anderson thanked his stars that the Sioux did not know of his plight.

When the supply train was sighted, he ordered Capt. James Greer, the post commander, to send a small unit out to escort it to safety. Greer issued his orders to Sgt. Jake Pennock. When Pennock's men were ready, he reported to the colonel, and was advised that Lieutenant Collins was going with the detachment.

Casper Collins, wearing a brand-new uniform, led the detachment out of the stockade gates. The drumming of the hooves on the bridge echoed up and down the creek bed, and the Indians were getting edgy as they waited for their opportunity. Right behind the Collins unit, ten more troopers, under Capt. Henry Bretney, crossed the bridge to keep an eye out for Indians and to support Collins in the event of trouble.

Some of the concealed Sioux recognized the young lieutenant and waved to get his attention, calling out for him to turn back. But Collins didn't notice, and rode on past while Young Man Afraid and Black Bear wrung their hands helplessly.

At the same instant, one of the officers in the stockade spotted some of the crouching Cheyenne and Anderson dispatched twenty more men. While the reinforcements saddled their mounts, Collins proceeded west along the road, and was already a half mile past the bridge. Hidden on either side, the Cheyenne and Sioux watched him pass.

A quarter mile ahead, several Sioux were gathered around the base of a telegraph pole. One of their number was busy cutting the telegraph wire. The small party bolted when it spotted Collins, who immediately left the road in pursuit. He was heading toward the main body of the Sioux now, and discovery of the trap was imminent.

As soon as the last of Collins's men turned north and left the road, the Cheyenne poured out of the brush. Collins kept his head and wheeled his men into a defensive line. But the Sioux swept out of the interlacing canyons. Collins was surrounded, his twenty-five men against two thousand warriors.

"Column . . . twos!" Collins shouted, then, "Retreat to the bridge!"

With such overwhelming numerical advantage, and combat at such close quarters, the warriors used clubs and lances rather than bows or the few guns they had. The troopers, their rifles only single-shot models, were almost instantly reduced to using their revolvers. Despite the horde of warriors, the troopers fought bravely, and managed to make it to the edge of the bluff from which they could reach the road back to the stockade. But several of their horses had been killed, and all the men were hit, four of them killed.

As Collins was about to lead the charge down to the road, one of the men, unhorsed, called out for help. Collins turned to see the Sioux and Cheyenne flood about to swallow the wounded man. Wounded himself in the hip, Caspar disregarded the pain and charged back toward the fallen trooper. An arrow slammed into his forehead and stuck, flapping as he rode on, firing a pair of revolvers at the advancing warriors. At the edge of the bluff, he fell from his horse, dead before he hit the ground.

The second relief detachment was armed with repeating Spencer carbines, the only ones in Anderson's command. Led by Captain Greer, the small unit poured relentless fire into the thousands of warriors, killing several and wounding many more.

The retreating troopers, those from Collins's command, and those from Bretney's, fell back toward the bridge under the cover of Greer's fire. The Indians were firing volley after volley of arrows, but the milling mass of warriors was sustaining heavy casualties not only from the Spencers but from the indiscriminate Indian fire, as well.

The retreating soldiers managed to cross the bridge, and Greer's Spencers laid down a constant fire, falling back behind the wounded men until the stockade gates closed around them. The combined Cheyenne, Sioux, and Arapaho forces, furious at their failure to annihilate the troopers, turned their anger westward as the supply train came into view. They swarmed over the wagons and, after a desperate siege, the last of the supply train troopers fell under the assault.

The battle for Platte Bridge Station was over. Despite killing twenty-eight bluecoats, the warriors knew their victory had been hollow. They left the lifted scalps scattered on the ground and rode off, unaware that, with the telegraph line cut, there would be no reinforcements and they could have taken the stockade itself with a little more time.

As the Sioux rode past the stockade one last time, Crazy Horse saw the body of Caspar Collins. The arrow still embedded in his forehead had snapped off at the skull an inch or so beneath the bloody patch where his scalp had been, or perhaps the warrior who had taken the scalp had snapped the shaft to make his work easier. Crazy Horse turned away. Collins had been a good and brave man, and it was a pity that their friendship had to end this way, he thought.

But it was the white men who had come to Sioux land uninvited.

# Chapter 16 ═══════

## August 1865

OLD MAN AFRAID WAS SORRY for the death of Caspar Collins. He was sorry because the lieutenant had been a good man, friendly to the Sioux in general, a man who seemed to see the Sioux as his equals, who was consumed by curiosity about their way of living, and who saw but did not judge. He had been friendly to all the Sioux, but especially to Old Man Afraid's own son and, even more, to Crazy Horse. He had died bravely, fighting a war he did not agree with, but, as a good warrior must, fighting when his chiefs told him it was time to fight. It had been a brave thing to go back alone for the wounded bluecoat, the kind of thing that Crazy Horse himself was known to do, the kind of thing that all great warriors do and that, one day or another, got most of them killed.

But Old Man Afraid saw something else that afternoon at Platte Bridge Station. He saw that Crazy Horse was right, that discipline was important, even essential, if the Sioux were to have a chance to win their war with the white soldiers. He remembered something from his youth, and paid a visit to one of the old men in his village, named Fights with a Lance.

The old man was glad to see him. Nearly blind, he had to lean forward, squinting across the fire in the center of his lodge to make out Old Man Afraid's features.

"It has been a long time since I have seen you, Old Man Afraid," he said.

Old Man Afraid nodded. "Too long. The fault is mine. I am sorry."

"You are busy with the things of the people. One old man is as nothing. I understand that and I do not blame you. In watching out for all the people, you watch out for me, too, and I am grateful."

Old Man Afraid smiled. "Do you remember, long ago, when the tribal council had seven men to make the laws?"

The old man nodded. "The Big Bellies," he said. "Yes, I remember. It was a good way, but we let it die."

"Tell me about it."

Fights with a Lance reached for his pipe, packed the bowl with shavings of willow bark, then tamped some tobacco on top, lit it with a slender twig from the fire, and puffed until he was sure the flame had taken hold. Then he passed the pipe to Old Man Afraid.

"I have heard that the white man does something like we used to do. But that does not mean that it is not a good thing to do. I think it was a good thing. It was not our way. Someone, I don't remember who, had learned it from the Blackfeet people. It was their way, and it worked for them, so we tried it, and it worked for us, too. It was better, because the people chose their leaders. That way, you did not have men trying so hard to be leaders that they forgot to lead. Always scheming, like now, trying to make friends to stay in front of the council. Red Cloud is one like that. He is a great warrior, and young men come from all the tribes to stay in his camp, to follow him on the warpath. But he is not satisfied with that. Always he is making plans to get more power. This is not a good thing. I think, if we could go back to the way you mean, to the Big Bellies and the shirt-wearers, it would be better for the people."

"I don't remember much about it. Who chose the Big Bellies? Was it the chiefs?"

"No. All the people. They could be chiefs themselves, and usually they were, because a chief is chosen for many of the same reasons. But not all chiefs make good Big Bellies. One must be wise and brave and unselfish. This is how they got the name Big Bellies, because they were older, with their bellies beginning to get fat, the way it happens with old men. Most of the time, their fighting days were behind them. But it was a way to use what they had learned for the benefit of all the people. Red Cloud is brave, but he is selfish, and sometimes he is not so wise as he is clever. And he is less interested in all the people than he is in Red Cloud."

"And the shirt-wearers, did the Big Bellies choose them?"

"No. The warriors chose the shirt-wearers. This was only right, since it was the warriors who had to follow the shirt-wearers, had to do the things the shirt-wearers wanted done. The shirt-wearers did not have *akicitas* to help them."

"Do you remember the ceremony? Do you remember how to make the shirt?"

Fights with a Lance grunted, then reached across the fire for the pipe. When Old Man Afraid handed it to him, he sucked contentedly for a few moments, letting the thick, fragrant smoke wreath his wrinkled face, then nodded. "My father was a shirt-wearer. I still have his shirt. It is a well-made thing and has lasted all these winters."

"Would you help me explain these things to the Council?"

"Why?"

"I think it is something we should do again. I think it is the only way we can survive."

Fights with a Lance smiled. "You learned this thing from Crazy Horse."

Old Man Afraid shook his head. "I have not discussed it with him."

"No matter. This thing he wanted to do at the bridge, that was the kind of thing the Big Bellies would do, and the shirt-wearers. Rules, discipline, that is why we had shirt-wearers. Crazy Horse knows this. Maybe he is the only one of the young men who does. But maybe he can teach the others."

"I would not want to have to teach them."

"Someone will have to. They love Crazy Horse and they will follow him. But he will need help. You can give him that help. You can convince the other chiefs how important it is."

"I have argued with them, but . . ." He shook his head.

"If you give up, then it is over. You cannot give up without a fight. Your son will help. So will Crazy Horse. If you convince the chiefs to do this thing, then . . . who knows what might happen? We know only what will happen if you cannot convince them."

"And what is that?"

"Our people will cease to be."

"Hou!" Old Man Afraid nodded his head wearily. It was true, and it was what he was trying not to face. But Fights with a Lance would not let him turn away from that truth. "Thank you," he said, getting to his feet.

And for three days, the chiefs talked about it among themselves. Day and night, sometimes all night long, taking turns adding fuel to the fire in the council lodge, they argued. And in the end, they did as Old Man Afraid suggested. They knew he was right, and they knew, too, that time was running out on them. One did not have to be a wise man to see that the buffalo were disappearing from their hunting grounds, that the whites were thick like grasshoppers on the summer fields, and that one day soon, if things continued to go as they had been going, there would be no buffalo and, not long after, no Lakota.

On the third night, they made their decision. They chose the Big Bellies not with joy, but with a sense of desperation, trying to pick the men who would be their last hope. And they chose well. Old Man Afraid was first among them, first to be chosen because he was the wisest and because he knew, better than any of them, just how heavy was the burden the Big Bellies would be asked to carry. Brave Bear was chosen, and Sitting Bear, too. But Red Cloud was passed over, and he was not happy not to be among the seven.

They began building the ceremonial lodge the

next day, in the center of the village circle, covering its enormous frame with painted skins that showed all the *wakan* things the Sioux held sacred. And when it was done, the sides were rolled up, so that all the people could see what would happen there. The newly chosen Big Bellies gathered then, sitting in a line across the center of the ceremonial lodge. The people gathered around the outside, filling all the space between the great lodge and the tipis in the village circle, spilling over into the space beyond the great circle, packed together, standing on tiptoe to see what would happen.

The warriors came then, riding in a circle, charging through until the people backed up to give them room. They circled the village, and called out the name of Young Man Afraid to be the first shirt-wearer. Young Man Afraid walked to the ceremonial lodge and sat down facing the Big Bellies. Behind him, he could hear the commotion as the warriors made a second circuit of the village. This time they chose Sword, the son of Brave Bear, and he, too, entered the ceremonial lodge.

After the third trip through, the women singing the praises of the two men already chosen, the warriors scanned the crowd, looking for their next shirt-wearer. They stopped in front of the opening facing the east and announced their choice. American Horse, the son of Sitting Bear, joined his fellow shirt-wearers. It now seemed clear. All three chosen were the sons of Big Bellies, which was, some said, as it should be. But others felt that it was only to be expected. Power, after all, they whispered, belongs to those who have it to begin with.

And for the fourth and final time the warriors circled the camp. Their faces were strained, deliberate, their eyes darting this way and that. It was clear they were looking for someone in particular, and having trouble finding him. Finally, one of the warriors spotted him, pointed, and called a halt—they had found Crazy Horse.

The people nodded their approval. He was the best, after all, and it was only right that the best warrior should wear the shirt. They had to coax him to leave the back of the crowd. He kept looking at his father, and Worm urged him to accept gracefully, to go to the ceremonial lodge, to take his rightful place.

When he joined the others, he took his place quietly, sitting cross-legged and looking at his knees.

An old man rose to speak, older even than Fights with a Lance.

"You are chosen by your people because you are brave," he said. "And because you know what is right and what is wrong. It is up to you to see that the old and the children, the women and the poor among us, are protected even as the strongest and richest are. If you do not look out for them, who will?"

He stared at each of the shirt-wearers in turn, almost daring them to disagree. None did, and he continued. "Respect everyone, and take nothing for yourselves. When you hunt the buffalo, give the best meat to those who need it most. You are young and strong. You can live on gristle and stringy meat. When the Crow attack us, look to the weak and do not worry about yourselves. Be wise and, above all, be kind. You are the best among us. Teach us to be as good as you are, and as brave."

"On a march, you will be our leaders. In camp, you will be our leaders. The warriors will do as you advise. And if they do not respect your words, then use more than words to make them respect you, but only when words fail."

Old Man Afraid called then for the shirts and they were brought in one at a time. Each was made from the skin of a bighorn sheep, dressed and cured to suppleness, finely wrought with beads and quillwork. The forelegs had been fashioned into sleeves and the hind legs dangled down free in back. Each shirt was fringed with hair, a single lock for each act of bravery, a friend saved, a coup counted, a scalp taken, a wound suffered. And the shirt for Crazy Horse had more than any other, more than two hundred and forty fringed locks dangling from its sleeves.

He held the shirt in his hands as if afraid to put it on. Young Man Afraid donned his, then Sword. American Horse laughed as he slipped his shirt on and then Crazy Horse, already known as one who took nothing for himself, stood and slipped the shirt over his head.

"Hou, Hou!" the people said, and it became a chant. Drums started to beat and the feast of buffalo meat and boiled dog was made ready.

Crazy Horse chewed on his lower lip, embarrassed by the attention, and slipped away to his father's lodge, where he could be alone and think about this new weight added to that already pressing on his broad shoulders.

# Chapter 17

**December 1865**

THE WINTER OF 1865 WAS THE HARDEST anyone could remember. The snows came early and often. The high plains were covered in drifts, the mountains covered deeper still. For the Sioux, hostile and peaceful alike, the toll was incalculable. Spotted Tail and his Brule were starving. Trapped north of the Platte by the hostilities, they had found the buffalo scarce when they found them at all. Red Cloud and his Oglala band also found the hunting paltry. Even for the Laramie Loafers, some of whom still clung to the security of the tails of the bluecoats, times were hard. The annuities were suspended due to the ongoing hostilities, all Sioux being punished by Washington for the depredations of some.

And the hurdy-gurdy of politics continued to grind, the crank turning slowly but surely, sending new monkeys in for old. Indian agents came and went over the years, arriving with empty pockets and leaving with the clink of silver to announce their departures. The turnover among the military men was just as frequent, and even more significant. The Sioux had no one to turn to, at least not with assurances that the same man would be there six months lator.

And as the personnel changed, so did the policy. Good intentions went back East with the few men who professed them, and newcomers, more often than not, were determined to show that they were the men to put an end to the Sioux problem notwithstanding the failures of their predecessors.

Col. Henry Maynadier had taken command of Fort Laramie. The colonel was the closest thing to a reasonable military man in the area since Colonel Collins had mustered out. Aware of the hardships the winter had been wreaking on the Sioux, he sent emissaries, including two Laramie Loafer chiefs named Big Ribs and Big Mouth, out among the hostiles with a request that the chiefs come in for a council.

At first, the results were slow in coming. But Swift Bear and his Brule band, their numbers reduced by heavy losses to cold and starvation among the women and children, agreed to come in. Old Man Afraid and his Oglala followed. They, too, had suffered severely under the harsh winter snows. Spotted Tail, too, agreed to come and talk. His daughter was desperately ill, and she had expressed the desire to be buried in the white man's cemetery at Fort Laramie.

When Spotted Tail asked if this could be done, Maynadier assured him that it could, and the great Brule chief agreed to bring his people to the council. The child, Yellow Buckskin Girl, was not yet seventeen, and died on the long trip to the fort. Maynadier was as good as his word, and at the funeral, he saw to it that all off-duty soldiers were in attendance.

Afterward, he met with Spotted Tail in his quarters. The chief, grieving at the loss of his daughter, was also moved by the kindness of the colonel.

Maynadier patted the chief's shoulder. "I am sorry for your loss," he said. "But the Great Spirit has taken your child to a better place. At night, the darkness of your lodge will be hard to bear, because it will remind you of that darkness in your heart where your daughter's light used to shine. It is hard to lose a child, but you must believe that one day you will see her again in that better place, when the Great Spirit sees fit to bring you to join her."

"It is like a dream," Spotted Tail said, "to sit here in such a room. This place is warm, and the feelings are of friendship. We feel that we have been done much wrong, and that justice has not been done to our people, but I am too sad to talk of such things now. I will wait until the council and the time when the peace commissioners from the Great Father arrive. Then we will discuss these things. But I thank you for your kindness."

Maynadier was not alone in his hopes that reasonable treatment and fairness would win the peace that guns and soldiers had so far been unable to impose on the fiercely independent Sioux. The head of the peace commission, the journalist E. B. Taylor, and the new agent for the territory, Vital Jarrot, were also committed to a satisfactory and just resolution of the impasse.

But Gen. John Pope, back in Omaha, was impatient. He knew that the plan of the commission was to bargain for a new road through the region to establish supply lines to the newly opened gold fields of Montana, and ordered troops into the Powder River country to establish two new forts. He placed Col. Henry Carrington, a career officer with no Indian experience, in charge of the construction, and ordered him into the field at the head of a column of seven hundred men.

The peace commission was scheduled to hold its first meeting in early June, but Carrington left on May 19, and word of his coming spread rapidly. By the middle of June, with the peace discussion already underway, and many of the major Sioux chiefs, including Red Cloud, in reluctant attendance, already at Fort Laramie, the talks had started to founder.

With the spring thaw, grass had returned to the plains, the hunting improved, and the Sioux, ambivalent at best about the white man's intentions, were beginning to doubt the wisdom of agreeing to any terms which would require them to cede still more territory to the whites. One of the chiefs, Standing Elk, got word that Carrington's column was approaching, and he rode out to meet the colonel.

Carrington received him hospitably, but was unprepared for the chief's direct approach. In a meeting in Carrington's tent, Standing Elk demanded, "Where are you going?"

"To build forts along the new road through the Powder River country," Carrington told him.

Standing Elk smiled. "The Sioux won't let you do that. The Indians in the Powder River country are wild Indians. They have no use for the white man, and they hate the bluecoats. There is no treaty that allows you to build anything there."

"I have my orders, Chief," Carrington said.

"You should wait for the treaty to be signed. Maybe then. But if you take the road before we give it to you, that will not be good."

Carrington shrugged. He wasn't sure what he ought to do, but orders were orders, and there was no time to send back to Omaha for Pope's opinion. Standing Elk tried once more to convince Carrington to hold off, but when he failed, he rode back to the peace council with his news.

The following morning, Carrington covered the last four miles to Fort Laramie. When he arrived, he was introduced to the chiefs at the council as the "White Chief" going to the Powder River country to build forts. The news did not set well with the Sioux chiefs. Red Cloud, especially, was annoyed. Only halfheartedly committed to peace to begin with, the arrival of Carrington struck him as one more instance of white deception.

He announced, "The White Father sends us presents and asks us to give him land for the new road, but other white men come to steal the road before we can give it to them."

The other chiefs gave an assenting "Hou!" They were distressed and angry, but Taylor and Maynadier tried to keep the talks going nevertheless. Red Cloud stalked out of the meeting. Over the next few days, he and most of his warriors left the campground near the fort and headed back to the Powder River.

Spotted Tail, the only significant chief among those remaining, signed the treaty, then left immediately for hunting south of the Platte River. But his warriors were in Red Cloud's frame of mind, and most of them headed north to join the Oglala chief, leaving Spotted Tail the chief of old men, women, and children.

Taylor, despite the obvious disaster over which he had presided, tried to put the best face on the affair, and wired East that a satisfactory treaty had been concluded. Then, quietly, he stored away the gifts and annuities intended for the Oglala, hoping that they would cool down and return. But it would be a long wait.

Carrington, in the meantime, pushed on toward the Powder River. Apprised that the treaty had been signed, he assumed that his men were going to spend most of their time in construction of the forts and their buildings. Red Cloud, though, had other ideas. Almost as soon as he'd left the fort, he and his Oglala, including Hump and Crazy Horse and Little Hawk, began a series of raids all along the route staked out for the new road.

Nothing and no one was safe. The telegraph again came under siege. Freighters carrying supplies to the mines were attacked almost daily. The stage lines and the wagon trains of new settlers came in for their own share of harassment. Over the next three months, hundreds of raids, resulting in hundreds of white casualties, were perpetrated. As always, the soldiers sent out to relieve those under assault were a day late and a dollar short.

Crazy Horse had been studying his adversaries, and now understood how to make the best use of the Sioux warriors. Although Red Cloud was nominally in charge, the warriors looked more and more to Crazy Horse for their leadership. Red Cloud was by no means a figurehead. Still a great warrior in

his own right, and a crafty politician, he was con-
solidating his dominance over not only his own
branch of the Oglala, but of considerable numbers
of Brule, Miniconjou, Sans Arc, and Hunkpapa
warriors, as well. It seemed as if the disaffected
warriors, regardless of their tribe, were gravitating
toward Red Cloud's band, in large measure because
Crazy Horse was there.

Carrington, in the meantime, had begun his construction. The first thing completed at the new Fort
Phil Kearny was the stockade. But wood was not
that easily available in the region, and it was necessary to send daily details out of the stockade for
more timber and hay for the cavalry mounts.
Whether Carrington realized it or not, he and his
men were in a very precarious position. Although
well armed with repeating rifles, seven-shot
Spencers, and even a few sixteen-shot Henry carbines, the whites at Phil Kearny were vastly outnumbered. And the Sioux were fighting for their
very survival against interlopers, an edge that
Carrington, not surprisingly, did not understand.

In July, Red Cloud led an assault that drove off
nearly two hundred horses. Over the next three
months, Crazy Horse led several raids that
destroyed telegraph communications and signifi-
cantly reduced the stocks of hay for the white soldiers' horses. The pressure was virtually nonstop.
Almost every day, either a work detail was
attacked, or word reached the fledgling fort of a
raid on other whites moving along the new road.

By the middle of September, the new fort was
under virtual siege. And his superiors were pres-
suring Carrington to do something to make the road

safe. The colonel complained almost constantly about his shortage of supplies and the lack of trained men. Most of his cavalrymen, to his amazement and dismay, knew next to nothing about horses. His infantrymen were untrained in the use of their weapons, poor shots who spent all their time sawing timber and building quarters.

And the number of hostile Sioux in the area continued to grow almost weekly.

Crazy Horse was growing impatient with the sporadic nature of the conflict. He sensed that a war of attrition was one the Sioux could only lose. Still convinced that the best, and perhaps the only way to defeat the bluecoats was to roll them back along the roads from west to east, taking one fort at a time, he collared Red Cloud one morning in late November.

"Always we go out," he said, "and we burn a few wagons, steal a few horses, maybe even meet the bluecoats and kill one or two of them. But it is not enough."

Red Cloud shrugged. "We cannot make them fight. If they will not come out to meet us, there is nothing we can do."

"We have used decoys in the past. We have tricked them, and it worked. It worked at the bridge over the Platte River, when my friend Lieutenant Collins was killed. It can work again."

"What do you want to do?"

"I want to put an end to this new fort. I want to drive the white men away, I want to defeat them so badly that they will count themselves lucky if they never see another Sioux warrior."

"And how would you do this?"

Crazy Horse outlined his plan. Red Cloud was skeptical as he listened. But he knew that many of the warriors would rather follow Crazy Horse than follow him, so it was better to go along. If the plan worked, then as chief he would get the credit. And if it failed, as he expected it would, he could shift the blame to Crazy Horse. The others would know whose idea it was. There was the risk that success would lure many of the best warriors away from him and into Crazy Horse's camp, but it was a risk he would have to take.

The other chiefs agreed, and Crazy Horse was given permission to outline his plan to several key warriors. He insisted that discipline was critical. "If we do not hold ourselves on a tight rein, then the bluecoats will know what we are planning, and it will not work. Remember at the Platte River bridge how well it worked. It can work that well again. But we must be patient. And this time we must position ourselves more wisely, so that we do not shoot our own warriors."

In early December, they were ready to go. In order to avoid making the whites suspicious, raids were continued against work details from Fort Phil Kearny, but they were just for show. The real battle plan would take a few days to set up. And Crazy Horse knew that they would have just this one chance to make it work. If the plan failed, then the Sioux would revert to the old ways of making war, and the war would be their last.

In the meantime, Colonel Carrington, feeling ever increasing pressure from his commanders, was finding that he had a handful of restless subordinates. Two of them, Captains Fred Brown and

William Fetterman, made no secret of their contempt for Carrington's timidity. Word of their dissatisfaction was filtering back to Omaha, and Carrington had already had his position curtailed. No longer commander of the Department of the Plains, he was simply post commander at Kearny, and plans were underway for his reassignment at the first opportunity.

One of the Sioux raids captured several dozen horses, and Captain Brown led a detachment out to recover the stolen animals. He encountered very little resistance and recaptured all the stolen stock. The success reinforced his belief that the Sioux were far less of a threat than Colonel Carrington believed.

Captain Fetterman, almost daily, would buttonhole the colonel. "Let me have a hundred men, Colonel," he'd say. "I can clear out the entire Powder River valley."

But Carrington was far too cautious to agree. Instead, he loosened the reins a little, and allowed both Fetterman and Brown to lead details out to relieve beleaguered work details. Beginning in the second week of December, the wood detail was attacked daily. There were never more than a few Sioux, enough to require reinforcements from the stockade, but not enough to frighten the troops.

Crazy Horse was walking a fine line. If he sent too many warriors, the troops would not leave the security of the fort. If he sent too few, they would be defeated handily, and it would cost lives. He was ready now to initiate the major engagement he had been planning for weeks.

On the morning of December 21, a small party of

Sioux attacked the wood train as it had every day in the previous two weeks. At the same time, Crazy Horse led another moderate-size band to a point within shouting distance of the fort. Carrington, apprised of the raid on the wood train, ordered a relief column to make ready. At the same time, Crazy Horse and his warriors taunted the troopers on the ramparts, shouting insults in English. "Come on out and fight us, you sons of bitches," they yelled, parading back and forth, sprinting their ponies and daring the troopers to come after them.

As the relief column was about to leave, Captain Fetterman demanded, by right of seniority, that he be allowed to lead the column. Spoiling for a fight, he was anxious to turn some of his words into action. Carrington agreed, but gave him strict orders to be careful. "Follow Piney Creek. When you reach the wood train, make certain that you don't go past the ridge. I don't care how many times the Sioux challenge you, let them go. Don't get out of sight of the stockade. Do you understand me, Captain?"

Fetterman nodded. "I understand, Colonel. I'll be careful. But it's about time we teach them a lesson. I have a feeling this is the day."

"Remember what I said, Captain."

Fetterman nodded again, swung into the saddle, and ordered the column out of the fort. The Sioux across the creek were still there, and Fetterman led his men that way, instead of taking the wood road. The troopers descended to the creek bed as the Sioux scattered. Carrington climbed to the rampart walkway where he could keep an eye on his sol-

diers. He saw Fetterman's men come back toward
the road, and left the platform, satisfied that his
orders were being obeyed.

Captain Fetterman saw the Sioux suspend their
attack on the wood train and head toward the creek
themselves. In the meantime, Crazy Horse and his
warriors fell back out of range of the soldiers' long
guns, exchanging sporadic fire but not pressing the
attack.

The war party from the wood train had too big a
lead for Fetterman to catch them, so he shifted his
attention back to Crazy Horse and his band, wheeling his column back toward the trees on the north
bank. Crazy Horse took off, following the tree line,
and Fetterman ordered his cavalry to take up the
chase.

The Sioux were following the Bozeman Trail to
the east of Lodge Trail Ridge, and Fetterman was
coming on hard. His cavalry was widening the gap
between itself and the infantry even as it closed on
the Sioux war party. The trail led through a shallow saddle, then swung to the northwest.
Following in the wake of the Sioux, Fetterman's
cavalry were now out of sight of the sentry platform at the fort. Scattered gunshots suggested to the
troops still in the stockade that Fetterman was
engaged in one more of those frustrating chases
that had punctuated the last several months.

The road then edged up the crest of a smaller
ridge parallel to Lodge Trail Ridge, and reached the
north end. Below, on either side of the slope, the
trap was waiting to be sprung. The decoys pushed
on past the north end of the ridge and down the
slope at its north end. The troopers followed.

Just as Fetterman's cavalry reached the northern-most end of the ridge, Crazy Horse looked back and, seeing that the entire party of bluecoats was within the gaping jaws of his trap, had his decoys ride back and forth, crisscrossing one another's trails, the signal for the trap to be sprung. The wait-ing warriors swarmed up both slopes of the small ridge. Cheyenne and Arapaho climbed up the grassy western slope while the Sioux broke like a tidal wave up and over the eastern slope. Fetterman was at the head of the infantry, almost a mile behind the cavalry troop. The two units were separated by a slight depression two-thirds of the way along the crest of the ridge itself. But there were so many warriors lying in wait on either side of the ridge that their sheer numbers swallowed both units.

As the attack commenced, the infantrymen ran for the nearest rocks and arrayed themselves in a circle, trying to fend off the assault and counting on their rapid-fire weapons to compensate for the overwhelming numerical superiority of the Sioux.

The cavalry, realizing it was cut off, did the only reasonable thing. The men dismounted and took up firing positions, facing the advancing horde head-on. Their repeating weapons repulsed the first assault, and the warriors were forced to fall back and regroup. After the first attack, the men ran for their horses again, but this opened them up to a murderous fire as thousands of arrows rained down on them like hailstones.

Trying desperately to reach the trapped infantry, the horsemen had opened themselves up to fire from all sides. Fewer than twenty of them reached the dug-in infantry, and now there was no way out. The infantry, unlike the horse troopers, were armed only with single-fire muzzle-loading Springfield muskets. The repeaters of the cavalry were strewn across the top of the ridge with the bodies of the cavalrymen.

Back at the fort, Carrington heard the thunderous fire and knew something was wrong. From the sentry box, he searched in every direction with his telescope, but could see nothing because Lodge Trail Ridge hid the battle site. Crazy Horse led charge after charge up the slopes, sometimes falling back when the fire was too heavy, sometimes thundering up and over the ridge, charging right through the rattled soldiers and down the opposite slope of the ridge.

Colonel Carrington, aware that Fetterman and his men were short on ammunition, hastily organized two relief units. Within minutes, he sent a detachment of thirty cavalrymen out to find Fetterman's command to reinforce them, followed a short while later by forty more men with wagons and additional ammunition.

The beleaguered troopers, in the meantime, were compressed into a tight mass by the relentless pressure from the waves of warriors. The closer they drew together, the easier they made it for the Indians, who launched arrows in clouds that fell among the soldiers in sheets.

One by one the guns fell silent. In some cases the men ran out of ammunition, in others they were too badly wounded to continue firing. The crest of the ridge grew deathly still. With bloodcurdling war whoops, the warriors swarmed up the slopes

and overran the survivors, smashing their skulls
with war clubs and slashing them with lances.
When it was over, not a single man was left alive.

Capt. Tenodor Ten Eyck, at the head of the relief
unit of cavalry, stopped in his tracks when he saw
the milling masses of Indians. He estimated later
that there were close to two thousand warriors in
the attacking force. Ten Eyck could see that the
Sioux were in total command. There was no sign of
Fetterman or his men, and he knew that to move
ahead could mean certain death for his men, many
of whom were also short on ammunition.

When the wagons of the second relief unit rum-
bled in behind Ten Eyck, the Sioux, thinking they
were howitzers, dispersed. By the time Ten Eyck
reached the ridge, there was not an Indian in sight.

And eighty-one soldiers lay dead.

# Chapter 18 ════

THE COUNCIL WAS GETTING ROUGH. They had been arguing for the better part of a week, and still there was nothing near a consensus. Instead of reaching some sort of agreement, the Sioux were finding themselves torn in two. The Big Bellies, largely compelled by the oratorical skill and the persuasive logic of Old Man Afraid of His Horses, were convinced that peace was the only viable option open to the Sioux.

"Every year," Old Man Afraid argued, "there are more and more whites. Every year there are more and more bluecoats. Every year there are fewer and fewer buffalo. Every year more of our warriors die, more of our children freeze to death, more of our women starve. That is no way to live."

"And would you have us hang around the forts like the Laramie Loafers? Would you want to depend on the white man for everything we need to live? Is it right that our land should be taken from us, and in exchange the white man gives us empty promises?" Red Cloud was angry, and his anger was fueled by the passion of the young warriors, stiffened by the resolve of Crazy Horse and the other shirt-wearers.

"Red Cloud makes big words, but what has war accomplished?"

"We won the fight at the bridge over the Platte River. We killed eighty-one bluecoats just last summer at the fort they call Phil Kearny. We cut their talking wire. We took their horses, burned their haystacks."

"And are there eighty-one fewer bluecoats now? Or more? Are the haystacks all gone? Where are the forts? Are they just ashes now, blowing away on the wind, covered over with spring grass? Or are they still there?"

Red Cloud shook his head angrily. "They are still there. You know that."

"Yes," Old Man Afraid said. "They are still there. They will always be there, because when we go to fight the bluecoats, they stay inside. They have their repeating rifles and their wagon guns. They have all the powder and balls they need. They have the new guns that shoot many times before they have to be reloaded. Their bullets go through our warriors the way a hot knife goes through buffalo fat. But our arrows do not go through their forts. We fire so many arrows that their stockade fences look as if they were made from the skins of porcupines. But when we run out of arrows, the stockade fences still stand, and the bluecoats still stand behind them, firing their repeating rifles."

"Perhaps if Man Afraid were more helpful, we would do better."

"Look at you, all of you," Old Man Afraid said, letting his gaze sweep around the council circle, pausing at each face, letting his eyes linger until the men, one by one, young and old alike, looked away. "You sit here and talk big words, and your deeds are paltry things, a handful of sand in a strong wind. We should make peace now, while we still have the strength to get something in return."

"The white man has nothing we want, nothing to give us."

Man Afraid clapped his hands together. In the sudden silence, the echo of the clap sounded like that of a gunshot far away. "The white man has our land. You said it yourself. Our land. And we are not strong enough to take it back from him. But we *are* strong enough to go to him and say, give us this land, and this and this, and we will make no more war. And he will listen because it is easier for him, because he wants his talking wire to be left alone, and the settlers to be unmolested on their way through the Powder River country. If we don't make peace now, soon we will have no food and we will have to crawl to the forts on our bellies and beg for food. Or we will die. All of us will die. We cannot eat words, no matter how brave. We cannot hunt buffalo that don't exist."

"If we ask for peace now, it is the same thing as crawling on our bellies. We are winning," Red Cloud insisted.

"We are *not* winning. All we are doing is hanging on by the tips of our fingers. Count the Sioux lodges. Count the people in them. Then think of the numbers of white men we have seen. You have heard the same stories I have heard, of armies with a hundred thousand men on each side, fighting for three or four days, until the dead were stacked like wood for a fire. I told you this before and you did not listen. But I say it again now. There are not enough of us to fight that kind of war."

Crazy Horse asked to be heard. The others leaned forward, knowing that he had the hearts and minds of most of the warriors. Red Cloud was the war leader, but it was Crazy Horse who knew what they felt inside, and he was not afraid to speak his mind.

"Man Afraid of His Horses says that we cannot win. But it is the warriors who decide that. It is the warriors who fight the bluecoats, and it is the warriors who hunt the buffalo. If we fight, we cannot hunt. If we hunt, we cannot fight. There are not enough of us to do both. But I think that if we fight the way the white man fights, we can win. If we let the bluecoats stay, next year there will be more, and more the year after that. One day there will be too many for us to fight. But not yet."

"They will come by the hundreds, more white soldiers than buffalo will cover the plains in swarms like the grasshoppers in summer. The great war they fought among themselves is over. They have the soldiers. All they have to do is bring them here," Old Man Afraid argued.

"But if we drive away the ones who are here, and burn the forts, there will be no place where they are safe. Our mistake was to let them come in the first place. We made things worse by letting them build the forts, where they could be safe. We let them bring ammunition and food to the forts, so that they always have enough."

"And how would you stop them, Crazy Horse?

You cannot go to them and ask them. But all your raids have not stopped them. Time after time we burn wagons, and still more wagons come."

"They come because we do not stop them."

"We *cannot* stop them. They are too many."

"We can, and we will. We said this before, but we did not do it. Always, when we beat the blue-coats, we ride away and dance the victory dance. We sing songs about each other, how brave this one is, how many coups that one counted. And while we sing and dance, new soldiers come to take the place of those we have killed. That is our mistake. When we fight, everyone fights and no one hunts. When we hunt, everyone hunts, and the war stops. We should do like the white man does. Some of us should fight, and some of us should hunt for food for themselves and for those who fight and their families. Then there will not be rest for the blue-coats. Wagons with supplies will not get through to the forts. They have many guns, but those guns cannot hurt us if they have no bullets. I say, stop the bullets and the guns fall silent. When the guns are silent, we burn the forts. Let the bluecoats leave peacefully if they will go."

"And if they will not?"

"Then we fight until there are no more blue-coats." Crazy Horse paused to look around the council fire as Man Afraid had done, looking at his comrades one by one.

Then, his head nodding a little to emphasize what he was saying, he went on. "If we don't do this, then soon there will be so many wagons on the Bozeman trail, it will be like the Holy Road, and the hunting will be ruined."

Old Man Afraid said, "I know Crazy Horse speaks for the shirt-wearers. I know he speaks for the warriors. And I know, too, that it is the warriors who hunt the buffalo. If they will not hunt for us, then . . . we have no choice but to try what Crazy Horse suggests. But I do not think it will work. I do not think we can win."

"Let us try," Crazy Horse said. "If we cannot win, we will know soon. And then we can do as you say. We will still be strong enough to do as you want. But if we give up without a fight, the white man will think us weak, and he will make promises to us and break them, just as he has always done, but it will be too late for us to fight then. And we will have lost everything we have and gotten nothing in return."

"Crazy Horse is stubborn," Old Man Afraid said. "But Crazy Horse is a great warrior." He looked at the other Big Bellies, and they whispered the "Hou!" of assent.

"We will make plans," Red Cloud said. "We will do as Crazy Horse suggests, and we will try to fight like the white man fights. But when we begin this time, we will not stop until the bluecoats are gone or the Sioux have been beaten."

And so Crazy Horse organized surveillance of Fort Phil Kearny once again. It seemed to him to be the key to the puzzle, the single most important piece, as Fort Laramie had been years before, when it was the westernmost installation the bluecoats had in Sioux land.

With Hump and Little Hawk along, he rode close to the fort, a spyglass looped over his shoulder on a buckskin thong. It was the middle of the

summer, and there were many wagons on the
Bozeman Trail, but Crazy Horse was not interested
in wagons. Chase away the soldiers and the wagons would go with them, this much he knew for
certain.

Watching the bluecoats through the spyglass, he
saw that things were not much changed from the
previous summer. The wood detail went out as
always, but now the soldiers had made a little
fence near a stand of pines. It would give them
some protection from the marauding bands of
Sioux and Cheyenne that sporadically hit the fort.
And a mile away was something new. The beds of
several wagons were arranged in an oval on the
ground, open at each end. There were even tents
inside. It was like a small fort itself. For two days,
he watched, not knowing why the wagon boxes
were there, or why they were arranged the way
they were.

On the third day, a band of Cheyenne swept
down out of the hills and attacked the wood detail.
The bluecoats were surprised, but they didn't
panic. They mounted their horses and rode quickly
to the wagon boxes, and took cover behind them.
They brought their horses inside, too. The
Cheyenne left off the attack quickly, but it was a
help to know about the wagon boxes.

The fort was too strong to be attacked head-on. It
was important to get the troopers outside the stockade fence, where the Sioux arrows would have a
chance. They could surround the fort and ride
around and around the stockade until their ponies
dropped in the dust and never get a shot at a single
bluecoat. Only when the bluecoats were outside

was it possible to do some real damage. Maybe then, with some trapped outside, if they could be killed or pinned down, the fort could be overrun. But the bluecoats had to be divided, so that even their guns would not be enough to repel the thousand or more warriors he would lead.

Crazy Horse came away knowing that fewer than thirty men lived in the tents inside the small fort of wagon boxes. And knowing, too, that even that frail thing might be enough if the soldiers had enough guns and enough bullets. But if he could decoy the troopers outside of the wagon box fort, then his advantage in numbers would be enough.

On the morning of August 2, Crazy Horse led the small decoy party, with Hump, Little Hawk, Little Big Man, and two other warriors. The plan was to wait until the woodcutters reached the pine trees. Then the decoys would attack, hoping to lure the men out of the wagon box fort. Timing would be critical. A thousand warriors would lie in wait on the far side of the hill between the pine trees and the wagon boxes. But if the bluecoats came too quickly, the decoy party would be badly outnumbered. If the warriors moved too quickly, the troopers would have time to get back to the protection of the wagon boxes.

Discipline was the key, and as often as Crazy Horse had tried to drive the point home, he had seen the warriors nod in agreement, only to lose their patience at a critical moment. Only in the Fetterman fight had the discipline been there. He hoped that it had not been forgotten.

The woodcutters reached the trees just after dawn. As soon as they started their work, the decoys made their move. Sweeping down off the hill, their war cries competing with the rasp of the workers' saws, they opened fire on the work detail.

One of the soldiers grabbed a rifle and fired at Crazy Horse as he led the raid. As if it had been a signal, the shot set off an avalanche of Sioux warriors rolling over the hill and down. In desperation, Crazy Horse looked back at the wagon boxes, and saw that the men inside had not even had time to get on their horses. And now, with the warriors thundering toward them, they would not leave the protection at all.

In order to salvage the moment, Crazy Horse turned his attention back to the woodcutters. More warriors joined the decoys, and after a short but furious fight, the work detail took to its heels. Crazy Horse plunged on after them. Behind him, he saw some of the warriors driving off the mule herd, while others milled around the wagon boxes.

Fifteen minutes later, he was alone. The woodcutters were still running, but Crazy Horse was the only Sioux still in pursuit. Angrily, he jerked his pony to a halt then wheeled around and raced back the way he had come.

Some of the warriors were sitting in the shade, eating food the woodcutters had left behind. Yanking one of the miscreants to his feet, Crazy Horse smacked him across the face once, then again, until Hump grabbed him by the arm. "You fools," Crazy Horse shouted. "You were supposed to wait. You were not supposed to move until the soldiers moved, and now look! They are behind the wagons."

Hump took him aside and tried to calm him down. "They cannot help themselves," Hump said. "You want them to fight in a new way. But it is difficult for them to understand. They have never fought this way before. You have to be patient."

"There is no time to be patient. There is no time to waste. Every day the bluecoats are here is a day less we have to drive them away. You understand that. Why can't they?"

"Because," Hump said, "we are fighting to save the old way. And for many of these men, it is the only way they know. They cannot see that new ways are necessary to save the old."

Crazy Horse shook his head in exasperation. He wanted to scream, or punch something, but he knew that his *kola* was right. He *was* asking a hard thing. But he had to ask and, if that did not work, then he had to insist. Old or new didn't matter. What mattered was that it was the only way.

"We will have to make them fire all their bullets," Crazy Horse said. He called the other shirt-wearers together, and explained that the warriors should circle the wagons, but not get too close, only close enough to draw fire. Then, when all the bullets were gone, they could sweep down on the small corral.

Young Man Afraid, Hump, and the others circulated among the warriors, explaining what had to be done. Then, with a sound like thunder, the thousand warriors galloped toward the wagon boxes. Around and around they went. One horse fell under the relentless fire from the corral, then another, and a third. And still the fire continued. Crazy Horse did not know that there were several wagon beds inside the corral with thousands of rounds of ammunition in them, positioned at key points on the perimeter of the makeshift fort. Only when a sixth horse went down and the fire continued unabated did he call off the circling warriors.

Dropping back well out of rifle range, they dismounted, thinking to approach on foot. But when this gambit was tried, the fire was like winter hail. The guns inside were not the old muzzle loaders. They were single-shot breech loaders, and could be fired almost as fast as arrows.

Attacking from only one side, the Sioux allowed the commander of the small stockade, Capt. J. N. Powell, to concentrate his men on one side. The Sioux in the rear ranks were unable to see over Crazy Horse and the others leading the assault, which reduced their effectiveness considerably. Most were unable to shoot their bows for fear of hitting the warriors in front of them, as had happened at Platte Bridge Station. And the wagon boxes were stopping those arrows which were fired.

Time after time, Crazy Horse led a charge, and time and again it was repulsed. He knew now that the soldiers were unlikely to run out of ammunition. Already, six warriors had been killed, as many as the bluecoats had lost, and still there was no chance to get any closer.

While he was deciding what to do next, Crazy Horse was summoned to speak to a scout, who told him that a hundred men had just left the fort and were coming on rapidly. A hundred men with such rifles, added to the nearly forty in the wagon boxes, was a force too formidable to be dealt with. Bows and arrows were no match for the firepower of the troopers.

Signaling for a retreat, Crazy Horse waited in the rear, knowing that there had to be another way, if only he could find it.

# Chapter 19 ═══════════

## October 1867

BLACK BUFFALO WOMAN had her third child at the end of the summer. Crazy Horse had taken to spending most of his free time around the lodge she shared with No Water. It didn't seem to matter to him what she was doing, it fascinated him no matter what. If she were scraping and tanning buffalo skins, he would squat nearby, not saying much, just drawing in the dirt with a twig, or watching the clouds, listening to the scrape of the skinning knife on the hide.

If she were pounding buffalo meat and herbs and berries together to make food stores for the coming winter, he watched her do that, too.

Her two older children played with Crazy Horse, and he seemed to enjoy the attention they lavished on him. No Water spent much of the time with a scowl on his face, but if he wanted Crazy Horse to leave, he never said so.

Sometimes Crazy Horse would go on one of his increasingly lengthy, and perpetually solitary hunts. No one knew when he would go, and once he left, no one was sure when he was coming back. White Deer and Worm worried about their older son on these solitary hunts. They knew that he paid little attention to their worries, and they had long since given up nagging him about their concerns. But still they worried.

Worst of all for his parents was the gossip. The women, whether Black Buffalo Woman was within earshot or not, wondered whether the two of them were thinking about running off together. It had happened before, and they knew it would happen again. Some of the sharper tongues among them suggested that since Crazy Horse had become a shirt-wearer, Black Buffalo Woman was beginning to think that she had made a bad choice for her husband. The theory was that Red Cloud, thinking to consolidate his power, had pushed her in the direction of No Water, not realizing that the warriors would pass him over in order to make his rival a shirt-wearer.

That struck some of the women as too cynical, but they nevertheless harbored suspicions that something was about to happen. Blue Elk Woman, in particular, thought that her friends were missing the point. "They love each other," she would say. "If anything happens, that will be why."

"What could happen?" Fights the Clouds would argue. "Crazy Horse knows that she is married. He is a shirt-wearer. He won't interfere."

"Lone Eagle was married, and that didn't stop his wife from running off with Three Bears."

"That was different. Three Bears is a scoundrel. He doesn't care about anyone but himself."

"And Gray Calf."

"And Gray Calf, yes."

"But he didn't care about Lone Eagle."

"Neither did Gray Calf." Blue Elk Woman laughed.

The others joined her, but there was an undercurrent of concern beneath the laughter. Lone Eagle was a brave warrior, but he was not crazy with jealousy like No Water. When his wife left him, he did what any upstanding Sioux warrior would do, he accepted the two horses Three Bears's family offered and forgot about it. It was no insult, no affront to his dignity. Women should not have to live with men they don't want to live with. They all knew that. And the custom made allowances for that fact.

"Besides," Fights the Clouds continued, after the laughter had died down. "Crazy Horse is a shirt-wearer. He is not allowed to take things for himself, or to make trouble. That is against his vows. And he is an honorable man. He won't cause trouble, no matter how much pain he is in."

"I am not worried about Crazy Horse," Blue Elk Woman said. "It is Black Buffalo Woman I am worried about. And No Water. You see how she teases Crazy Horse, flirts with him. It is shameful, and she doesn't seem to care. And if she goes to Crazy Horse and says she wants to live with him, what do you think he can do? Can he close his lodge and send her away? I don't think so."

"And then No Water will lose control of himself. Already he walks around with his face darker than any rainstorm. It won't take much more for him to get really angry—angry enough to do something foolish."

"Crazy Horse will kill him, then."

"Crazy Horse has to worry about his responsibility as a shirt-wearer. He also has to worry about No

Water's brother, Black Twin, who is now a shirt-
wearer himself."

"It will work out," Fights the Clouds said. "It
always does."

"I wish I could be so sure," Blue Elk Woman
said.

But Crazy Horse ignored it all. If he had any
plans concerning Black Buffalo Woman, he was
keeping them to himself. In late September, with
the sky a thickening gray, he rode off on one of his
solitary hunts. Little Hawk had volunteered to
accompany him, but the bleak look on his brother's
face was enough to convince him that Crazy Horse
wanted to be alone.

He mounted his horse after kissing White Deer
goodbye and telling his father that he would be
gone for a while. Once more, Worm was left behind
to worry. Little Hawk tried to convince him that his
brother would be all right. "He always comes back,
doesn't he?" he asked.

Worm nodded. "Yes. He always comes back. But
one day he won't."

"That day is a long time off," Little Hawk said.
"You know his vision. You know that he cannot be
killed by an enemy." He walked across the village
and stood watching his brother slowly shrink away
on the horizon. As Crazy Horse climbed a long,
gentle slope, then reached the top and headed
across the top of the ridge, he looked almost like a
shadow etched against the gray. Little Hawk wanted to turn to look behind, to see where the figure
was who had come between the light and the gray
sky. But he knew there was no one there.

Rolling easily down the far end of the ridge,

Crazy Horse rode without thinking. There were so many things he didn't understand, so many sources of confusion in his life. And somehow they all seemed to be jumbled together, so that he couldn't even separate out the pieces of the half-dozen puzzles. Nothing seemed to fit together with anything else. The bluecoats, Black Buffalo Woman, No Water, the Crows, puzzles, every one.

He rode all day, stopping only once for some dried buffalo meat and a little water, while he let his pony graze a little and slake its own thirst in a small, cold creek.

The trees were starting to lose their leaves now. Some were already just black sticks against the sky, while others were still full of red and orange massed like flames. They were beautiful, but so were the desolate, blackened trees in their own way.

When he camped for the night, he lay down and wrapped himself in a buffalo robe. He knew that it would be cold during the night. It was even possible that the creek beside which he camped would have a silvery skin of ice in the morning. The first snow was not that far off, and even now the air smelled as if it might snow during the night.

He built a small fire and sat watching the flames dance restlessly for an hour or so before the wood was exhausted and the flames slowly died down. He lay there watching the sky, wondering where the stars had gone. He could hear the crackle of the coals, and now and then sparks in a slender column would climb a few feet into the air where they'd hang for a few moments, as if trying to compensate for the missing stars, before winking out altogether.

Beside him, he had the buckskin sheath White Deer had made for him, covered with beadwork in red and blue. Fringed with strips of shredded buckskin, it was seldom out of his sight, especially on his lonely hunts. Inside it was the Springfield rifle Caspar Collins had given him.

He thought about the young lieutenant, how brave he had been in the last moments of his life. He remembered watching the battle at the Platte River bridge then, when he saw that it was Caspar at the head of the bluecoats, running into the open and waving his arms desperately, like a grouse trying to lead a coyote away from its chicks. But Collins never saw him.

And the Brule were too angry to stop and think. Collins was not well known to them in any case, but had they known, they would almost certainly have stopped their attack.

But that hadn't happened, and now Caspar Collins was dead nearly two years. Crazy Horse had good memories of the young bluecoat, and although he would have prevented Caspar's death if he could have done so, he was pleased that it had been a courageous one. And he thought that Caspar was pleased, too. They had talked much, and during these long, lonely hunts, Crazy Horse often recalled entire conversations the two had had.

And it made him understand something that long had puzzled him. He knew Frank Grouard, the old white scout, and liked him. He knew Peter Bordeaux, the half-breed trader. And he knew Caspar Collins, the bluecoat soldier. They were white men, and he liked them. They had liked him, too, and respected him. He understood now that it was not white men whom he hated, but the white man, that abstract thing that represented greed and violence, contempt for the Sioux and hatred of all things Lakota. It was a small difference, but it was an important one.

He fell asleep almost reluctantly, more than once sitting bolt upright as he tried to ward off the sudden surge of weariness that seemed to sweep over him like dark water, threatening to drown him.

In the morning, he awoke to find the ground already dusted with snow, and as he looked up, he could see that it was going to be a heavy storm, maybe snowing all day long. He broke camp quickly, as he had a thousand times before, and mounted up with one eye on the heavens.

For a moment, he thought about turning back. He knew how suddenly the earth could be swallowed up in a blizzard on the plains. Even though it was early, not even winter yet, he could find himself trapped in a foot or more of snow. Crazy Horse nudged his pony along the edge of the creek, staying out of the water, but inside the straggling line of trees that marked the creek bottom as it zigzagged across the valley floor.

This hunt would not be a long one, he promised himself. He did not want to find himself cut off from the village, but he did not want to go back empty-handed. There were too many people who depended on him. The old ones, especially, needed the meat he would bring in. As always, he gave them the best cuts of meat, keeping only the tough, stringy haunches for himself. It was enough for him, and he thought it might even make him stronger. The old ones with few teeth needed the tender cuts, and he was more than happy to see to it that they got what they needed.

And there was a new widow in the village now. Old Three Stones had died the week before, and his wife had no one to provide for her. He knew that Three Stones had been a great warrior in his day, although he had already been an old man by the time Crazy Horse had met him. But the old man had been kind to him, and loved to tell stories to all the children about the old days, the days before the bluecoats had come, when war was what it should be—a fair fight with mortal enemies. Three Stones liked to tell stories especially about the Pawnee, who he said were far worse than the Crows, crueler and more dangerous warriors.

It was at his knee that many of the young men, including Hump and Young Man Afraid, had heard the hero stories, and tales of the trickster. Three Stones knew them all, and more than once, the boys had spent all night in his lodge while the old man smoked his pipe and took requests for favorite tales. His own sons were both dead, killed in a great battle with the Pawnee.

It was partly out of a sense of duty, and partly to pay homage to his fond memories of the old man, that Crazy Horse wanted to find something before turning back, maybe a deer, if not a buffalo.

It was snowing harder now, and his vision was drastically impaired by the sheets of snow fluttering all around him. He followed the creek bed for more than a mile before finding a sign. The small depressions in the snow were already nearly filled in, and it wasn't possible to tell whether they had been made by a deer or a small elk. But either one would do, he thought, as he stared across the creek, where the animal had gone.

He followed the tracks, leaning forward over his pony's neck in order to keep his eye on the shallow depressions in the snow. The trail wound uphill for nearly half a mile, then angled across a ridge. His pack horse was fighting him, tugging on the follow line, almost as if it sensed something that frightened it. But he kept pushing on. The snow was picking up, and on the face of the ridge, the snow all but obliterated the tracks. Breaking over the ridge, he started down the other side. Trees loomed up suddenly, the black shapes startling him when he caught a glimpse of them through the swirling storm.

When he reached the trees, he had some protection from the wind, and the thickly needled pines, as well as those trees still leaved, held off the snow, and the trail was much easier to follow. He could hear running water somewhere ahead, probably a creek at the bottom of the hill. If he were fortunate, the quarry, which he could now tell was a deer, would be huddled somewhere in the trees trying to keep away from the worst of the blizzard.

He could see the dark water now, and the tracks in the snow made straight for it. At the edge of the creek, the tracks moved laterally, following the watercourse rather than crossing it. Sensing that his prey was close, he squeezed the pony between his knees, urging it to move a little faster. He remembered hunting with Caspar, and how the lieutenant had done so poorly with the bow and arrow, but had laughed at himself. And how Caspar had practiced and practiced, until he could shoot the bow well, not like Sioux, but well enough for a white man.

And there it was, a big doe, one of the biggest he had ever seen. The deer was in a cluster of small pines all but free of needles, deprived of sun by the taller pines around it. In places, he could even see the needled floor, barely dusted with snow. Without dismounting, he pulled the rifle Caspar Collins had given him and thumbed back the hammer on the single-shot breech loader.

He sighted carefully then realized that it would be better to shoot from a more stable platform, and he slipped from the pony's back, his feet barely louder than the whisper of buckskin on horsehide. The doe looked up as he sighted in again. He squeezed the trigger and the doe went down while the echo of the gunshot rattled among the trees for a few moments before dying away.

Then there was nothing but the hiss of snow and, high above him, the wind in the branches. On foot, he tugged his pony forward, then tethered him to a tree while he hoisted the doe onto the back of his pack horse, tied its legs together, and swung back onto his mount.

It took him several hours to make his way back to the village. The snow stopped as suddenly as it started, and by midafternoon, the sky was a crystal blue, and the snow underfoot was already melting. It was nearly sundown as he approached the camp, and it was obvious that something had happened.

He went to the lodge of Three Stones's widow and gave her the deer, then went to his father's lodge to find out what the trouble was.

"Things are getting out of control," Worm told

him. "This afternoon, two women were fighting about whether or not we should go to Fort Laramie to get the white man's gifts. Then a scout came and asked for Red Cloud. He said he had come from the white man general, Sherman, and that the general wanted to talk to Red Cloud about making a peace."

"But Red Cloud is not even a Big Belly. Why do they ask for him?"

Worm shrugged. "I don't know. But they asked for him."

"Will he go?"

"I don't know. I don't think so. Red Cloud said he would not talk peace until the forts in the Powder River country are taken away. But the scout said General Sherman is willing to talk about the forts, maybe even to take them down."

"I will believe that when I see it."

"Stranger things have happened, son. But maybe the things you have fought for for so long will come to be. And soon."

# Chapter 20 ════════

**January 1868**

REBUFFED BY RED CLOUD and the rest of the wild
Sioux, General Sherman nevertheless went ahead
with his plans for a peace conference in late 1867.
He met first with Sitting Bull and other Hunkpapa
leaders, then with Spotted Tail and his Brule
advisers. But this represented little in the way of
progress in the Powder River country.

Spotted Tail had long been peaceably disposed,
and any concessions he might make would not
lessen hostilities to any significant degree. And
Sitting Bull's people had been all but absent from
most of the conflict. They had stayed farther north
and east, away from the Bozeman Trail and the
forts Colonel Carrington had built to defend it.

After those conferences, Sherman headed to Fort
Larned, in Kansas, and held a large peace council
with representatives of the eastern Apache, the
Arapaho, the southern Cheyenne, the Comanche,
and the Kiowa. He bargained hard, but he was prepared to make concessions to be, if not conciliatory, then at least flexible, to get what he wanted.

But that flexibility was no softening of his notori-
ously hard heart when it came to Indian affairs. It

was rooted in pragmatism, nothing else. Sherman knew that his forces were spread dangerously thin. The entire United States Army numbered fewer than sixty thousand men. Of those troops, more than half were tied down in the Confederacy as occupiers and preservers of peace. More were assigned to coastal defenses, and of the remainder posted to the frontier, ten percent comprised the garrisons of Forts Reno C. F. Smith and Phil Kearny.

The forts were relatively secure, but they were isolated. Supply runs were extremely hazardous, and the troops were all but confined to the forts themselves. The numbers of Sioux and northern Cheyenne warriors available at any one time exceeded three thousand, and that was only a part of the total forces of hostile northern plains tribes. Most of them were concentrated in the valley of the Powder River and its tributaries, where the last of the great buffalo herds could be found.

Sherman was as much concerned with completion of the Kansas Pacific Railroad as he was subduing Red Cloud and Crazy Horse, and he knew he couldn't do both. In a meeting with Ulysses S. Grant, then head of the army, he argued for a new approach.

"General, I don't have enough men to clear the hostiles out of the Bozeman Trail area. Red Cloud and the others refuse to talk until we abandon Reno and the other forts in the area."

"You have to do something, Bill. I'm getting pressure from the Congress and the President. The worst thing that could have happened was for somebody to find gold in Montana Territory. But somebody did, and there's nothing to be done about it."

"General, you know as well as I do that we have all we can do to keep the men in supplies and ammunition. You know what it was like at Kearny. What happened to Captain Fetterman was no accident. The only reason it hasn't happened again is that most of the commanders won't take their troops out of the forts except when they have overwhelming numerical superiority. And that's damn seldom."

"I know what you're up against. The trouble is, the Congress doesn't know or, if it does, it doesn't care. And there's a powerful pro-Indian faction in and out of Congress."

"Have you told them how bad morale is? Do they realize the Indians are getting fat on the buffalo, and our troops are lucky to get one solid meal a day? Ammunition runs low, and we have a hell of a time getting more in. Anything moves along the Bozeman, the Sioux are all over it, cavalry escort or not. Out in the open country, it's the Sioux who run things. All we really have is what's inside the forts. The rest of the Powder River valley belongs to the hostiles."

Grant nodded. He stroked his beard, chewing on his lower lip. "I know the situation, Bill, but you have no idea what these congressmen are like. I'd sooner run naked through a field full of bees than have to go to the Capitol."

"Maybe we can buy some time. Maybe if they see some progress on one front, they'll be patient."

"I'd like to think so, but they all have personal axes to grind. The man from Iowa doesn't care what you do for the man from Kansas. And vice versa. They all want what they want and everybody else be damned. Getting elected is more important than anything else. If they can go home and say the army will put a lid on things, they come back next year. This is a lot tougher than the Civil War, I'll tell you that. And there's all those Indian lovers out there who say we're being too hard on the Sioux. Hell, they say that about every tribe. And sometimes I think they might be right. They didn't ask us to come into their territory. We did that on our own. Can't hardly blame them for putting up a fight. I sure as hell would, if I was a Sioux or a Comanche. And so would you, Bill."

"That's true, but it doesn't make much difference what we think. The settlers want protection. And you know as well as I do, General, that the railroad is the most important thing. I got some concessions from the southern plains chiefs. If they stick to their word, then we can get the railroad through without real trouble. There'll be some young bucks looking for trouble, and we can accommodate them, but I can't have a full-scale war north of the Platte. Not yet."

"When? Damn it, Bill, I have to give them something to hang their hats on."

Sherman shrugged. "I don't know. Maybe next year, or the year after. Once the railroad gets through, the buffalo hunters will follow. I think our best chance is the extermination of the buffalo herds. If those redskins don't have anything to eat, they'll be a hell of a lot more tractable. If the demand for buffalo skins and tongues holds for another couple of years, there won't be enough left of the herds for the Sioux to keep body and soul together. They'll be damn glad to have our handouts then."

"I don't know if Congress'll wait that long. As it is, I'm scaring 'em off with the numbers. I already spread the word that a full-scale war with the Sioux might cost four hundred million dollars. That took the wind out of their sails for a bit, but I don't know how much longer I can hold them off. The funny thing is, that's a realistic estimate of the cost."

"It might be a little short of the true cost, actually, General."

"Short or no," Grant snorted, "right now, they think it's too high. But that could change from week to week."

"What do you want me to do, then? You have the Congress to deal with, and I don't envy you that job. But I have thousands of soldiers, General. Their morale is lower than a snake's belly. They spend most of their free time getting drunk on cheap whiskey and playing poker. That's when they don't have the energy for a good old-fashioned donnybrook. I have to tell *them* something, too."

Grant leaned back in his chair. He seemed to be staring at the ceiling. Sighing heavily, he shook his head. "The only thing you can do, Bill. Give in. . . ."

"You mean . . . ?"

"That's exactly what I mean. Give them what they want. Clear the hell out of Reno and Smith and Kearny. That should buy us some time. Maybe then we can get things on track in the South."

"That won't sit too well with the goddamned settlers and miners."

"To hell with the settlers and the miners. Sometimes they're more trouble than they're worth. I can only fight one war at a time. And somebody's got to pay for it before I can even do that."

"I can't move those troops in the middle of the winter. We've lost a lot of men to the winters out there."

"As soon as you can, then. And make sure Red Cloud and Crazy Horse know it. Maybe that'll settle things down some in the meantime."

"If they believe me. But I don't have too much hope of that."

"Make them believe you, Bill. Do whatever it takes, but make them believe you."

Sherman headed back to Omaha. He was anxious to get started, but the weather was something he couldn't control. It seemed that the spring thaw would never come as January dragged into February. Finding the Sioux would be half his problem, and he had to give plenty of time for the messengers to find their quarry, and allow still more time for the chiefs to make their way in. Near the beginning of March, the weather finally began to cooperate, and Sherman sent runners out to all the Sioux, asking that Red Cloud and Old Man Afraid and the other leaders meet him for an important conference at Fort Laramie in April.

The chiefs straggled in, each leading his own band. Sherman gave them permission to establish a village a few miles from the fort. Old Man Afraid was there, and Spotted Tail. But not Red Cloud.

The general knew that Red Cloud was the single most influential war leader at the moment, and knew, too, that a treaty without his signature was useless. The other chiefs were already in favor of peace, and those warriors who followed them were similarly disposed. The more warlike of the Sioux and Cheyenne were another matter, and they did not care a whit what Spotted Tail said, or what terms he might agree to.

Sherman fumed for two months, and still there was no sign of Red Cloud. By June, Sherman was furious, but he couldn't afford to let it interfere with his purpose. He began the conference, hoping that Red Cloud would come in before it concluded.

Sitting in an open lodge large enough to accommodate the chiefs and the peace commissioners were Generals Harney and Terry, as well as N. G. Taylor, the new Commissioner of Indian Affairs and former Methodist minister, and Commissioner John B. Sanborn, the principal civilian negotiators. Taylor and Sanborn were firmly committed to reaching a fair settlement with the Sioux and, surprisingly, General Harney was very sympathetic as well. The Sioux remembered him very well from the Ash Hollow fight with Little Thunder's village, and the idea that such a man could be advocating a peace that was favorable to the Indians swayed more than a few to believe that this treaty just might be worth accepting.

Sherman took pains to outline the geographical provisions with clarity.

"The Sioux people," he said, "will have forever, as long as the grass shall grow and the waters shall run, all the land in South Dakota west of the Missouri River, including all of the Black Hills. In addition, they will have the right to hunt in all the land west of the Black Hills all the way to the Bighorn Mountains."

He was ceding the entire Powder River country, and the Sioux leaders were pleased, but tried to keep their enthusiasm in check. There was a catch, though, which was not explained. The Sioux right to that hunting ground would last only so long as there were enough buffalo to sustain them. Once the buffalo were gone, the Sioux would be expected to become "civilized," settle down, and take up farming. If the chiefs understood this, they must not have believed that the buffalo would ever run out, because it did not deter them.

In addition, Sherman agreed that no whites, for whatever reason, would be allowed into Sioux lands, including the Powder River country, without Sioux permission. This almost clinched the deal, although Old Man Afraid was skeptical that it would be enforceable, assuming, which he did not, that the whites were even willing to try to enforce it.

The forts, though, remained a big sticking point. They were almost stunned, then, when Sherman also announced that the three forts along the Bozeman Trail—Reno, C. F. Smith, and Phil Kearny—would be abandoned within a few weeks.

The chiefs conferred among themselves for two days and, when they could find no reason not to agree, informed Sherman that they would touch the pen.

Red Cloud and Crazy Horse were still absent, but Sherman was determined to get whatever he could, so the signing ceremony went ahead, and the general left behind a copy of the treaty for Red Cloud, should he ever decide to come in.

On July 29, the troops marched out of Fort C. F. Smith. On a ridge overlooking the fort, Crazy Horse and a large band of Sioux watched in amazement, and more than a little disbelief. The bluecoats were actually leaving, just as they had said they would.

The last guidon had barely fluttered out of sight when Crazy Horse and his men swooped down on the fort and set it ablaze. Every building was torched, as was the stockade fence. The Sioux could hardly believe their good fortune, and held an elaborate victory dance to celebrate the departure of the hated white soldiers.

All that remained now was for the whites to keep their word that Sioux lands were inviolable. But Crazy Horse would believe that when he saw it.

# Chapter 21 ═══════

**October 1870**

RED CLOUD HAD FINALLY MADE IT to Fort Laramie in the fall of 1868. General Sherman had been gone for almost six months. If Red Cloud was sorry to have missed the bluecoat general, he kept his disappointment a close secret. It was more than enough compensation that the forts had been abandoned, as the treaty said they must be. The hunting was good, so good, in fact, that the buffalo, without the rapacious white hunters to decimate the herds in the rich grazing land of the Powder River valley, seemed to be increasing. It was the first time that anyone could remember that the numbers of the great beasts had grown larger, rather than smaller.

And with no settlers or miners careening along the Bozeman Trail, the wild Sioux were free to turn their attention elsewhere, to more ancient enemies, men who knew how to fight the Sioux way, using weapons that were familiar, and tactics that both sides could understand.

Crazy Horse seemed to relish the renewed opportunity to harass the Crows. He had gone straight to Crow country before the smoke from the incinerated buildings of Fort C. F. Smith had been cleared by the summer breeze. Even as he rode west, he had kept glancing back over his shoulder in the broad valley, as if expecting to see the bluecoats coming back, as if it had all been a trick.

But after a battle with the Crows, which saw him garner nearly fifty horses, he swept by the ruined fort one more time. It was still there, its ruins etched in the ground like ugly scars. The heaps of blackened timbers, little more than mounds, were surrounded by sprouting grass. And as he rode slowly through the center of what had once been a bastion of the bluecoats, he was pleased to see blackberry and strawberry sprouting, their tangles draping the ashen heaps with green garlands. If it had been a trick, it had been a good one indeed.

Red Cloud, too, relished the renewed freedom to pursue old habits. In the late summer of 1869, he had mounted a great war party to punish the Shoshoni, another ancient enemy, a people the Sioux called the Snakes.

All of the warriors seemed to find a youthful exuberance, as if the familiarity of a long-forgotten way of life had suddenly exploded in their memories. They embraced it the way they embraced a brother, long missing and presumed dead. There was a certain joy in the war whoops, an exultation in the victory celebrations that had long been absent.

Red Cloud, though, was getting along in years. Soon, he would reach that age when his job would not be to paint his face and adorn his horse with feathers and daubs of bright color. He would stay at home, waiting for news of younger men, men who were following in his footsteps, men like Crazy Horse and Hump and Little Hawk and Young Man Afraid.

The war against the Shoshoni had taken a lot out of him. He still counted his share of coup, but he was so renowned, that one more would do little to burnish an already brilliant reputation. Crazy Horse was the future, the veteran war leader knew, partly because he was so firmly committed to the ways of the past. That, after all, was what the war with the bluecoats had been all about—preservation of the old ways.

Crazy Horse, more than any of the young warriors, perhaps even more than most of the older warriors, loved the old ways. They seemed to breathe life into him, and he was never happier than when he could shower his pony with those few paltry handfuls of dust, daub a few hail spots on his chest and shoulders, and tie the small stone under his arm. It was almost as if Crazy Horse were a figure out of the tribal past, an embodiment of an ideal, a warrior's warrior. Red Cloud was vain, with the kind of vanity only the great seem to have, that vanity that might resent one who was superior but which was so deeply rooted in a set of values that it could do nothing other than pay homage to that superiority. And he knew better than anyone how great a man Crazy Horse had become.

Politically astute, Red Cloud was coming to realize something else: Despite Crazy Horse, despite the treaties of 1851 and 1868, the assurances of

General Sherman, and the blessing of the Great
Father in Washington, the past might not be res-
cued. It galled him to think so, but if there was any
possibility that Spotted Tail was right, that the
whites would be back, and they were too powerful
to be held off much longer, then it behooved him to
think how he might make the best of so dreadful a
prospect.

His concerns were exacerbated in the fall of
1869. Long deprived of the white man's addictive
goods, like coffee and sugar, and in need of ammunition for their weapons, the Sioux spent several
months amassing huge stores of buffalo hides. They
knew that the hides still brought high prices, and
hoped to be able to trade their stores for supplies
they needed. Packing up their entire village, Red
Cloud's Sioux commenced their exodus to the
Platte River valley. Crazy Horse refused to go along,
preferring to stay and hunt where he felt he
belonged and where he felt all the Sioux belonged
with him.

But Red Cloud was to be disappointed and Crazy
Horse credited with superior understanding.
Arriving at the Platte, the Sioux were welcomed
rudely. Several warriors were fired upon, and two
wounded by troopers. Under a white flag, Red
Cloud visited the military commander, and was
advised that the terms of the treaty were quite
explicit: the Sioux were to stay in Sioux lands,
either in Dakota or in the Powder River country.
They were not welcome at the Platte, and they
were not to be allowed to trade with anyone, even
willing traders, and most particularly were they not
to be allowed to obtain ammunition.

And the traders were strongly cautioned that they would not be permitted to take their wagon loads of goods to the Sioux, even in their own country. The treaty was just as explicit on that point. White men were prohibited from entering Sioux territory. Furious at what he took to be a betrayal, Red Cloud returned to the Powder River. A few hardy, or reckless, traders, almost all of them half-breeds, defied the ban and made surreptitious journeys to the hostiles, but they risked confiscation of their goods and imprisonment if they were to be detected by the military authorities.

In a matter of months, Red Cloud came around to Spotted Tail's position, and sued for peace. Unwilling to come under the latter's authority, Red Cloud asked for his own agency, separate from that of the Brule chief, and his request was granted. Half of his followers went with him to the White River, where the agency was christened the Red Cloud Agency. But the other half of his warriors, feeling that Crazy Horse had been right all along, went back to the Powder River to join forces with the man who was now the single most influential hostile Indian leader on the North American continent.

Red Cloud had read the cards and, not liking the hand he'd been dealt, took what seemed to him the only viable route. But it was not long before the hazards of peace made themselves felt. In a matter of months, Red Cloud had a list of grievances as lengthy as his list of coups. An able politician, he made his complaints known in the only place where they might be addressed—Washington, D.C.

No less astute as a politician, Ulysses S. Grant, now President, sent an invitation to Red Cloud, Spotted Tail, and Crazy Horse, asking that they come to Washington. The ostensible purpose of the visit was to explore the outstanding conflicts between the whites and the Sioux. Red Cloud, recognizing an opportunity to enhance his standing, hastened to accept. Spotted Tail also agreed. Crazy Horse, though, wanted nothing to do with the white men. He was content to stay in the Powder River and live his own life according to standards more powerful, and more attractive, than any gift the white man had to offer.

Their journey took the Sioux chiefs first to Omaha, where they saw for the first time buildings of four and five stories, far more imposing than any structures they had seen on the frontier. If the buildings themselves were not enough to intimidate the Sioux, the sheer numbers of whites in Omaha added their weight, and Chicago, their next stop, all but sealed the impression.

Once in Washington, Grant lost no time in trying to harvest some hay of his own. He accompanied the bewildered chiefs on an endless round of meetings and conferences with congressional leaders, businessmen, and assorted policymakers. One afternoon, the Sioux were taken to the shores of the Potomac for a demonstration that was not explained ahead of time. Grant, knowing that this might be the chance to fire the last shot of the Sioux wars, had arranged for a fifteen-inch Rodman cannon to be present.

When the huge gun was fired, the chiefs were terrified by the thunderous report. Spotted Tail clapped his hands over his ears, his eyes searching Grant's face for an explanation. Red Cloud stood, arms folded across his chest, watching the heavy artillery shell skip across the Potomac's rippling surface several miles away. When the last arcs of silver spray had collapsed back into the river, Red Cloud had made up his mind—for him, the warpath was a thing of the past.

If the cannon were not enough, the next stop on the carefully planned journey was New York, where the teeming crowds brought home to the chiefs the accuracy of the grasshopper metaphor which had dominated so much of the berating, cajoling, and dire warnings the Sioux had received from every white politician, soldier, and agent. The chiefs now knew for certain that their people were unbelievably outnumbered.

Red Cloud, dressed in the white man's clothing, with a vest and a high-crowned hat, made a speech at the Cooper Institute on June 16. It was an eloquent presentation of the Sioux plight, a passionate summary of red-white relations on the great plains and, as might be expected, it accomplished nothing. Red Cloud returned to the agency, and the problems continued. He never put on a warbonnet again, choosing instead to devote his life to the political machinations which seemed to the great chief the only way for the Sioux to survive. He knew he could not control the more passionate of the young warriors, but closed his eyes because it was easier not to see.

Later that year, Crazy Horse, following his own path, turned his eyes westward, and led war

parties against the Crow and the Shoshoni. He
was doing what he loved best, and he had the
companionship of his best friend, Hump, to ward
off the loneliness. He was in love with Black
Buffalo Woman, and she with him. She had gone
so far as to ask her husband to release her, but
No Water flatly refused. War was the only comfort left him.

At the head of a small war party that included
Hump, He Dog, Little Hawk, and Good Weasel,
Crazy Horse went in search of the Shoshoni. It was
the middle of November. So far, the weather had
been kind, but the party left in a drizzling rain. As
they pushed westward, the rain turned to sleet, and
then to snow.

Underfoot, thick slush began to accumulate.
Crazy Horse was concerned about the weather.
Pulling alongside Hump, he said, "I don't like this.
The horses are already having trouble in the slush.
Maybe we should turn back. It could get a lot
worse."

Hump laughed. "Do you remember what happened the last time we turned back from a war
party at this spot?"

Crazy Horse nodded. "I remember."

"Do you want the same thing to happen? Can
you stand the teasing? We have to think of our
reputations. This time there will be a fight. There
has to be. Go home if you want to, but I will go
on."

Crazy Horse was ambivalent. "Your rifle is fine. I
have a good gun, too. But look at the others. Their
rifles are old. They are better off fighting with bows
and arrows. This is no place for a fight, and the

weather only makes it worse. But if you insist, we will fight."

Hump laughed again. "At first, I thought you were turning into one of the Loafers. You were starting to sound like Spotted Tail. I'm glad you're staying." He clapped his *kola* on the shoulder, then nudged his horse ahead, still laughing.

An hour later, they stumbled on a Shoshoni hunting party. The slush had deepened, clinging to the hooves of the horses like translucent glue. The ground under the slush was slippery and soft, making matters all the more treacherous.

Crazy Horse and Hump led the attack, but the Shoshoni band was larger, and well armed. Charge and countercharge, the horses of both sides slipping and sliding as they careened across the slippery ground, led to a standoff. Hump was getting frustrated, and got out ahead of the others on his next pass. A flurry of gunfire crackled, the Shoshoni warriors like shadows in the driving sleet and snow.

Hump went down, then scrambled away from his horse. He waved to Crazy Horse to show that he was unhurt. Crazy Horse galloped toward him with Good Weasel right behind. He had already sent the others home, and planned to keep the Shoshoni busy while his own men made their escape.

Back on his horse, Hump realized the pony had been wounded in the leg and was nearly lame. "We're in for it now," he shouted.

Crazy Horse nodded. They charged ahead once more, Hump's horse limping along behind the other two ponies. The Shoshoni held off the charge, then pressed their own attack. Trying to turn, Hump's horse went down again. This time, the great warrior was too close to the enemy, and the Shoshoni charge swallowed him up. Desperate, Crazy Horse charged back, but he couldn't get close enough. He saw the frenzy of the Shoshoni as they swarmed around his friend.

Then, like a shadow from beyond, Hump broke through, staggering. Even through the swirling sheets of rain and sleet, Crazy Horse could see the blood streaming from a wound in Hump's shoulder. One arm hung limply, as if a bone had been broken, or a tendon severed.

Once more Crazy Horse charged toward the Shoshoni phantoms. The enemy warriors kept disappearing in the mist and slashing sleet, only to reappear as they turned their horses and bore down once again on Hump, who turned now to raise his one good arm. Unable to use a bow, he was reduced to fending off the charge with a lance.

Crazy Horse loosed arrows in a frenzy, his horse circling the swirling mass of Shoshoni braves and ponies. One Shoshoni fell, an arrow protruding from his chest, and Hump finished him with a stab of his lance. Another went down, then a third. Hump leaped on the last, snapping the shaft of his lance with a vicious thrust.

Crazy Horse made a headlong charge as the Shoshoni wheeled their mounts one more time and thundered past Hump with arms flailing. And then it was over. Hump staggered backward then fell over on his side, four arrows in his chest. Hump was gone. Crazy Horse heard the disembodied voices of the Shoshoni as they vanished in the mists for a moment, the whoops of triumph growing suddenly louder as they turned once more and came charging back. Forced to give ground and then to run, he couldn't even recover the body.

It seemed an omen of things to come.

# Chapter 22 ══════════

**August 1871**

THE SUMMERS WERE ALMOST FUN AGAIN. Crazy Horse
was staying on the Yellowstone River, now at the
head of a small village of his own, no more than
fifty lodges in winter, but swelling to four and five
times that size in the warm weather, when half of
Red Cloud's people left the agency to hunt and live
the old way.

Most of the warriors saw him as the last and
best war leader, and had elevated Crazy Horse to
membership in the Crow Owners *akicita*, and
made him a lance bearer, charged with the protection of the sacred medicine lances of the Oglalas. It
was a high honor, and one he took seriously. In
August, after a good hunting season, it was time to
pay some attention to the Crows, who had an agency of their own far to the west, where they
camped, like Red Cloud's people and the people of
Spotted Tail, under the very muzzles of the bluecoats.

But, like the Sioux, the Crows were not fully
adjusted to the new ways. Some of their warriors
resisted so easy a peace with the whites. They
loved the hunt, and they loved stealing ponies from

the Sioux. Crazy Horse, his village swollen with the summer soldiers from Red Cloud Agency, put together a war party to go in search of the Crows. It was to be an old-fashioned war party, with women along to cook and lighten the long hours.

Four days west, they found a Crow hunting party, a large one, almost as large as their own. Camping in the next valley, they made ready, the whole village buzzing with excitement as the warriors painted their ponies and their faces. The women, after making sure that the camp was in order, followed the warriors, as Crazy Horse and He Dog, now a shirt-wearer and lance bearer like his friend, rode toward the crest of the high, distant hill dividing the warring camps, holding the sacred lances aloft and waving them to encourage the warriors.

The women streamed up the hill behind them, then strung themselves in a long line across the ridge as the warriors plunged down into the valley full of Crows. The men were whooping and waving their bows and lances, their shields sometimes soaring above their heads as they drove one another on with shrieks and earsplitting howls.

Behind them, they could hear the women taunting the Crows, daring them to come and get a real woman, one who was so much better in the buffalo robes than any scrawny Crow hag.

The Crows responded, and charged out to defend their village. The two forces met near the grazing Crow herd, and some of the Sioux split off a sizable portion of the ponies and drove them back up the hill, while the rest of them thundered through the ragged Crow lines. Warriors on both sides were flailing with their bows and war clubs, leaning out to count a coup. There was some gunfire, but most of the contending warriors seemed to prefer the old way.

Crazy Horse was in the thick of it, and the Sioux could see his lance waving high above the seething mass of painted men and horseflesh. The Crows broke first, and started to fall back, as the stolen ponies were pushed on up and out of sight.

From his pony, Crazy Horse could see the Sioux women cheering him on, and seemed almost carefree, relishing the battle as he had not in a very long time. The Crows regrouped, and some of them mounted a counterattack, charging across the long slope of the hill and cresting the ridge where they recaptured a few of their stolen ponies.

Emboldened by their modest success, the Crows drove the recaptured horses straight toward the mass of Sioux warriors now commanding the valley floor. But Crazy Horse led a breakneck charge that split the Crow force in two, scattering the enemy ponies and sending both halves of the attacking force spilling down the slope and across the river to their village.

The Sioux preened a little, the warriors now echoing the insults of their women, daring the Crows to come back. But their taunts fell dead in the water. If the Crow heard them at all, they were in no mood to be provoked, and headed up the far hillside.

Crazy Horse and He Dog wanted to pursue them, but the rest of the warriors wanted to take their plunder and go home.

"I want to chase them," Crazy Horse insisted.

"Me, too," He Dog said.

Little Hawk volunteered his services as well and the three kicked their mounts into a trot heading for the river as the Crows straggled up the far side. Watching the bearers of the sacred lances run after an overwhelming number of enemies, the warriors realized they had better go along to protect them. The lances were big medicine, important to the Oglala people, so it would not do to have them fall into enemy hands. And no one wanted to challenge Crazy Horse for their possession.

With whoops as much of joy as bloodlust, the Sioux swarmed across the river, their ponies' hooves churning the shallow water into mud as they drove on through the abandoned Crow village and on up the hillside. The Crow were running for their lives, and sent a rear guard back behind the main body to slow the Sioux pursuit.

For two days, taking their time and settling into a steady rhythm, the Sioux ponies kept on, stopping only for nightfall, when the Crow themselves would halt their flight to make camp for the night. By first light, the Crow were on the move again, the Sioux right behind them. The all-out warfare of the first day had dribbled away, and was replaced by an occasional skirmish which the Crow seemed to enjoy every bit as much as the Sioux.

Neither side had lost a man, although two Sioux warriors had been wounded by arrows, one badly enough that he might not survive the injury.

By noon on the third day, the buildings of the Crow agency at the Little Bighorn River came into view. Crazy Horse called a halt at the last ridge above the permanent Crow village, urging his pony to rear up while he let out a final whoop and waved his lance high overhead in triumph over the hated Crows and defiance of the even more hated bluecoats.

The fun was over, and it was time to go home. Crazy Horse fell back, taking his place at the end of the line while He Dog led the triumphal caravan back to the Yellowstone. It took five days, and each night in camp Crazy Horse would wonder how much longer the old way could survive. He thought back to his youth, not that long ago, when one could go almost anywhere without seeing one of the white man's long-knife soldiers. Now, it seemed that everyone, Sioux and Crow, Shoshoni and Pawnee, lived in the white man's shadow. Hands out, the pacified Indians lived on the white man's charity, afraid to take food for themselves, afraid to go where they wanted, to hunt, to make war, or just to ride out into the vastness of the plains to soak in some of the comforting solitude that could be found best under the big, open sky.

He would sit beside the fire until its orange light faded to a barely visible smear on his skin, its heat no longer enough to ward off the late-night chill. He watched the flames as if he were looking for something in them, waiting for something, or someone, to appear to him, dancing among the darkening tongues.

The third night, He Dog sat up with him, saying nothing, knowing that his friend didn't really feel like talking, but knowing, too, that he needed someone there in case he should feel the need to talk, whether he wanted to or not.

It was well after midnight when he said, "I miss Hump. I can't believe that I'll never see him again."

He Dog nodded. Taking a deep breath, he said, "What bothers you is not recovering his body. You feel as if it is your fault."

"He should have had a proper burial. He should be lying on a scaffold in the Paha Sapa. I would have taken him there myself."

"There was nothing to be done. I was there. I know what it was like. The Shoshoni were too strong."

Ignoring the comfort He Dog was offering, Crazy Horse contemplated his pain in silence for a long moment, then, digging his teeth into the meat of it, he said, "When I went back, there was just a skull. Even the bones were gone. Wolves and coyotes had taken . . ." he choked off his recitation then looked at He Dog, tears running down his face. "Hump was one of the great ones, not just as a warrior, but as a *man*. There will never be one like him."

He Dog clapped his friend on the shoulder. "He is happier now. There are plenty of buffalo where he has gone. It is never cold, and there are always Crow ponies to steal. It is where we will all go someday. You will see him again there."

Crazy Horse shook his head. "I do not think so."

"You have to think so. It is the only reason to keep on going. The only reason we have to live at all."

Crazy Horse nodded sadly. "I hope it is a good enough reason." He turned then and looked at his old friend. "Good night," he said, leaving no doubt that he wanted to be alone now.

The rest of the trip, He Dog watched Crazy Horse closely, unable to suppress the feeling that something was very wrong, something that Crazy Horse himself felt but did not understand. He Dog didn't understand it either, and knew that he would be of little help unless he could somehow find the key to unlock the chains weighing so heavily on his friend.

When they reached the Yellowstone again, Crazy Horse seemed better, more lighthearted than he had been, and led the triumphal procession around the village. The celebration started immediately and, as usual, Crazy Horse faded into the background. He left it to the others to sing of their heroic deeds, tell tales of coups counted and Crows humiliated. He knew what he had done, and the knowledge was enough. Uncomfortable, as always, he stayed as far as possible from the center of attention.

After the victory celebration, a kind of tranquillity settled on the village. Life returned to normal, with small hunting parties searching for buffalo, and bringing home deer and elk that Wakan Tanka saw fit to place in their paths.

Beside the Oglala, there were small contingents of Miniconjou, Sans Arcs, and Hunkpapas. The northernmost groups of Lakota had been relatively isolated from the white men. They had kept to themselves, far off the Oregon and Bozeman trails, far from the iron road of the white man's trains. They lived the old way because it was the only way they knew. They had no taste for coffee and sugar because they had never been exposed to the white man's seductive blandishments.

Crazy Horse was in his element. And it seemed to agree with him. Black Buffalo Woman was there with No Water and her children. But even this did not seem to disturb the serenity that seemed to have enveloped Crazy Horse.

The winter went quietly. So far from the white soldiers, there had been nothing to disturb the Sioux, and when the first rush of melting snow filled the rivers, making them foam and the waters snarl like cornered cougars, so loud you could hear them a mile away, Crazy Horse started making plans for another war party against the Crows.

Little Hawk signed on, so did He Dog. Even No Water and his brother, Black Twin, agreed to go. When the waters had subsided in late spring, the war party left in high spirits. The previous summer had been the best in years, and all the warriors had their hearts set on getting a few Crow ponies for themselves.

The party left early one morning, Crazy Horse, as before, in the lead. They rode long and hard, this time making good time because the women were staying at home. After midnight, Crazy Horse slipped onto his pony and rode back the way he had come.

When he reached the village, just before sunrise, Black Buffalo Woman was already waiting for him. She had entrusted her three children to the care of her family. Her possessions were packed, and Crazy Horse slipped from his pony just long enough to sweep her into his arms for a moment before swinging her onto her own mount and springing to the back of his pony.

By noon, the village was far behind. They were alone at last. When they had ridden far enough, they camped for the night, not bothering to erect the lodge. That could wait for morning. There were more important things to do.

The sun rose well before the runaways. It was nearly noon before they awoke. Before eating, they went for a swim in a branch of the Yellowstone, squealing like children as the frigid water pebbled their skins and numbed their limbs. Crazy Horse had never felt so free.

For three days, they lived the life that Crazy Horse had only dreamed about and that Black Buffalo Woman pretended to live with No Water. They talked almost nonstop. She thought he was a different man, so voluble, chattering like the boy she remembered from their childhood, the boy she thought had long been cast aside by the warrior like a snake casts aside its skin, a useless shell of something he would never again be. But there he was, right beside her, day and night. And it was better than she had hoped when she had agreed to run away with him.

Black Buffalo Woman felt occasional twinges of guilt about her children, but she would see them again. She didn't know when, only that she would. Life without them was too horrible to contemplate. And there would be more, with the man beside her their father.

That night, with so much just beginning, they sat beside the fire in their lodge, talking about the future.

"We can live anywhere you want," Crazy Horse said.

"I want to live someplace where No Water can't find us."

"I'm not afraid of No Water."

"You don't know him. You don't know what he might do."

"What can he do? You have done only what it is your right to do. He will have to live with it. Later, when things settle down, I will send him horses, and the past will be where it belongs. Behind us."

He stopped then, hearing something outside the lodge. Putting a finger to his lips, he reached for his bow and notched an arrow. Suddenly, someone tapped on the entrance flap. "Crazy Horse, it's me, Little Big Man."

Crazy Horse let his breath out in a long, slow whistle, then shook his head. "Come in," he shouted.

The flap moved aside and Little Big Man stooped to enter the lodge. He took a seat beside Crazy Horse, and Black Buffalo Woman, not without a look of resentment, said hello.

"No Water is looking for you," he said.

"Of course he is."

"He's furious."

"I imagine so."

"No, you don't understand. I've never seen anyone so angry. He'll kill the two of you if he finds you."

"Let him find us, and then we will see what happens."

"The Big Bellies are angry, too. They say you have shamed yourself and all the shirt-wearers."

"There are things that are more important."

"Not for a shirt-wearer."

"It is only a shirt. I can live without it." He regretted saying it immediately, and knew in the deepest part of himself that it wasn't true, but it was too late to call back the words.

# Chapter 23 ===

**April 1871**

THE ENTRANCE FLAP FLEW BACK as if a great gust of
wind had caught it. No Water burst in, a revolver
clutched in his right hand. His teeth were
clenched, and Crazy Horse could see the knuckles,
squeezed white, of No Water's fist. He started to
rise, jerking a knife from its sheath.

"No!" Little Big Man shouted. He tried to get to
his feet, grabbing Crazy Horse by the arm as he
rose. No Water charged toward the men as Black
Buffalo Woman screamed.

Struggling to free his arm, Crazy Horse turned
toward his friend for a split second. In that
moment, the gun went off.

The bullet slammed into Crazy Horse, piercing
his upper lip just beneath the nose, breaking several teeth and the left side of his upper jaw before it
exited. Black Buffalo Woman had her hands to her
face, framing black eyes that seemed to be escaping
from their sockets, then she ran as Crazy Horse
pitched forward into the fire.

Little Big Man grabbed Crazy Horse by the legs
and started to drag him out of the flames as No
Water turned and chased after his wife. The sizzle

of blistering skin, the too sweet smell of cooking flesh filled the lodge.

Crazy Horse was bleeding badly, and his skin, still lighter than any Sioux, was turning dark red. In some places it was almost black as Little Big Man dragged him from the lodge and stumbled toward the river. When he reached the sand along the shore, he lowered his friend to the ground, then dragged him into the shallows, where the cold water bubbled and swirled around the burned chest and shoulders of the heavily bleeding warrior.

In the distance, Little Big Man could hear the pounding of hooves as Black Buffalo Woman fled for her life and No Water galloped after her. Another gunshot shattered the silent darkness, and Little Big Man instinctively ducked. Crazy Horse rolled his head from side to side as the water burbled around him. In the darkness, it was difficult for Little Big Man to see just how bad the wound might be. He felt for the shattered jaw with blind fingers, and Crazy Horse moaned as he turned his head away.

It was bad, and the warm, sticky mess clinging to his fingers told Little Big Man that something had to be done, and done quickly. Dragging the bleeding man out of the river, he turned his attention to the bleeding. Like most Sioux, he knew more than a little about healing, but not enough for a wound this bad. He had to get help, and knew that Crazy Horse was in no condition to ride. He'd have to hoist his friend up and drape him over a pony. Traveling at night was dangerous under the best of circumstances, and when one man had to worry about an unconscious companion, the risk was greater still.

But there was no question that morning might be too late. It took ten minutes to pack the gunshot with a paste of mud and herbs, makeshift at best, but at least it would keep the bleeding to a bare minimum. Once that had been accomplished, Little Big Man got Crazy Horse onto a pony and tied his ankles together under the horse's belly, then let the now unconscious man fall forward, where he could tie him in place. The trail would be rough and the ride would have to be fast if Crazy Horse was going to survive.

It was late morning by the time the village came into view. The women swarmed around the two riders, and Little Big Man was forced to nudge his pony through the crowd, shouting at the top of his lungs for people to get out of his way. He kept one eye open for any of the Bad Faces, No Water's clansmen, and when two of them tried to push their way through the milling throng, Little Big Man drew his revolver and pointed it in their general direction. "Go home," he said. "Go back to your lodges, unless you want me to use this. There's been enough shooting already."

The two men mumbled, but stayed where they were. Little Big Man finally got through, and kept glancing over his shoulder as he made his way to Worm's lodge. Crazy Horse would need protection while he healed, if he were still alive, and Little Big Man was determined to see to it that the convalescence was insured.

Little Big Man slipped from his horse and stuck the bridle rope into an extended hand without looking to see who it was. Pulling his knife, he moved to Crazy Horse and cut the ropes holding the wounded warrior on his pony. Taking the full weight of the unconscious Crazy Horse on his shoulders, Little Big Man staggered to the entrance to Worm's lodge. Only then did he stop for a second and look around. He saw Worm then, standing right beside him, his face a stoic mask. Without a word, he accepted half the burden and stooped to back through the flap and into the lodge.

White Deer screamed when she saw her son, then rushed forward to hold him, but Worm shook his head and turned his body to keep her away. Laying Crazy Horse on a buffalo robe by the fire, he said, "Find Chips. Hurry."

He then sat beside the unconscious body of his son. "What happened?" he asked, without taking his eyes away from the bloody face.

"No Water . . ." Little Big Man said, then stopped without knowing how to continue.

"I was afraid of this. I knew it. I knew . . ." He shook his head again. Drawing a deep breath he held it for a moment, then puffed out his cheeks, forcing the air to hiss as he expelled it between compressed lips. Looking at Little Big Man, he said, "Thank you for helping my son."

"I should have been able to stop it."

"No one could stop it. It was . . ." He paused again, his voice thickening until it clotted in his throat and words were no longer possible.

Chips hurried into the lodge without waiting for an invitation. Kneeling beside Crazy Horse, he unslung a deerskin bag from his shoulder. White Deer hovered over him, and he sent her for water.

"I will need a lot," he called after her, then started to peel away the mud and herb plaster Little Big Man had laid on.

Worm gasped as the full extent of the wound was revealed. "Will he live? Can you save him?"

Chips shrugged. "I will do what I can, but . . . he has lost much blood. Maybe too much. I don't know. It is fortunate for him that the bullet passed out the cheek, but . . . I will try."

When White Deer returned with three bowls of water, he instructed her to heat some, while he used the rest. "As hot as your hands can take it," he said, then turned his attention to the unconscious man before him.

Worm got to his feet, stood over Little Big Man for a moment, then reached down. Little Big Man seemed almost oblivious of the offered hand, and only slowly looked up. His own hand moved in slow motion as it sought the older man's grip, curled into it like the hand of a child into a grandfather's fist, and got up slowly.

"Let's leave Chips to his work. You and I have to talk," Worm said. "I have to know exactly what happened to make certain that this business is over. It will get very bad if it is not stopped now."

"I'll tell you what I can," Little Big Man whispered. "I . . ."

Worm tugged the limp arm in his grasp. "Outside. We will walk for a bit." He moved toward the entrance, bent to exit, and pulled Little Big Man through after him. The latter seemed to be sleepwalking, and followed in the holy man's wake as if he had no will of his own.

Chips spent several hours bent over his charge.

Sending everyone away, even White Deer, he worked slowly and deliberately, not sure whether all his efforts would come to nothing. It was nearly sundown before he knew that Crazy Horse could live, but it would be longer still before he knew for certain whether he would.

After his talk with Little Big Man, Worm had gone to the lodge of Old Man Afraid. He needed the chief's help to avert a bloodbath. The Bad Faces were angry at Crazy Horse, and even the shooting might not satisfy them. But Worm was afraid that a prolonged dispute would tear apart the fabric of the tribe in a way that could never be repaired. It was up to him to make certain it didn't happen.

Crazy Horse lay in the silent vacuum of the buffalo robe for two days and nights. From time to time, he would see things going on around him, but they seemed too far away when he would reach out to touch them. Noises drifted to him wrapped in thick robes, muffled and meaningless. Light would come and go, as if the sun were somewhere high above him, and between him and it stood a tall oak, its layers of leaves swallowing most of the sun's rays. Now and then a blade of light would lance through, so bright it almost hurt, but he couldn't tear his eyes away, afraid that he would slip back into darkness and never come back.

He was unaware of anyone around him, but White Deer and Worm both were there; sometimes alone, sometimes together, they watched over him, silent prayers pounding noiselessly in their skulls while they waited and hoped.

Chips came often to change the dressings he was using on the wound. The bleeding had stopped, but

the wound looked as if it would never begin to
heal. Chips had heard how the white medicine
men sewed sundered flesh together with needle
and thread, but he had neither, and had to force the
tears in the meat of Crazy Horse's face together as
best he could, in the hope that it would knit. There
would be a terrible scar, that much he knew, and
there was nothing to be done about it.

He knew that Crazy Horse would live now, but
said nothing, not wanting to raise hopes only to
find them dashed when Wakan Tanka changed his
mind. Of all the hard things he had to do, being
certain was the hardest.

Outside the lodge, things were happening that
Crazy Horse would have run from, if he could. The
Big Bellies were angry, and they wanted back the
shirt. It was Old Man Afraid who brought the news
to Worm.

"My friend, it pains me to tell you this, but it is
right and it must be. Crazy Horse can no longer be
allowed to be a shirt-wearer. He has broken the first
rule. He should not have brought disruption to the
village. That was forbidden above all else, and yet
he has done so. And for a woman . . ."

Worm nodded. "I understand."

"But will your son?"

"My son knows better than anyone what it is to
be a shirt-wearer. He has done it better than anyone, given more and taken less than any other
shirt-wearer. He will understand, and he will give
up the wearing of the shirt. You should know this."

Old Man Afraid nodded. "I do know this. But I
have my job to do, just as Crazy Horse had his. The
Big Bellies are much divided on this point, but

there is no way to undo what has been done. I wish it could be some other way."

"If it were some other way, then the wearing of the shirt would be meaningless."

Old Man Afraid nodded. His lips moved, but he said nothing, as if he were unwilling to speak such a painful truth aloud.

Worm had his own work to do, and he was doing it well. The Bad Faces were angry, but not so angry that they could not see that there was wrong on both sides, as well as right. No Water was wrong to shoot Crazy Horse, just as he was wrong to prevent Black Buffalo Woman from leaving him, as was the right of every Sioux woman. But Crazy Horse had been wrong in bringing conflict to the village. He should not have tried to take Black Buffalo Woman for himself. It would have been better to deal with it another way.

There would be bad feelings for a long time, but it was important to begin dealing with them.

The following morning, Crazy Horse regained consciousness. He could not speak, but he could sign, and the first thing he did was tell Worm that Black Buffalo Woman should not be punished. She had done nothing wrong, he signed. That afternoon, No Water's brother appeared at Worm's lodge.

Black Twin invited the holy man outside, and there presented him with three horses. "These are the best horses No Water owns. His best roan, his best bay. I offer these horses in payment for the wrong he has done."

"It is a great wrong," Worm said.

Black Twin nodded. "I know this. Crazy Horse is

a great warrior, a brave man, and my brother was wrong, even cowardly, to do what he did. But I know, too, that Worm understands that we cannot fight among ourselves. The world is too much against us to allow that to happen."

Worm nodded. "Black Twin is very wise for his years. It is unfortunate that his brother is not so wise. But I accept your gift with thanks. There will be no trouble from my son or his friends, I promise you. Crazy Horse has said as much."

"Then he is an even greater man than I thought."

Black Twin went away slowly, turning once or twice to look over his shoulder at the older man, almost as if debating whether or not to mention one final thing. But soon he was lost to view, and Worm went back inside to tell Crazy Horse what had happened.

The wounded warrior was asleep, but he was twisting violently from side to side. He kept waving one arm, as if trying to pull it free from something, and mumbling "Let me go. Let go of my arm."

Worm wondered whether it was the dream coming back to haunt his son, or if it had something to do with the shooting. Or both.

That evening, Crazy Horse was outside for the first time since the shooting. He was sitting beside the lodge, watching a handful of boys chase one another around the fort like a competition among whirlwinds.

He heard a commotion at the other end of the village, and got unsteadily to his feet. A crowd had gathered, and he could hear the women beginning to wail. Someone had been hurt. Or worse. His legs were unsteady, but he managed to make his way toward the center of the uproar. The crowd, sensing his presence, turned and, when they recognized him, parted. A hush fell over the village.

Lone Bear, streaked with dirt and a smear of blood on his left shoulder, saw Crazy Horse. He straightened up and took a step forward.

"What's wrong?" Crazy Horse asked.

"It's . . ." He shook his head and turned away.

"White men," Lone Bear mumbled. "Miners. They . . ."

Crazy Horse took Lone Bear by the shoulders and stared into his eyes. "What is it? Tell me."

"Little Hawk. It's Little Hawk. He's . . . he's dead."

# Chapter 24

**August 1872**

CRAZY HORSE SAT ON THE HILLTOP. He watched Sitting Bull climb slowly toward him. The older man stopped every so often to turn and look at the thick grass rolling away like huge bolts of the white man's green velvet cloth. It seemed to Crazy Horse that Sitting Bull was not just looking at the world, he was absorbing it, taking it into him and making it a part of himself. The great medicine man was so thoroughly entwined with the world around him that there was no way to tell where the one left off and the other began. That was what had drawn Crazy Horse to him in the first place. And the more time they spent together, the greater became the younger man's respect.

Sitting Bull understood the old ways. He knew them inside out, but more than that, he respected them. He saw why they were the best ways. The relationship between the Sioux and the world in which they lived was more than a simple dependency. Each needed the other. The Sioux needed the plains, the open sky, the cold, rushing waters of the rivers, and the buffalo. But all those things had special meaning in relation to the Sioux. It was the people who gave them their value. That was what made the Sioux so different from the white man. The whites had no respect for the earth. It was just something you stabbed and slashed and tore apart, ripping things from its insides the way a thief ripped things from a torn pocket.

Crazy Horse valued his friendship with the medicine man the way he valued no other human connection, not even that which he'd had with his *kola*, Hump, or with his brother Little Hawk. It was stronger even than his attachment to Worm, the man who had given him life and raised him to be what he was.

But the admiration was mutual. Sitting Bull was a brave man and a great warrior. And he saw that Crazy Horse shared those qualities with him, and felt the same devotion to the old ways. In some way that he couldn't articulate, he realized that he and Crazy Horse were like two parts of the same organism, heart and brain of the same beast. Without either, the beast would die. And without either man, the Sioux were lost. What Sitting Bull feared, and what he had tried so hard to explain to Crazy Horse, was that the Sioux might be lost in any event.

As he drew closer, he raised a hand to acknowledge the younger man, then turned once more to look out over the valley, the blue-white band of the river like a strip of the white man's shiny ribbon curling off to the southeast. A hawk cried high above the hill, and Sitting Bull looked up to watch it glide, its wings motionless as it rode the warm air rising from the valley floor. The great bird cried once more, and Sitting Bull waved toward the sky.

Crazy Horse wondered whether man and bird were communicating, or if the wave was just an accident that had nothing to do with the hawk.

Turning once more to look uphill, Sitting Bull climbed the last two hundred feet and sat on the grass beside Crazy Horse before saying a word. He was only seven years older than the young warrior, but he seemed almost ancient. It was not that his physical powers had begun to desert him. Far from it, they were at their peak. Not even forty years old, he was still vigorous, his broad shoulders and solid trunk almost like a slab of granite. He seemed so much more powerful than his young friend.

"It's a beautiful day," he said, by way of opening the conversation. They sat this way often, when time and duty permitted, and talked about whatever crossed their minds. Most of the talks had to do with the plight of their people, because neither man could afford to let his thoughts wander far from the impossible bind in which the Sioux had found themselves.

"The village looks so small," Crazy Horse said. "When I was a boy, I used to make tiny tipis out of willow branches and scraps of buckskin. I could hold three or four in the palm of my hand, like a tiny village. I could make it float high above my head, where nothing, not even the dogs, could get to it."

"We are in a greater palm," Sitting Bull said. "Wakan Tanka holds us in his hand. But sometimes I worry that he will forget that we are there and clap his hands together to kill a fly, or roll his hand into a mighty fist. Maybe it will be something simple, as simple as a wave to a friend. But whatever it is, it will be the end of the Lakota people."

"I worry more about the white man. I can't interfere with what the Great Spirit will or will not do," Crazy Horse said. "But the white man can be stopped."

"I have heard that he is building another iron road. There are soldiers, too. Many of them. They are coming into the Yellowstone country, and soon there will be too many of them to stop or to drive away."

"I have heard that, too. I think it is time we tried to do something about it."

"The young men have their heads full of foolishness. It is hard to teach them to do things in a way that the white man won't understand. They have no discipline. And Long Holy is filling their heads with his nonsense."

"Long Holy has strong medicine."

Sitting Bull nodded. "I know he does. I understand medicine. You know that. But I don't think he knows what he is doing. He tells the young men he can make them bulletproof."

"I have heard that he gave a demonstration."

"He did. I saw it. He shot a gun again and again. And the young fools tried to catch the bullets in their palms."

"And what happened?"

"The bullets bounced off. They made bruises, but did not break the skin."

"But you don't believe his medicine is powerful?"

Sitting Bull snorted. "Always, the young men want to think that they are bulletproof, or that a knife cannot cut them. They want to think that their heads are so hard that a war club will not break their skulls like melons. And that is a good thing. It is important to believe that you are powerful, that you have strong medicine to protect you on the warpath. It lets you do things that you would not do if you were afraid of getting hurt. But Long Holy's medicine is a fraud."

"You said the bullets bounced off."

"They did. But I know it is because we do not put as much powder in our bullets as the white man does. If there is not enough powder, the bullets don't hurt. You have seen it yourself, how sometimes we shoot a bluecoat or a Crow and he does not bleed. That is because we don't have enough gunpowder, and we weaken the bullets. But the white man has all the gunpowder he needs. If the young men ride in front of his guns thinking they will not be harmed, they will be killed."

"Have you told them this?"

Sitting Bull shook his head. "I have told them. But they don't listen. They hear me and they smile and they shake their heads. Then, behind their hands, they say 'Sitting Bull is jealous of Long Holy.' I am not jealous. But I am not a fool. I know what I know and what the young men do not know."

"Maybe it is better that they believe in Long Holy's medicine."

"Sometimes I think so, but then I think what it will be like in the lodges when the women learn that their young men were wrong . . ."

Crazy Horse nodded his head. "Hou!"

Sitting Bull stood then, and started down the hill. It was a long walk, and Crazy Horse watched the medicine man every step of the way. He felt a great weight on his shoulders and noticed that his friend's shoulders, too, seemed to sag under some invisible burden.

When Sitting Bull started across the flats toward the village, Crazy Horse looked out across the valley. He saw the herds of ponies, their heads bowed as they tugged on the lush grass. He saw the dogs lapping at water by the river's edge. He saw the children running along the riverbank, sometimes falling, sometimes slipping into the water and kicking great silver arcs of spray into the air with their bare feet. The sight made him sad, and he wondered if it could be saved or if one day the valley would be full of the white man's white-painted buildings, with the white man's fences carving the earth into tiny squares. He didn't know the answer, and it frightened him.

As he got to his feet, he noticed some movement on the ridge across the valley. One, two, then three riders broke over and down, pushing their ponies at a full gallop. Crazy Horse started to run. Soon he was going so fast that he dared not stop for fear of falling over. The effort made his lip hurt where the bullet scar was a ragged slash of lightning, and his lungs felt as if they were full of fire.

Something was happening, and he raced to the village, reaching the first lodge as the riders slipped from their ponies.

The riders were scouts, and they were beside themselves. "Bluecoats," they shouted. "Many bluecoats. On Arrow Creek."

The word spread rapidly, and the Sioux warriors were infuriated by the invasion of their territory. Crazy Horse looked for Sitting Bull, and saw him on the opposite side of the circle thickening around the excited scouts.

Slipping through the throng, he eased in beside the medicine man. "We should make a good plan before we ride out to meet these soldiers," he said.

Sitting Bull nodded. "We should, but I don't think the hotheads will listen."

"We can make them listen."

Sitting Bull shook his head. "No, all we can do is go with them, and try to save them from themselves. You'd better get your rifle and pony."

The ride took three days. Each night in council, Crazy Horse pleaded for restraint, for careful planning, for an understanding of the white man's way of fighting. And each night there was an argument. Sitting Bull argued on the side of Crazy Horse. Other warriors, too, like White Bull and Two Bows, were in favor of planning the attack. But the younger warriors, even Lone Bear, were too agitated to listen and to learn. Long Holy had filled their heads with his ideas, and they wanted to test his medicine.

On August 14, the word came back from the advance scouts. There were many bluecoats, horse soldiers and foot soldiers, maybe four hundred, maybe more. Crazy Horse tried one more time to create a reasoned attack, but the younger men were not to be restrained. They urged their ponies ahead and all Crazy Horse and Sitting Bull could do was follow them.

The vanguard swept over the last ridge above the mouth of Arrow Creek, a mile from where it met the Tongue River, and thundered down on the bluecoat herd. They succeeded in driving off some

American horses and some beeves, but the attack
was too spontaneous to have much impact on the
soldiers. Under the command of Maj. E. M. Baker,
they quickly mounted a defense. Their superior
weapons drove off the attackers with little to show
for their efforts, and with all chance of a surprise
swept away.

When the attackers fell back to rejoin the main
body of Sioux, Long Holy announced that he and
seven of his followers were going to ride up to the
bluecoat defenses and circle around them four
times. He told the warriors that all eight of them
would return unharmed. "Maybe then," he challenged, "you will see that what I have been saying
is true. Maybe then you will believe."

With that, Long Holy climbed onto his pony and
led a charge. Long Holy had taught his followers a
song, and they bellowed it at the top of their lungs
as they circled Baker's men. A hail of fire poured
out from the defensive positions. One by one, the
circling warriors were hit until four of the eight
were wounded.

Sitting Bull, unable to bear it any longer, charged
into the open space between the Sioux and the
white soldiers. "Stop!" he shouted. "Stop this foolishness! You'll all get yourselves killed." He saw
the blood streaming from the four wounded Sioux
and could not restrain his contempt for Long Holy
and his pride.

But Long Holy was not ready to give up. "I
brought them here to make war," he shouted. "Let
them do it!"

Sitting Bull paid no attention, and argued with
the young warriors. Frightened by the results of

their first foray behind Long Holy, and more than a little in awe of the great Sitting Bull, they obeyed.

For two hours, the two sides exchanged shots at long range, neither side causing much damage. Then, in an attempt to provoke pursuit, Crazy Horse drove his pony down toward the bluecoats and rode slowly across the entire width of the soldiers' line. But no one came out to chase him. Instead, the bluecoats blazed away to little effect, and when he returned to the Sioux line, Sitting Bull was annoyed. He felt that Crazy Horse was getting too much attention for his heroics.

Dismounting, he took his pipe and walked slowly across the open field until he was about midway between the opposing lines, at the edge of the effective range of the bluecoats' carbines, then sat down. Using a flint and steel, he lit the pipe and casually puffed away, until a wreath of smoke swirled around him. Turning to look over his shoulder, he shouted, "Anyone who wants to join me in a smoke, come on."

Several warriors took the dare and came out to join him until six or seven were arrayed in a line. Sitting Bull handed the pipe to White Bull, who puffed hurriedly, then passed the pipe along. The others smoked as fast as they could while bullets whistled and sang around them, swarming like bees, but hitting no one.

When the pipe had finally made its way back to him, Sitting Bull took one more puff, and, when the others who had smoked had scampered back to safety, he got out his cleaning stick, scraped the bowl clean, and put the pipe into its beaded sheath. Then, slowly, he got to his feet and walked back to join the others, a broad smile on his face. The whole war party was in awe. This was certainly the bravest thing any Sioux had ever done, they thought. Admiration spread like a flood among the warriors.

Then Crazy Horse played his trump card. Springing onto his pony, he called to White Bull, "Let's make one more pass," and he was off, charging across the open field toward one end of the bluecoat line. White Bull was behind him as he galloped the full length of the line, every soldier firing at him as he raced past. At the far end of the line, he turned back toward the Sioux, with White Bull, who had not gone as close, now in front of him.

Crazy Horse was almost home when a bullet caught his pony, killing it outright under him, and spilling him to the ground. Scrambling and crawling, he raced back unhurt, his face wearing a smile even broader than that of Sitting Bull.

The medicine man nodded his approval, and returned the smile. "That's enough for today," he shouted. He might not have been outdone, but he had certainly been matched.

# Chapter 25

CRAZY HORSE WAS GROWING more and more withdrawn. His moods were deep and black, and there was not much that could overcome them. His friends were worried. They knew there was much on his mind, and they knew how much each of those things hurt. But they also knew that he had to let go of the sorrows. The loss of Hump, the loss of Black Buffalo Woman, the loss of Little Hawk—each one a blow from a heavy hammer, and each one had done its share to flatten him, to pound him down as if he were a piece of soft metal.

He Dog was probably his closest friend now that his *kola* and his brother were gone. He thought long and hard, trying to find something, some idea, no matter how wild, that could help cheer Crazy Horse a little, that could bring back the friend who seemed to be slipping away from him.

On an overnight hunt with Red Leaf, He Dog stayed up late, poking the campfire with a stick, watching the swirling sparks swarm like fireflies. Red Leaf, too, was close to Crazy Horse, and he knew what was on He Dog's mind.

Joining his friend at the fireside, he grabbed a stick of his own and started to poke the coals.

"What are you doing?" He Dog asked, looking up after a moment.

"The same thing you are," Red Leaf told him. "Looking for a way to lighten Crazy Horse's heart. He is gloomy too much of the time."

"His heart is broken," He Dog said.

"I know that. And I know why. He misses Little Hawk."

"And Hump."

"Yes, and Hump. And Black Buffalo Woman."

He Dog snorted. "She had another baby, I have heard. And the baby has light skin like his. And light hair."

"Does he know?"

"He knows. How could he not?"

"What will he do? Will he try to take the baby to his own lodge?"

He Dog shook his head. "No. He knows it would make trouble again, and he doesn't want that."

"He needs a woman. He needs someone he can talk to about those things he keeps between his heart and his ribs, those secret things that we talk to our women about."

Red Leaf was right, and He Dog had been thinking the same thing, but one couldn't just decide to get a friend married and then make it happen. Or could he?

"Your sister is about his age, isn't she?"

"Black Shawl? I don't know. I suppose so."

"And she isn't married, either."

Red Leaf laughed. "She has a strong back and a will to match. No man is good enough for her. Or that's what she thinks. It's how she acts, anyway."

"She is a good-looking woman."

Red Leaf was skeptical. "You've seen the way the girls look at Crazy Horse. They follow him with their eyes when he goes past. They stop working, sometimes their hands hang in the air like hawks, barely moving, until he disappears, then they start working again just as if they had never stopped. Crazy Horse could have anyone he wants."

"Except Black Buffalo Woman."

Red Leaf nodded. "Yes, except Black Buffalo Woman."

So it was decided. No one bothered to tell Crazy Horse until the arrangements were well under way. If he was pleased, he didn't show it. If he was annoyed, he didn't show that either. His expression barely changed when He Dog gave him the news, and then there was just a momentary flash, as if a fleeting pain had stabbed somewhere deep in his body. He Dog knew it was a memory of Black Buffalo Woman, but said nothing.

The marriage was low key, and Black Shawl seemed happy with it, as if the right man for her had somehow fallen out of the sky, despite the fact that he had been there all along.

Crazy Horse settled into the match, and it wasn't long before Black Shawl was expecting. Crazy Horse spent the long evening hours by the fire, playing with the village children, as if preparing himself for impending fatherhood. He had always liked children, and had never been too busy to take time out to spin a tale or give a lesson.

Now, though, he seemed to relish the role of teacher. His hunts were not so solitary as he took one or two of the boys with him, teaching them everything he knew about the habits of the deer and the elk, the rabbit and the duck and, of course, the buffalo. He taught them to make bows and how to fashion arrows, fixing the points perpendicular to the feathers for use in war, so they could slide more easily between a man's ribs, and parallel for hunting.

In the evenings of the long winter, the boys gathered in his lodge, sitting in a circle at his feet as he told them tales of the heroes and of times long ago, those times he was trying so desperately to preserve for them. The children never seemed to get enough. One of them, a boy named Black Elk, seemed to pay special attention, as if he were not just listening to the words, but soaking them up, absorbing sound and meaning through every pore.

And finally the baby came. She was a girl, and he named her They Are Afraid of Her. She seemed to fill the huge void in him the loss of friend, brother, and lover had created, one small, frail child to take the place of three people, and yet she was enough.

Black Shawl watched him cuddle with They Are Afraid of Her, and smiled as she worked with skin and bead. She made moccasins and shirts, breechcloths and buffalo robes. Her mother had come to live in the lodge, and she helped with They Are Afraid of Her, leaving Black Shawl free to tend to the tipi and the food. According to Sioux custom, Crazy Horse was not permitted to look at his mother-in-law, but it presented no problem since the older woman was used to the tradition.

Hunting as always, and as always providing for those who had no one else to care for them, to supply them with food and horses, Crazy Horse seemed even more the shirt-wearer now that the title had been taken from him. He still went on occasional forays against the Crows and, sometimes, led small war parties to harass the bluecoats down on the Yellowstone, where the iron road was growing like a snake that had no head and no tail, just stretching every day longer and longer, winding its way through the valleys. The Northern Pacific was another nail in the Sioux coffin, and Crazy Horse seemed to realize it, but for the moment he was content to be the family man.

Sometimes at night he would wake up suddenly, jerking his arms as if some invisible force were holding them. He would hear Hump laughing or see Little Hawk lashing his pony to get out ahead of his older and more famous brother, anxious to catch up, to build a reputation as great as Crazy Horse's own.

And sometimes, not often, but sometimes, he would wake up crying. Black Shawl knew that it was those times when he missed Black Buffalo Woman, but she said nothing, contenting herself with wrapping her grieving husband in her arms and helping him forget. She loved her husband, and knew that he had come to love her, too. That helped ease the pain, but didn't expunge it altogether. Time would do that for Crazy Horse, she thought. And sometimes she prayed that time would work its magic soon.

But there was a shadow on the horizon, one that

Crazy Horse and Sitting Bull watched the way they would watch the advance of a tornado's funnel. The bluecoats were pushing deeper into the Yellowstone country. With them were surveyors who were busy plotting the next stretch of track for the Northern Pacific.

Scouts kept track of them, and the two leaders spent several days planning their response. The best approach would be an ambush, and Crazy Horse made two surveillance trips, looking for the perfect place. It was obvious that the surveyors wanted to plot a track that would require as little trouble with the mountains as possible, and once that was clear to him, Crazy Horse found the perfect place.

In early August of 1873, Crazy Horse, Sitting Bull, and three hundred and fifty warriors crouched in wait as the bluecoats set up their camp at the mouth of the Tongue River. Looking down on the camp from the top of a bluff, Crazy Horse saw the commander dismount, unsaddle his horse, and proceed to remove his red shirt, then bunch it up to cushion the hard leather of the saddle which he used for a pillow. While Crazy Horse watched, the officer lay down to nap in his long underwear.

Through a spyglass, he watched the sleeping man for a moment, then handed the telescope to Sitting Bull. "The long-haired one does not seem to be afraid of the Sioux," he said.

"Maybe we can teach him," Sitting Bull answered, as he peered through the glass.

Crazy Horse took back the glass and scanned the terrain ahead, on the far side of the sleeping officer and his camp of eighty-five cavalrymen. A stand of timber, easily large enough to conceal all three hundred and fifty Sioux, was the best place from which to launch the attack.

The cavalry mounts were grazing, unsaddled, and ambling through the lush grass. The timber stand was upstream, and Crazy Horse suggested that a small party of warriors try to stampede the horses. The bluecoats would have to follow to get them back. If all went well, they would chase their animals into the trees, where the advantage of their new rifles would be neutralized to a degree.

It took some time to maneuver the warriors into the trees after a long detour, and when they were ready, it was early afternoon. The unrelenting sun was hot and the air filled with dust and swarms of flies. Crazy Horse led five warriors on a dash toward the American horses, but one of the half-drowsing pickets spotted them as they neared the herd, shouted the alarm, and opened fire.

With surprise lost, and the fire heavy, the decoy party was forced to fall back. Most of the soldiers, even though they were on foot, rushed toward the Sioux, and their repeating rifles made any approach hazardous. Even the sleeping officer, still dressed only in his long underwear, woke up, grabbed a rifle, and sprinted toward the herd.

The Sioux returned fire, but they were few, and had only ancient weapons. Crazy Horse had a newer rifle than most of the others, but even it was no match for the new guns of the bluecoats. When the decoy held its ground, the officer dressed

quickly, then detailed twenty men to chase down
the Sioux, and led them in their chase.

The decoy team rode confidently, never allow-
ing itself to get too far ahead of the pursuing bluecoats. The closer they came to the trees, the more
wary the soldiers became. Three of them sprinted
out ahead while the rest of the detail watched. The
decoys moved a few dozen yards, then stopped.
The three soldiers stopped, too. When the decoys
moved, the soldiers moved. By this point, it was
obvious to Crazy Horse that the plan would not
work. The bluecoats were either too nervous to follow him, or they suspected a trap.

For several minutes, the two parties stared at one
another. There was no exchange of insults, as was
usual in such confrontations.

The warriors in the timber included a few
Cheyenne. One of them recognized the officer,
and whispered to another, "Remember him? From
the Washita? It's Long-Hair! The one they call
Custer."

The word spread rapidly among the Cheyenne.
Many of them had been at Black Kettle's camp.
Some had even been there as children with Black
Kettle at Sand Creek. That massacre burned in
their guts like water from an alkali spring. And
memories of the Washita attack stoked the fire.
There was no holding them back as they broke into
the open, firing their guns and launching a shower
of arrows.

If the ambush had had a chance, even for a few
of the bluecoats, that chance was gone now.

Custer wheeled his horse and galloped back
toward the rest of the pursuit detail, looking over

his shoulder. He wasn't watching the Cheyenne, though. His gaze was locked on the pale Sioux with a single hawk's feather in his light brown hair. We'll meet again, he thought. I can feel it.

# Chapter 26

**July 1874**

CUSTER LED AN EXPEDITION into the Black Hills in the summer of 1874. There were rumors of gold and, in the aftermath of the Panic of 1873, whites were desperate for more of the precious metal. Despite warnings that the Black Hills were sacred to the Sioux and that any entrance would provoke hostilities, Custer had been ordered in, to accompany a geological team. It didn't seem to occur to anyone in Washington that the Black Hills had been declared permanent Sioux territory by the treaty of 1868, and that by its terms, no whites were permitted to enter the region without Sioux permission.

The column consisted of ten cavalry and two infantry companies, accompanied by one hundred Indian scouts, mostly Arikaras. The supply train was one hundred and ten wagons long. Smoke signals filled the air along the route of march, a sure sign that the Sioux knew he was there.

But if Custer was worried, the natural beauty of the region more than assuaged his fears. He wrote reams of letters to his wife extolling the perfection of the Hills. He hunted every day, doing more than his share to supply fresh meat for the command,

and he fell in love with the region. And when gold was discovered in unimaginable volume, all fears of the Sioux, and any concerns about violating the treaty's terms, were forgotten.

But unexpectedly, Custer and his command encountered only a small band of Sioux, and they were peaceful residents of the Red Cloud Agency, under the leadership of Red Cloud's son-in-law, Stabber. Custer tried to enlist Stabber as a guide, but he was refused, and that was the last he saw of the Sioux during his three-week exploration.

The one the Sioux now, like the Cheyenne, called Long-Hair gathered animals for his traveling zoo, while the troopers roamed through the valleys gathering flowers by the armful. So smitten was he with the Edenic riches that he had the company band play a concert in the middle of a valley filled from ridge to ridge with flowers.

Crazy Horse and Sitting Bull were far to the west, in the Powder River country. If they knew of Custer's intrusion, they made no attempt to stop it. Crazy Horse was so wrapped up in his family, spending hour upon hour with They Are Afraid of Her, that he was seldom away from the village for more than a day or two to hunt.

Sitting Bull spent the idle time making speeches, trying to rally the hostiles for another war on the white soldiers, but Crazy Horse paid little attention to politics, preferring to stay in his lodge and play with his daughter. She had brought him a serenity he had never known, and he relished it.

In early July, he stirred himself just long enough to lead a small war party westward to raise a little havoc among the Crows. On his return, he found that the village, near the Little Bighorn River, had moved after he left. Pointed sticks on the ground at the village site led him toward its new location on the Tongue, and he pushed his pony and his men hard. He wanted to get home, to resume the tranquillity that increasingly absorbed him.

The next two days seemed to take forever, and he drove himself harder and harder, desperate to cover the last few miles. Finally, the smoke from campfires came into view, and Crazy Horse lashed his pony into a full gallop.

Slipping from his pony as he entered the village, he raced toward his lodge, but Worm intercepted him, grabbing him by the arm and holding on, despite Crazy Horse's attempt to pull free.

He knew then that something was wrong, and searched his father's face for some clue.

Worm lowered his eyes and shook his head. Clearing his throat, he whispered, "They Are Afraid of Her . . ."

"What? Tell me, Father . . ."

Worm sighed, then shook his head once more. "The white man's sickness, the one they call cholera. She . . ."

Crazy Horse ripped loose then and dashed into the lodge. Black Shawl looked at him and her face was a mask of grief. Her eyes were red and swollen, and she fell apart as he rushed to her. Kneeling on a buffalo robe, she reached up to her husband, and Crazy Horse sank to his knees beside her. He wrapped his arms around Black Shawl and she buried her face in his shoulder. Sobbing uncontrollably, she tried to tell him the details, but couldn't stop the quavering of her voice. Crazy Horse patted her back and stroked her hair, but she continued to tremble, the sobs wracking her body again and again.

"Where is she?" he asked.

Worm had come into the lodge, and he reached out to touch Crazy Horse on the shoulder. "You can't go to her scaffold, son. It is too far from here, deep in Crow country now."

"Where is it?" Crazy Horse said, without looking around. "I want to know."

"If I tell you, I know you will go there, and . . ."

"Where *is* it?" Crazy Horse snapped. It was the first time he had ever used such a tone with his father. Both men seemed to recognize it, and Crazy Horse turned then to look at his father, tears streaming down his face. "I have to know."

Worm started to speak, then thought better of it. He knew that he could not forbid his son to go. They were way past that. And he knew that he could not ask his son for a promise that Crazy Horse would be unable to keep. "I'll tell you," he said. "But you must promise to take someone with you. Don't go alone, please."

Crazy Horse nodded. He said nothing, but the shake of his head was enough. He had given his word.

He left in the morning. With him was Frank Grouard, the old white scout. The two were friends, and Grouard knew enough about Sioux customs, and about his friend, that he made himself invisible on the seventy-mile ride. Crazy Horse said not a word on the two-day trip.

Near sundown on the second day, they found the scaffold right where Worm had said it would be. Etched against the darkening sky, solid black as if drawn with a piece of charred wood on gray paper, the scaffold frame trembled when Crazy Horse climbed up, wrapped himself in a buffalo robe, and lay down.

For three days, he lay there. Grouard moved a mile away, to camp near a small creek. Each night, just before sunset, he would climb the hill. But when he drew close enough to hear Crazy Horse sobbing, he would turn and head back down the hill.

Lying there motionless, except for the quaking of his body during the fits of weeping, the great warrior stared at the sky. It reminded him of his vision quest, how he had lain so long on the rough rock overlooking the lake, how the blue seemed to grow deep and still, how the clouds drifted slowly across his field of vision, changing shape like magic creatures from some other world and, at night, how the stars had seemed so cold and far away.

His serenity was gone now, as distant as those stars, and replaced by a rage as deep and dark as the night sky. They Are Afraid of Her was so tiny, and she had brought him such peace, and now she was gone, a victim of the white man every bit as much as if she had been killed by a soldier's gun. She had never hurt a soul, never done anything but give him joy, and she had been taken from him.

Someone would pay for her loss, and pay dearly.

Crazy Horse ate nothing and drank nothing for those three days. Instead he fed on the rage that tormented him, even as it fed on him, burning its way toward the surface from someplace deep inside, a place where nothing and no one except They Are

Afraid of Her had ever been able to touch before,
and no one would touch again as long as he lived.

On the morning of the fourth day, he climbed
down from the scaffold. His eyes were dry, and his
face was made of stone. Only the scar above his lip,
whiter than usual over the clenched muscle of his
jaw, betrayed what he was feeling.

Leaving the buffalo robe on the scaffold, he
looked once more at the platform where his daughter lay, then at the sky as if giving it one last chance
to explain the unexplainable, then he turned and
walked downhill. Behind him, still almost black
against the pale blue sky, stood his daughter's burial platform, like a grim monument to his tranquillity. That tranquillity was dead, too, a thing of the
past, and only the willow poles and small, frail
body of They Are Afraid of Her remained. Soon
they would be gone, too.

He saw Grouard waiting for him, saw his pony,
Grouard's horse, the pack horse, the small fire, but
most of all he saw Grouard's skin, darkened by the
sun, but still white. For a moment, the rage boiled
up inside him and he wanted to hurl himself on the
old scout, wrap his fingers around Grouard's throat
and throttle him until his tongue lolled, turned pur-
ple, and his eyes protruded from their sockets.

But he caught himself. Grouard had done nothing to hurt him, or to hurt They Are Afraid of Her.
He remembered seeing the little girl, even smaller
alongside the tall, lanky white man, her little hand
wrapped in Grouard's gnarled fist, as they walked
to a creek to go fishing. And he understood then
that it wasn't the whiteness of a man's skin that
made him an enemy, but the blackness of his heart.

And there was no way to tell that until you gave him a chance to get close, close enough to do you damage. That only made the hurt worse. And he thought then of No Water, who had hurt him, too, and No Water wasn't a white man. The secret then was not to make choices on the color of skin, but to keep everyone at arm's length, to hold them far enough away that they couldn't reach you at all, couldn't touch you in the only place that mattered.

Grouard nodded. He said nothing as he looked up at the warrior, and only then did Crazy Horse notice the twin strands of silver filigreeing the old man's weathered cheeks. The tears laced and interlaced as they wound their way down to his chin and dripped onto the buckskin shirt, making patches of dark wetness on the pale beige of its chest.

Crazy Horse felt his own eyes well up, and made no attempt to stop the tears as they ran down his cheeks. Neither man spoke, neither made a sound. But the grief was shared, and Crazy Horse knew again that Frank Grouard was a friend.

They broke camp in silence, and rode the seventy miles in silence, stopping only twice, neither time for more than a few minutes. Only the steady clop of the horses' hooves broke the stillness, and it seemed to Crazy Horse that it was like a drum beat, or the beating of his own heart, some inescapable rhythm that would be with him until the day he died.

When he returned to the village, Black Shawl greeted him warmly, but there was a reserve about her now, as if the place where They Are Afraid of Her used to be was now some unbridgeable chasm, a great void across which they could see each other but where even shouted words were swallowed by the yawning silence.

He returned to the old ways, going off alone for days, even weeks at a time. No one knew when he would leave and, once he had gone, no one knew when, or if, he would come back.

The people started to hear stories about miners found in the Black Hills, dead, a single arrow stabbed into the ground beside their stiffened corpses, their hair still intact. Most Sioux took scalps. But Crazy Horse did not, and the people all seemed to understand, without one of them saying a word, that this was the revenge of Crazy Horse, his way of exacting payment for the incalculable loss of his little girl.

Black Shawl tried to get him to talk, to tell her if it were he who was leaving the bleak reminders strewn across the holy ground of the Paha Sapa, but he said nothing.

While Sitting Bull tried to rouse the people, Crazy Horse kept to himself. He made plans when there was a war party, but said nothing more than was necessary to make those plans understood. The rest of the time, he kept to himself, alone in his lodge with Black Shawl and her mother.

Red Leaf accompanied him on hunts once or twice, but felt isolated, even when riding beside the man he idolized. After the second time, Crazy Horse went alone. No one knew where he went. They knew only that when he came back, he had food for the old ones.

And they saw that in battle he was a different man. More reckless, they said, worse than Little Hawk. Worm heard the stories from He Dog and

Red Leaf and Little Big Man, and he knew what drove his son. It was not vengeance so much as the unspoken wish that something would put an end to his pain, that a white man's bullet or a Crow arrow would send him off to be with Hump and Little Hawk and Lone Bear again. And, most of all, where he could sit under a tree beside a perfect stream, with They Are Afraid of Her curled in his lap, her tiny head on his shoulder.

And Worm lived in fear that that wish would be granted.

# Chapter 27 ═══════

**June 1876**

IN LATE 1875, the government in Washington, aware
of the huge potential of the gold fields in the Black
Hills, decided to induce the Sioux to sell them.
Custer's preliminary enthusiasm had proved to be
well-founded, and the rush of prospectors into the
forbidden territory was proving difficult to stop.
Once again, a commission was appointed in an
attempt to gain concessions from the Sioux without
telling them the true worth of the land they were
being asked to surrender.

But the chiefs were no longer so gullible. They
had been through a number of treaty negotiations,
and they had seen how willing the white men were
to lie and cheat and, when neither of those options
worked, to take by force what the Sioux would not
give up. Spotted Tail took a tour of the Black Hills,
and while there, talked to several miners and the
new agent for the territory. All the whites he spoke
to told him the same thing—the Black Hills were
worth at least thirty to fifty million dollars, possibly more. But they also told the Brule chief that
such a figure was more than the government in
Washington was likely to pay.

Red Cloud did some figuring of his own, and came up with seven million dollars, which he wanted put in an account to generate interest, which would be distributed annually without ever drawing on the principal. At the same time, he asked for a number of regular goods distributions, everything from food to the erection of houses, for seven full generations.

In its counterproposal, the commission, headed by William B. Allison, the senator from Iowa, and once again including Gen. Alfred Terry, made an offer of six million dollars for outright purchase or perpetual rental at an annual payment of four hundred thousand dollars.

But there was no consensus among the Sioux. The young warriors were outraged that their chiefs would even consider selling the sacred land of the Paha Sapa. The older chiefs, Spotted Tail and Red Cloud in particular, thought they were being more practical, trying to get something for their people in the belief that if the Hills were not sold, they would be taken by force.

But the anger of the young men, which threatened the commissioners, led to talks being broken off without a firm deal having been made. The talks crumbled, and the commission rode off, followed by angry warriors who outnumbered the commissioners and their cavalry escort by more than ten to one.

Once the negotiations terminated, the army, which had been trying to stem the tide of miners seeking to enter the gold fields, backed away. They no longer made any effort to prevent incursions into the lands which had been guaranteed to the

Sioux under the treaty of 1868. While the young warriors had been right to be angry, Red Cloud and Spotted Tail had proved to be prescient.

If there was to be any preservation of Sioux title to the Black Hills, it would have to be achieved on the warpath.

For a short time after the talks were terminated, the Sioux squabbled among themselves. Those from the agencies were trying to convince the wild Sioux of the Powder River country to accept reservation life. They told tales of the wonders of the agencies.

"Every five days," Red Bear said to a council of hostiles and agency Sioux, "the white man turns loose hundreds of cattle. We take to our horses and hunt them like we hunt the buffalo. The women butcher them just like they did the buffalo. But it is better than the buffalo hunt, because there are always cattle. Before, when we lived free, sometimes we had to go weeks without finding a buffalo herd. That can't happen with the cattle."

Crazy Horse and Young man Afraid were anything but convinced. Young Man Afraid argued a bit, but Crazy Horse preferred to sit stony faced, letting the tame Indians talk of their lives, but not caring what they said. Spotted Tail and Red Cloud stayed silent, too, knowing that their words were suspect. They were too closely identified with the white man now, worse than Laramie Loafers in the eyes of some, and nothing they had to say would carry any weight with the hostiles from the Powder River.

But there was one Sioux present who could speak with authority, and who still had the respect of the hostile leaders. Touch the Clouds asked to be heard, and when he was recognized, he looked slowly around the council circle, choosing his words carefully, framing them before speaking.

"I have lived in the Powder River country," he began. "And I have tried living at the agency, too. Red Bear talks about hunting the white man's cows. He says it is like the old days, like running down the buffalo. But it is not. When we rode to hunt the buffalo, we were free men, and the buffalo were free, too. It is true that sometimes we had to ride far, looking for the herds, farther and farther now that the white man is here. But it is not true that hunting the white man's scrawny cows is like hunting the buffalo. The cows are kept in cages, and so are the agency Indians. White man cages. Both of them."

Red Bear started to argue, but Touch the Clouds held him off. "I am not finished," he said. "The food they give us at the agency is not fit to eat. The flour is bad, the corn is full of worms, even the cattle, which Red Bear likes to hunt, are diseased. The agents are thieves and cheats. They sell things intended for the Indians and put the money in their own pockets. They don't care what happens to the Indians under them, as long as they can get rich at Indian expense. That is not how free men are supposed to live. That is not how Sioux warriors are supposed to live. That is not how I want to live. And I will not live that way. I will not go back to the reservation unless the white man holds a gun to my head. And even then I might not go. Red Bear can do what he wants to do. He is a free man, whether he knows it or not. But so am I."

Touch the Clouds didn't bother to resume his seat. Instead, he stepped through the council circle and went on out of the lodge. Inside, no one said a word. Even when the pounding of Touch the Cloud's pony's hooves faded away to nothing, the council lodge was silent.

Then, without a word, Crazy Horse got to his feet and walked out of the lodge. Behind him came Sitting Bull, then Young Man Afraid. For all practical purposes, the council was over. There was nothing more to be said, and no one of influence among the hostiles there to say it in any case.

But Gen. Philip Sheridan, the commander of the Department of the Missouri, was determined to force compliance. While the Sioux argued among themselves over the winter and into the spring of 1876, Sheridan was assembling a formidable army. He sent three columns into the field, each under an experienced commander.

Gen. George Crook led over a thousand soldiers and nearly three hundred Shoshoni and Crow scouts north from Fort Fetterman, heading toward the Little Bighorn River valley. Gen. Alfred Terry, with Custer in his command, led two thousand, seven hundred more troops. Terry was following the Yellowstone from the east. The third, and smallest, contingent was heading along the Yellowstone from the west, its four hundred and fifty men having left Fort Ellis in Montana Territory under the command of Gen. John Gibbon.

As the troops slowly converged on the Sioux, the Indian numbers had begun to swell. Near starvation at the agencies, many of Red Cloud's and Spotted Tail's people headed northwest, where they could still find buffalo and where they would feel safe. The troop movements near the reservations had frightened some and made others angry. Neither emotion was sufficient to uproot lodges by the dozen and send their owners streaming into the hostiles' country.

By the end of May, with the troops rapidly closing, there were as many as two thousand lodges in the great camp on the Rosebud Creek. The number of warriors might have been as high as four thousand, and possibly even higher. Not even Crazy Horse and Sitting Bull knew. But what all the Indians, Sioux and Cheyenne, Arapaho and Assiniboine alike, agreed upon was that this was their last, best chance to send the white men packing. Some had already resigned themselves to defeat, and were determined to have one last summer of freedom to live the old way. Others, and Crazy Horse was chief among them, were determined that victory was the only permissible outcome.

Sitting Bull led a sun dance at what all agreed was the largest gathering of plains Indians the continent had ever seen. The mood was decidedly celebratory, with feasting nonstop, endless dancing, gambling, and horse racing, but there was an elegiac undercurrent for the fatalists among the Sioux and their allies.

Terry and Gibbon joined up on the tenth of June at the mouth of the Rosebud. Their scouts were convinced that the hostile camp was somewhere to the south, between their joint command and Crook's column coming up the Rosebud from the south. Neither Terry, Gibbon, Custer, nor Crook knew where the Indian village was located.

But Crook was not so lucky. The Sioux had found him. Camped in the valley of the Little Bighorn, their scouts had stumbled on Crook's column and hastened back with word of the approach of the man they called "Three Stars."

Crazy Horse hastily assembled a force numbering nearly fifteen hundred warriors. But it had taken more than a little argument on his part to deploy his forces in a way that made sense to him.

Some of the other chiefs wanted to send the entire force of warriors to the Rosebud to smash Crook's column once and for all. Even Sitting Bull was in favor of the idea.

"And who will protect the women and the children?" Crazy Horse argued.

"If we kill all the bluecoats, they will not need protection," Lone Eagle countered. "You have heard of Sitting Bull's dream. You know that he saw bluecoat soldiers falling upside down into our village. You know that means a great victory will be ours."

"Yes, I know of the dream. But I also know that there are many bluecoats, and if we are not careful, that dream might not come true. The bluecoats send soldiers from many different directions. Does Lone Eagle know for certain that there are no soldiers to the east? Or to the west? Or to the north?"

"It does not matter. As long as we are willing to fight, we will win."

"It *does* matter. Someone must stay behind to defend the village. Ask those who were at Ash Hollow when Harney came. Ask those who were at Sand Creek. Ask those who were at Washita, when Long-Hair came. How many times have we come home to find the lodges reduced to ashes, the women and children dead on the ground, our horses gone, our food destroyed? Once would have been too many, but it has been more than once, and Lone Eagle knows this."

"Crazy Horse is right," Sitting Bull said. He was weak from the sundance, in which he had had fifty pieces of flesh sliced from each arm. The loss of blood had reduced him to near invalid status. But his word was still powerful, and with him and Crazy Horse in agreement, no one wanted to argue.

So Crazy Horse assembled his force of fifteen hundred warriors and led an all-night march on June sixteenth. The Sioux crossed the divide between the Little Bighorn camp and Rosebud Creek, moving in a military-style column, with scouts out ahead and the *akicita* warriors guarding the flanks and the rear. Crazy Horse was determined that this time tempers would be on a tight rein, and the younger men would be held in check. He sensed that this might be the last real opportunity to inflict significant damage on the bluecoats and would not let a lack of discipline spoil it.

At dawn the following morning, the warriors reached the banks of the Rosebud, where the horses were allowed to graze while the warriors donned their war paint. By eight thirty, the Sioux were ready to move again.

At the same time, Crook called a halt to his march, which had begun at 4:00 A.M. His troopers unsaddled their mounts while Crook conferred with Washakie, the great Shoshoni chief who was leading the contingent of scouts.

"There are many Sioux ahead," Washakie told him.

But Three Stars was confident. "We are many, too," he said.

Washakie shook his head. "Too many Sioux. We should send scouts to see exactly where they are. And how many."

Crazy Horse was on the west side of the Rosebud valley. Creeping to the top of a hill, he could see the creek below, and the huge column, its members scattered on both banks. He saw the horses unsaddled and grazing. The north end of the valley narrowed dramatically, the walls getting progressively steeper, and a heavy stand of timber filled the gap. If he could get the Sioux into the timber without being spotted, it would be an ideal place from which to launch an ambush.

But as he was about to back away from the crest, a small band of Crow scouts stumbled on the advance party and, when they saw the massed Sioux might, broke back for the column, shouting the alarm.

The Sioux poured over the ridge in pursuit of the scouts. There was no time for strategy. The troopers, broken into smaller units by the terrain, started to lay down heavy fire, but the hordes of Sioux and Cheyenne kept on coming. The pockets of resistance fought fiercely, but the Sioux and Cheyenne were every bit as fierce. They swarmed in masses over and through the clumps of troopers. The fighting was hand to hand much of the time, the warriors pressing their assault instead of staying at a distance where the repeating rifles of the bluecoats were more deadly.

The pockets of battle became swirls of limbs and lances as the warriors kept the troopers off balance. Pressing, charging, falling back and charging again, the Sioux never let up. Crook's men were fighting for their lives, and they knew it. Much of the combat involved knives and clubs. At such close quarters, the soldiers were unable to make efficient use of their long guns.

Limbs were severed, eyes gouged out, throats slashed, and blood splattered on Sioux and soldier alike. It was like nothing the troopers had ever seen. And they weren't prepared for it.

Crook tried to mount a counterattack, but Crazy Horse was everywhere, leading charge after charge. Wherever it looked as if the tide was about to turn, Crazy Horse took the lead. Good Weasel, Black Twin, and Kicking Bear, *de facto* lieutenants for Crazy Horse, followed his lead, taking command of large contingents and rallying the warriors to keep the pressure on.

Convinced that the main hostile camp was downstream, Crook made a tactical error. He dispatched Col. Anson Mills, at the head of eight cavalry troops, to find the village, capture it, and hold it.

From the very heart of the battle, Crazy Horse saw the horse soldiers moving away. He waited until they were too far to offer support to Crook's main unit, then began to mass warriors on the left flank. At the same time, he sent a large contingent to the rear of the remaining portion of Crook's column.

At the last minute, Crook realized he was being outmaneuvered and sent a runner to bring Mills back. When Mills's cavalry troopers reappeared, Crazy Horse broke off the engagement, pulling his warriors back and abandoning the valley of the Rosebud.

Crook withdrew from the field, claiming a victory, but he was unable to get word through to Terry's command. Terry had no idea either where Crook was or that he had encountered a huge force of Sioux and Cheyenne warriors. The most critical failure of communication was that Terry and his commanders, including Custer and Gibbon, were unaware that Crazy Horse had taught the hostiles a new method of engagement. The massing of warriors and the constant pressure at close quarters were unheard of in Indian warfare, and Terry's ignorance of that development would carry a high price tag.

# Chapter 28

THE SIOUX WERE JUBILANT. They had overwhelmed the huge force of Three Stars and, although they had sustained some losses, they had also inflicted significant casualties on the bluecoats. But Crazy Horse was more restrained in his enthusiasm. Sitting Bull, too, was worried.

"I don't like what happened yesterday," he said, sitting on a hill overlooking the sprawling village. The Little Bighorn River glinted in the sun, and he watched the waters for a long time, waiting for Crazy Horse to answer. When Crazy Horse said nothing, the medicine man poked him with an elbow. "You're very quiet this morning."

Crazy Horse nodded. "Yes, I am."

"You are worried about yesterday, too, I can see that."

"I have a feeling there are more bluecoats. I don't know why, but something tells me there are many more."

"And you don't think we can beat them?"

"I don't know. I want to think so, but it is just because I want it so much that I wonder if we can. I am afraid the younger men will get reckless now,

286

they will think they can't be beaten and that reck-
lessness will *get* them beaten."

"You don't believe in my dream, then?"

"I didn't say that. But how do we know that your
dream was not about yesterday's fight? Maybe all
the bluecoats we will kill were killed yesterday.
The dream was not precise."

"It said they would fall into our camp.
Yesterday's fight was not like that. I still believe in
the dream. I believe that it is still to be realized."

"Then it will be other bluecoats. The ones from
yesterday went south, where they came from. They
are still moving south, and . . ."

"Where are the other bluecoats, then?" Sitting
Bull asked.

Crazy Horse shrugged. "Close, somewhere close.
I can feel it. I can almost smell them."

"We will continue to send out scouts. If they are
near here, we will find them."

Four days later, Gen. Alfred Terry met with
Custer. The combined command, numbering over
three thousand troops, had been waiting for word
from General Crook, and when it hadn't come,
Terry started to worry.

"The Crow scouts say there are many Sioux out
here somewhere. We have to find them. We can't
let them slip away. Not this time. With Crook coming from the south, we have them trapped. It's our
best chance to put an end to this bloody business."

Custer nodded. "That's why we're here, General.
What do you want me to do?"

"I want you to follow the Rosebud. You know
about the trail Major Reno found a few days ago?"

"I do."

"When you strike that trail, I want you to follow it. See what you can find. Make sure you keep checking your flank. When you get to the mouth of the Tongue River, head for the Little Bighorn. I can't tell you exactly what to do, because I don't know what you'll find, if anything. If the Crows are right, there's a big camp out there. If you stumble across the Sioux, you'll have to use your judgment."

"When do you want me to leave?"

"This afternoon. I can let you have four troops of the Second Cavalry, and the gatling guns. General Gibbon and I will follow along shortly."

Custer smiled. "Won't need them, General. The guns'll just slow me down. And I have more than six hundred men in the Seventh. I can't imagine needing more than that."

"Are you certain?"

"Yes, General, I am. The faster we move, the sooner we'll find that village."

Four hours later, to the strains of Custer's favorite song, "Garryowen," the 7th Cavalry paraded past Generals Terry and Gibbon. As Custer passed and snapped a crisp salute, Terry said, "Now, Custer, don't be greedy, but wait for us."

Lowering his hand, Custer shouted over his shoulder, "No, I won't."

The 7th followed Rosebud Creek for twelve miles before camping for the night. The following day, with a full day's march, they made thirty miles, and thirty more the day after that. Signs of the Sioux were everywhere. Huge patches of grazed land, the grass down to the nub, trampled patches of muddy ground along the creek bank, the ashes of the burned sun-dance lodge. Everywhere they looked, the scouts found traces. And they knew the Sioux party was a large one.

On the twenty-fifth, they found the remains of a camp, complete with sand paintings showing the details of Sitting Bull's vision. Bloody Knife, Custer's favorite Arikara scout, showed him the paintings and explained what they meant, but Custer shrugged it off.

When they found the trail of the village once more, it was almost a mile wide. The travois poles, thousands upon thousands, had plowed the ground into raw furrows. They were getting close, and Custer was determined to find the Sioux quickly. On the twenty-fifth, the 7th marched another ten miles after midnight. His men were getting beaten down by the relentless pace, but he pushed them still harder, sending scouts out ahead to try to locate the village itself, which he knew couldn't be too far away now.

Bloody Knife found the village, and what he saw terrified him. Hurrying back to Custer, he tried to convey the size of the village. "More Sioux than we have bullets," he said. "The ponies are like nothing I have ever seen. They fill the valley. The white lodges are like snow, everywhere lodges and more lodges."

Custer thanked the Arikara, but didn't seem disturbed by the news. Mitch Bouyer, a white scout who had been there with Bloody Knife, tried again to impress the significance of the discovery on Custer. "General, it's the biggest village I ever seen. Maybe the biggest there ever was. I been here thirty years, and I never saw nothing that even come close."

Custer saddled his mount and rode out with Bouyer and Bloody Knife to see for himself. But by the time he reached the vantage point, fifteen miles from the Little Bighorn, a haze had settled into the valley, and he could see almost nothing. Moments later, advance scouts reported that the village was getting ready to move. They also reported that Sioux scouts were heading toward the column, and were certain to discover it.

Custer had the bugler trumpet Officers' Call, and when his commanders assembled, he said, "The largest Indian village on the North American continent is ahead, and I am going to attack it. Gentlemen, make sure your men have plenty of ammunition. A minimum of a hundred rounds each. Captain Benteen, I want you to take three troops, H, D, and K. Major Reno will take three also, M, A, and G. We'll leave B Troop to defend the ammunition train, and I'll take the remaining five troops myself."

As the 7th moved out, Crazy Horse, Sitting Bull, another Hunkpapa chief named Gall, and Two Moons, the leader of the Cheyenne contingent, were kept apprised of the cavalry movements. They knew an attack was coming, but not where or when. The village was relatively calm, with most of the people, even the warriors, unaware of the impending battle. Children swam in the cool waters of the Little Bighorn, young men kept watch on the huge pony herd, and women were out gathering berries and wild turnips.

The advancing cavalry had split into three columns, with Captain Benteen on the left, Major Reno in the center, and Custer on the right. Behind them came the ammunition train, with its single troop of defenders. At noon, Custer found a solitary lodge standing on a hilltop. He ducked inside and found a funeral scaffold with a single warrior laid to rest. He ordered the tipi burned, and pushed his men on harder, thinking that the Sioux were making a run for it.

One of the scouts spotted a great cloud of dust and when he reported his discovery to Custer, the colonel sent Benteen south, parallel to the Little Bighorn, to get in position to prevent the Sioux from escaping in that direction. Then he sent a courier to order Major Reno's command to charge ahead, and attack the village, while he took his own units northward, keeping a line of bluffs between him and the village.

The Sioux had failed to spot Reno's column, and when his three troops of cavalry appeared, they were taken by surprise. Crazy Horse had been keeping his warriors in check, waiting for Custer, because he knew exactly where Long-Hair was. But Reno, for some reason, despite having surprise on his side, failed to charge the village as ordered. Instead, he dismounted his command and had the men fire at long range, causing little damage, but succeeding in stirring up the opposition.

Many of the warriors wanted to charge Reno, but Crazy Horse sprang onto his pony and headed them off, riding back and forth across their line of advance and insisting that they hold fast. Reno started to fall back, and Short Bull, a noted warrior, called out to Crazy Horse, "You're too late. You missed the fight!"

Crazy Horse laughed and pointed to the north.

"There's another one coming, a big one. And I won't miss that one," he shouted.

From a hilltop at the northern end of the village, Custer could see Reno's men. He planned to take advantage of the second surprise and push into the camp from the rear. When the Sioux realized their families were in jeopardy, their forces would be split and they would run for it, fighting defensively while the women and children tried to make their escape.

Calling to his trumpeter, Custer said, "Go to Captain Benteen. Tell him we found the Sioux and that it's a big village. Tell him to come quick, and to bring the ammunition packs."

Crazy Horse saw Custer and his men disappear behind the bluffs, and he pulled his men back, leaving just a few to harass Reno's command, already falling back. The troopers with Reno were exhausted, and Crazy Horse saw that most of them could barely stand. Sitting Bull noticed it, too. "They are shaking like cypress limbs in a strong wind," he said.

Crazy Horse nodded. "We can hold them off easily." Then, pointing to the north, he said, "There is our real fight." Realizing that Custer was trying to outflank him, he sprang back onto his pony and yelled, "Ho-ka hey! It is a good day to die! Strong hearts, brave hearts, to the front! Weak hearts and cowards to the rear!" Waving his rifle overhead, he kicked the pony and charged to the north. Behind him, more than a thousand warriors surged like flood waters, their shrieks and war whoops echoing off the hills. The thunder of their ponies' hooves made the lodges tremble as the warriors charged out to meet Custer and his men.

As Crazy Horse rushed to outflank the advancing cavalry, Gall and fifteen hundred warriors blocked Custer's approach, forcing him to turn to the right and head for high ground. At this point, he must have realized that he was in for the fight of his life. The sheer number of Indians confronting him was more than he expected, and he now realized that he had badly miscalculated.

Heading away from the village now, Gall right on his tail, he galloped toward a hill at the northern end of the bluffs. He hoped to dig in and hold off the Sioux hordes until Benteen could arrive with reinforcements. They were well on their way up the hill, and Custer knew that with more than two hundred men with repeating rifles, he could hold the hilltop indefinitely. But as the hilltop drew ever closer, Custer, charging at the head of his command, saw a lone warrior, Crazy Horse, suddenly break over the ridge and take command of the hilltop. Behind him swarmed another thousand warriors. Custer was trapped between two huge forces, and with the Sioux commanding the hilltop, he was completely cut off from a viable defensive position.

For a moment, the earth seemed to stop spinning. All sound vanished into a void. The swirling colors of the warbonnets, shields, painted ponies and, most of all, the thousand Sioux warriors, seemed to hang motionless in the air. A stiff breeze whipped the feathers wildly and then, in a single instant, Crazy Horse gave vent to a war cry, and the world exploded into bloody chaos.

Crazy Horse led his warriors over the crest of the ridge and down toward Custer. The thunder of gunfire echoed from every direction. A cloud of gunsmoke gathered on the hillside then mingled with dust as two thousand Sioux and Cheyenne ponies charged around and around, slowly closing on the shrinking circle of cavalrymen. One by one the troopers fell, Custer running this way and that, rallying his troops until he stood alone, the last man to fall.

Then it was over, and peace descended once more, bringing with it silence that, like a funeral shroud, wrapped within it the bodies of two hundred and twenty-six officers and men of the 7th Cavalry.

# Chapter 29 ═══════

**September 1877**

THE BATTLE AT THE LITTLE BIGHORN RIVER was the single most impressive victory by the Plains Indians, indeed by *any* Indians in the long, bloody history of American westward expansion. But it was also the last hurrah of the Sioux. The smoke had barely cleared when the women began to break down the lodges and assemble all their possessions on the travois. The warriors were exultant, but their leaders were frightened.

When they became aware that General Terry was nearby, the Sioux and Cheyenne broke into smaller groups and headed south, away from Terry's column, then doubled back, Sitting Bull leading his Hunkpapas in a great circle and heading for the Grandmother Country, Canada.

Crazy Horse led his people toward the Black Hills. Some Cheyenne lodges were part of his encampment, and he spent the rest of the summer and fall of 1876 harassing the miners beginning to disembowel his beloved Paha Sapa. He seemed to sense that the end had come, and still spent much of his time on solitary hunts and leading an occasional small war party against the whites, but he no

longer harbored hopes of a permanent victory over
the bluecoats.

The uproar in the press over Custer's defeat led
to an uncharacteristic flurry of activity in the capi-
tal, and Congress acted to take control over Indian
affairs away from the Indian Bureau and put the
army in charge. The general officer corps was
ecstatic at the change. It was something they had
long argued for, and now that the opportunity had
been presented to them, they were more than willing to take advantage of it.

There was just as much turmoil on the reservations. Spotted Tail and Red Cloud, both now adept
at scheming and intrigue, anxious to acquire power
and quite comfortable in wielding it, moved to consolidate their authority at their respective agencies.

The army, knowing that Crazy Horse and Sitting
Bull were on the run, and knowing, too, that there
was little food for their people and no place for
them to hide, enlisted the aid of the two agency
chiefs. Each sent runners out to the various fugitive
bands of hostiles, but the runners were rebuffed.

A military engagement at Slim Buttes, which
saw the last significant war leadership of Crazy
Horse, ended with more defections from the hostile
camps. Crazy Horse was adamant that he would
not surrender, but changes in the laws now made it
illegal for the Sioux to be anywhere but on the
reservations. Unable to persuade the Sioux to sell
the Black Hills, the government simply took them.

Still Crazy Horse would not surrender.

When winter came, it was brutal, worse than
anyone could remember. The buffalo were all but
gone from the Black Hills region, and the bitter

cold and deep snow made it all but impossible for the Oglala band to get to the last buffalo hunting grounds in the Powder River country.

In early 1877, He Dog, convinced that there was no point in continuing to resist, tried to convince his friend to accept the inevitable.

"This winter is too hard on the people," he said.

"Do you think I don't know that?" Crazy Horse barked. "I have seen the starving children, the women who are wasting away. I know how hard it is. But you saw what happened when you tried to surrender—-they shot at you. They will shoot us all, if we give them the chance. I can't let that happen."

"Have you thought about the Grandmother Country? We could go to Sitting Bull."

"It is even colder there. There is little food and we would be worse off. Besides, the women and children could not make such a long march in the bitter cold. There is little to eat as it is, and if we march north we will need strength. Without enough food we would never make it."

The argument continued off and on for months. One small group of defectors tried to leave the Crazy Horse camp, but he caught up with them shortly after their departure, ordered their horses shot, and brought them back. He was afraid for them, and thought they would be punished by the whites if they surrendered.

The Cheyenne under Dull Knife and Little Wolf had surrendered and were taken to the desert of the Indian Territory, where there was no food and little water. They were starving, because the white man delivered promises by the wagon load, but nothing else. Tall Eagle, a Cheyenne warrior who had been at Little Bighorn, had sneaked away from the reservation and headed north to rejoin the hostile Sioux. He made it quite clear that the white man was in no mood to dispense mercy.

But the winter took its toll, and it was a heavy one. More than a dozen babies froze to death in their mothers' arms. Others died of starvation. Women, too, were crushed under the weight of the winter. Some warriors slipped away from the camp and made their way south, but few were willing to make the trip alone, and many of those who did never made it to the agencies.

Things improved a bit with the beginning of the spring thaw, but everyone knew that the days of roaming where they would across the plains were over. And the thought of another winter like the one just ending was more than Crazy Horse could bear. He couldn't watch another child die, hear another mother grieve for a dead infant, see another warrior crazy with grief as his family slipped away into death.

So, when runners came from Three Stars, he listened. He knew better than to trust everything he heard, but the people came first, and he had to decide what was best for them. Runners also came from the agencies, dispatched by Lt. William Clark, the officer the Sioux called White Hat.

Then Col. Nelson Miles sent runners of his own. It seemed that every officer in the bluecoat army wanted to be the one to accept the surrender of Crazy Horse. They were making promises they could not fulfill, but that didn't seem to matter to any of them. As long as they could get Crazy

Horse to come in, their careers would be enhanced and what happened to the Sioux was of no importance.

Crazy Horse was skeptical of each and every promise. They were just words, after all, and words were as nothing to the whites. Even when written on the treaty paper, they were brushed aside like grains of sand from a sleeve, and when they were gone, it was as if they had never been there at all.

And still the words came. Always words and more words. But there was nowhere to turn. So when Spotted Tail and a contingent of his Brule found the Crazy Horse camp in late March, Worm told the chief that although Crazy Horse was not there at the moment, he had left word that he would come in to surrender as soon as the weather permitted his people to travel. Spotted Tail brought assurances from Three Stars that the people would be well cared for.

But when White Hat heard that Crazy Horse had agreed to surrender to Crook, he sent another committee, this one headed by Red Cloud, to negotiate different surrender terms. Red Cloud had brought large supplies of rations with him, and distributed them to the hungry Sioux.

Crazy Horse talked with Red Cloud in his lodge.

"It is a long time since we have ridden together to fight the bluecoats," Red Cloud began.

Crazy Horse smiled sadly. "Perhaps if you had not given up so early, we might be riding against them still. Perhaps we could have won the war against them."

Red Cloud shook his head. "No, we could not have won. It would have taken longer for us to lose, but that would only have meant more suffering for the people, and it is of them that we must think now."

"I have never stopped thinking of the people. You know that. The people, and the old ways. These white men take what they want from us and give us nothing in return. They say the Paha Sapa will belong forever to the Sioux, and then they change their minds. When they ask us to sell and we say no, as it is our right to do, they take them anyway."

"It is true. And I tried very hard to get something for the people in exchange. But I have been to Washington to see the Great Father. I have been to Omaha, and to Chicago and to New York. You have no idea how many white people there are. The Sioux could not resist them. They would have overwhelmed us, killed us all."

"Have you yet met a white leader who told you the truth? Who made promises to you and then kept them? And is the slow death of the reservation better than dying in battle to protect what is ours?"

Red Cloud made no answer. There was none to make, and both men knew it. But Red Cloud made the promises White Hat had told him to make, and Crazy Horse, because he could do nothing else, agreed.

On May 6, Lieutenant Clark and a military escort met the advancing caravan of Crazy Horse's people two miles north of Fort Robinson, the army post adjacent to the Red Cloud Agency. The leaders of the Sioux band dismounted and sat in a row on the ground, then gestured for Clark to come forward. One by one, the leaders shook hands with White Hat, Crazy Horse last. He took Clark's extended hand with his left, and said, "Friend, I shake with this hand because my heart is on this side; the right hand does all manner of wickedness; I want this peace to last forever."

It was Sioux custom to surrender a warbonnet to a victorious commander, but since Crazy Horse had never had one, He Dog offered his own, placing it on Clark's head, tugging it into place, then offered his shirt and pipe in token of capitulation.

It was time for the march to Fort Robinson and the two-mile-long column was led by Crazy Horse and his chiefs, painted for war and riding at the head of the long, straggling caravan. As the buildings of the fort came into sight, the chiefs began to sing. The chant was picked up by the warriors, then the women, and finally the children.

One of the officers, standing in awe, said, "By God, this is not a surrender. It's a goddamned triumphal march!"

Red Cloud, looking on, knew that Crazy Horse might have surrendered but that he had not been broken.

Crazy Horse settled into agency life with dignity, but the magnetism of his personality, which captivated not only the Sioux but even the army officers, was a source of concern for the scheming Red Cloud, who wanted to be the leader of all the Sioux in captivity the way he had never been when they had been free.

Rumors that Crazy Horse was planning to head

north again as soon as his people recovered their strength began to circulate through the camp. Spies were everywhere, spies for Clark, spies for Crook, spies for Spotted Tail, and spies for Red Cloud.

The army men began to frequent Crazy Horse's lodge, where they talked about hunting and the battles they had shared. He showed great dignity and generosity, and a sly sense of humor, although he talked little. He drew close to Clark, and invited him to several feasts at his camp. And the growing respect with which Crazy Horse was regarded was a burr under Red Cloud's saddle.

And already, Washington was reneging on some of its promises. Crazy Horse had been told that he could have his own agency, in the Powder River country, where his people would be able to live the old way. But there was no real intention to honor that pledge. In fact, General Crook was making plans to send Crazy Horse to prison at Dry Tortuga, off the coast of Florida. Experience should have made the politicians realize that so abrupt a change in climate would be unendurable and probably prove fatal, but they were unlikely to worry about Crazy Horse in any case.

If Crazy Horse was aware of the intrigue swirling around him, he made no attempt to escape. He even had the post surgeon, Valentine McGillicuddy, begin treating Black Shawl, who was seriously ill. Rebuked for using the white man's medicine, Crazy Horse pointed out that the Sioux medicine men had been unable to help his wife, and he would do whatever it took to see her well again.

He seemed to like McGillicuddy, and in one conversation summed up his feelings regarding the cultural clash between the Sioux and the white man.

"We did not ask you white men to come here," he told McGillicuddy. "The Great Spirit gave us this country as a home. You had yours. We did not interfere with you. The Great Spirit gave us plenty of land to live on and buffalo, deer, antelope, and other game; but you have come here; you are taking my land from me, you are killing off our game, so it is hard for us to live. Now you tell us to work for a living, but the Great Spirit did not make us to work, but to live by hunting. You white men can work if you want to. We do not interfere with you, and again you say, why do you not become civilized? We do not want your civilization. We would live as our fathers did, and their fathers before them."

It was an argument that was hard to counter, and McGillicuddy didn't even try. Instead, he said, "You should go to Washington like the soldier chiefs say. You can tell this to the Great Father."

"I do not want to go to Washington. Red Cloud went to Washington, and all he did was learn to sell what belonged to the people for nothing of value. I do not need to learn that. Red Cloud already knows. He has already given away everything the Sioux own."

McGillicuddy tried again to persuade him, but Crazy Horse was insistent. McGillicuddy did not know that Red Cloud was spreading stories, all variations on the theme that if Crazy Horse went to Washington, he would be clapped in chains and

thrown in prison. And, of course, the stories were
based on truth. Crook still planned to ship the
Oglala leader to Dry Tortuga.

Many of the Sioux, at both Red Cloud and
Spotted Tail agencies, were getting restless. They
missed the open plains and the freedom to ride
where they wanted. When Crook asked for volun-
teers to ride as scouts in his hunt for the Nez Percé,
who had fled their Wallowa Valley en route to
Canada to join Sitting Bull, many signed on. They
were issued new repeating rifles and bluecoat uni-
forms. Crook hoped to get Crazy Horse to join him,
but was rebuffed. Crazy Horse would not lift a finger to help the white man enslave other Indians,
and he secretly believed that Crook's real intention
was to push on north and capture his friend Sitting
Bull.

All of the intrigue and scheming crystallized in
early September. Anxious to get away from the
backstabbing and slander, Crazy Horse rode off to
the Spotted Tail Agency, but when he arrived, he
was arrested. Spotted Tail had him thrown into the
guardhouse at the agency. When the news spread,
the wild Sioux were on the verge of erupting, and
Spotted Tail had Touch the Clouds, one of Crazy
Horse's staunchest allies, lead the great chief out
onto the parade ground, where hostile and agency
Sioux had squared off, to show that no harm had
come to him.

Crazy Horse explained that he only wanted to
get away from the mischief at Red Cloud Agency,
and agreed that he would return the following
morning, September 6. He left in the morning for
the forty-five mile ride, accompanied by Touch the

Clouds. All the Sioux at the agency had assembled in the twilight, and the newcomers had to wait for a path to be made though the throng.

He Dog approached Crazy Horse and whispered, "Watch out. You are heading into a dangerous place." But Crazy Horse pushed ahead.

As he neared the guardhouse, Little Big Man slipped up on his right hand. Little Big Man was now determined to be a leader at the agency, and he was jealous of the influence Crazy Horse had among the warriors.

Early snow covered the parade ground, crunching under their feet as they moved forward. Little Big Man escorted Crazy Horse through a door, and when he realized it was a prison cell, Crazy Horse turned and drew a knife he had hidden in his clothing. He tried to back out, but Little Big Man grabbed hold of him. Crazy Horse tore loose and rushed out into the cold where a sliver of moon cast its pale light on the snow.

Once more, Little Big Man grabbed him from behind, and one of the soldiers shouted "Stab him! Stab the son of a bitch. Kill him!"

One soldier stepped forward, a bayonet fixed to his rifle, and thrust it toward the great Sioux war leader. Struggling to free himself from Little Big Man's grasp, Crazy Horse was unable to ward off the bayonet, and it sliced into his side. Another thrust pierced his kidney.

He fell to the ground, and Little Big Man and a couple of troopers reached for him, but Crazy Horse waved them away. "Let me go, my friends. You have got me hurt enough," he said.

The soldiers wanted to put him in the prison

cell, but Touch the Clouds forbade it. "No!" he thundered. "He was a great chief and cannot be put into a prison." Instead, the seven-foot warrior bent over and picked up his friend's body and carried him to a bed in the office of the post adjutant. McGillicuddy came running, and Worm rushed out of the crowd and into the office, where he knelt by his son's side.

"Son, I am here," he said, leaning over the gravely wounded man.

Crazy Horse whispered, "Father, it is no use to depend on me. I am going to die."

An hour later, with only Worm and Touch the Clouds in attendance, Crazy Horse breathed his last. He had said not another word.

Sighing heavily, Touch the Clouds got to his feet and stepped out into the cold, where the moonlight sparkled on the snow, and the collective breath of the silent throng hung like a cloud in the air over its head.

"It is well," he said. "He has looked for death and it has come."

The assembly melted away into the night, confused, hurt, angry and, most of all, certain that the way of life they had known and treasured had come to an end at last.

# Afterword

CRAZY HORSE WAS AN EXCEPTIONAL MAN, and his life is, in many ways, emblematic of the entire history of conflict between white civilization and the broad gamut of other cultures with which it came into contact. That each and every one of those cultures was beaten into submission, its people brutalized and compelled to accept a way of life it had no interest in adopting is one of the more deplorable aspects of American history. More deplorable still is the unremitting highhandedness with which those cultures were dealt by a succession of greedy, insensitive, and often corrupt politicians, agents, and military officers.

It is one of the paradoxes of the "Indian Wars" that the most evenhanded treatment experienced by the conquered peoples was often (though not always, as the case of Crazy Horse clearly demonstrates) that at the hands of the soldiers themselves. George Crook, for example, while he was dishonest and calculating in his treatment of Crazy Horse, seemed to have learned something of value from his experiences of the Sioux Wars. When he later went West to fight Geronimo in the Apache Wars, his conduct was honorable and even progressive.

Nelson Miles, barely a participant in the preceding story, also seemed to have learned something and although he was the man who accepted the surrender of the great Nez Percé Chief Joseph, he was also the man who fought for more than twenty years to win for Joseph and his people the right to return to their homeland in the Wallowa Valley of northeastern Oregon. It is unfortunate that Crazy Horse had no such honorable adversary, for he surely deserved as much.

In some ways, certainly in the best sense of the word, Crazy Horse was a conservative, a man devoted to a way of life and willing to do whatever it took in order to protect it from unwelcome change. That he failed does not make his effort less noble or less admirable. Almost classical in its tragic contours, the life of Crazy Horse is even today instructive and edifying, as are his courage and generosity.

The Sioux are, perhaps, more written about than any other Native American people, in part because their fight was the most effective and of the longest duration with the single exception of that of the Apache. But terrain was on the side of the Apache the way it was not on the side of the Sioux. The inhospitable territory of the southwestern mountains and deserts welcomed the white invaders even less than its residents did, and that is the only significant difference. Even so, Geronimo and his people were able to hold out for only ten more years, and with their surrender in 1886 the "Indian Wars" were over.

Among the more useful books on the subject of Crazy Horse and his people are the biographies by Mari Sandoz and Stephen Ambrose, the latter a

joint study of Crazy Horse and his most famous
adversary, George Armstrong Custer. Stanley
Vestal's biography of Sitting Bull is also fascinating. George Hyde's studies of Spotted Tail and Red
Cloud fill in many gaps, and are as good as we have
on those two Sioux chiefs.

The Sioux War of 1876 has been much studied,
and there are several volumes available on that
campaign. Some of the more significant battles of
the entire epic struggle of the Sioux and Cheyenne
against white domination, such as the Fetterman
fight, Sand Creek, and the Washita battle are
explored in individual books by Dee Brown on the
first and Stan Hoig on each of the latter two.

Custer, of course, comes in for his share of
scrutiny. Edgar Stewart's *Custer's Luck* and Jay
Monaghan's *Custer* are both excellent places to
begin for those who want to know more about
Long-Hair. The battle for the Black Hills is not
over, and Edward Lazarus's *Black Hills, White
Justice* explores the ongoing legal fight.